Pat

In he[art]

   I choose to welcome

In Spirit

   I choose to share

In memory

   I choose to smile.

Green Rising

<u>www.azkelvin.com</u>

To Alicia —

Cheers !

A Kelvin

The bookshelf of

AZ Kelvin

The Altered Moon Series
Rise of the Altered Moon
Curse of the Altered Moon
Apogee of the Altered Moon

The Druids of Arden
Green Rising

Projects in the works:

The Druids of Arden
Southern Winds

Here We Ghost

For more information on *The Druids of Arden* and other projects
AZ is working on be sure to visit:
www.azkelvin.com

The Druids of Arden: Book One

Green Rising

Written by

AZ Kelvin

This story is a work of fiction. Names, characters, businesses, places, vessels, events, incidents, and every other scrap of this story are the products of the author's vivid imagination. Any resemblance to actual persons, living or dead, or actual events and locations is purely coincidental. All rights are reserved.
Written and published in the USA.

Green Rising

Published by Lee Companies, LLC. Copyright 2017

Edited by Nikki Busch/nikkibuschediting.com

Original cover design: CJ Lee * Story Wrangler: Sunny Lee

First edition 2017 paperback ISBN: 978-0-9913050-2-5

Library of Congress Control Number: 2017914442

Lee Companies, LLC. Kalamazoo, Michigan

For Pat,
A childhood friend,
Who fought to the end.

Contents

Foreword

Greetings reader,

Welcome to the first book of the Druids of Arden Series and thank you for reading. *Green Rising* is a fantasy fiction story about a multicultural group of people banding together to form the Druidic Order of Arden and rise in defense against the Disciples of Nemilos who would see the ancient watersheds and old growth forests of their world poisoned and destroyed.

Green Rising has a cast of characters with speech patterns and dialects originating from the different geographical locations across the northern and southern continents of their fictional world, Arden.

Five locations and six dialects are involved with *Green Rising*: Vakere to the southeast of the northern continent, Shaan along the south and southwest, Raskan to the northwest and north, and Kalnu to the north, with Onomala River Basin the sole location from the southern continent.

Human speech patterns can range from crisp and precise to sloppy and clipped, but usually one can be geographically identified by inherent accents and dialects. When I began writing *Green Rising*, I used very heavy phonetic accents and felt it hindered the story flow, so I backed off until I found a good mix of accent and readability.

Below you will find the same conversation written out in all dialects used in the story to serve as an example of the differences. As for the characters in the story, I will leave the flavoring of the vocal tones and the depth of the timbres up to your imagination.

I hope you like the story as much as I do. Cheers! - AZK

Sample dialog:

"Yes, I heard you, but I will not be going to the festival tomorrow."

"You have to go. It is the last festival before the end of the season."

"No, I tell you, I cannot. I do not have the time if I am to finish my lesson."

"Ugh, you do not have to do that now, do you? You know there is nothing better than wandering around a festival."

Vakerian:

"Yes, I heard you, but I will not be attending tomorrow's festival."

"You have to go. This festival offers the chance to bid farewell to the season."

"No, I must say again, I cannot. I have not the time if I am to finish my lesson."

"Ugh, the need for that is secondary, yes? You know nothing beats wandering around a festival."

Shaanlander:

"Yi, I heard ya, but I won't be goin' ta the festival tomorrow."

"Ya have ta go. It's the last festival before the season's end."

"Ni, I tell ya, I can't. I don't have the time if I'm ta finish me lesson."

"Ugh, ya don't have ta do that now, do ya? Ya know there's nothin' better than wanderin' around a festival."

Raskanish:

"Aye, I heard ye, but I'll nae be goin' ta the festival on the morrow."

"Ye have ta go, 'tis the last festival afore season's end."

"Nae, I say, I cannae. I dinnae have the time if I am ta finish ma lesson."

"Eck, ye dinnae have ta do that now, do ye? Ye know there's naught better than wanderin' around a festival."

Kalnuvian:

"Yah, I hear you, but I'll not be a'going to the festival tomorrow."

"You have to be a'going, love. It be the last festival afore the end of the season."

"Nah, I told you once already, I can't be. I don't be having the time if I am to finish my lesson."

"Och, you don't be having to do such at this very moment, do you? You know there be nothing better than wandering around a festival."

Gwylari:

"Yay, I hear thee, alas the morrow's festival must suffer mine absence."

"Thee must go. 'Tis the festival which endeth the season."

"Nay, I tell thee, I cannot. Mine lesson must reach completion 'ere the opportunity to do so expireth."

"Ugh, thou dost not need to complete such at present, dost thee? Thy knowest nothing is better than wandering around a festival."

Onomali:

"Yes, I did hear you, but I will not be going to de festival tomorrow."

"You have to go. It will be de last festival before de end of de season."

"No, I have said, I cannot. I do not have de time if I am to finish my lesson."

"Ugh, you do not have to finish dat today, do you? You know dere is nodding better dan wandering around a festival."

Well, now, I hope your imagination is fully engaged and you are settled in a nice comfortable spot. You are about to embark upon a journey with the druids as they travel across the Arden countryside fighting foes to save the environment from destruction while making new friends, forgiving old ones, and even finding love.

Now, for your reading enjoyment – *Green Rising*.

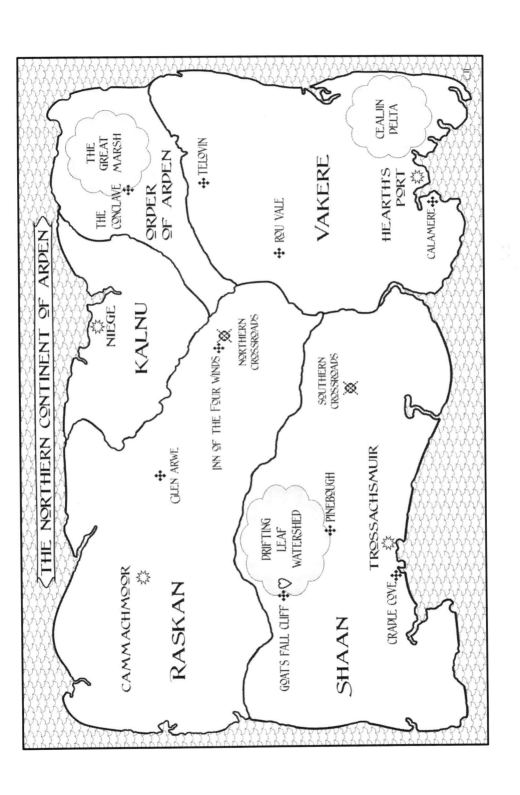

THE NORTHERN CONTINENT OF ARDEN

THE GREAT MARSH

THE CONCLAVE

ORDER OF ARDEN

TELOVIN

RIU VALE

VAKERE

CEALIIN DELTA

HEARTH'S PORT

CALAMERE

NIEGE

KALNU

NORTHERN CROSSROADS

INN OF THE FOUR WINDS

SOUTHERN CROSSROADS

GLEN ARWE

CAMMACHMOOR

RASKAN

DRIFTING LEAF WATERSHED

PINEBOUGH

GOAT'S FALL CLIFF

TROSSACHSMUIR

SHAAN

CRADLE COVE

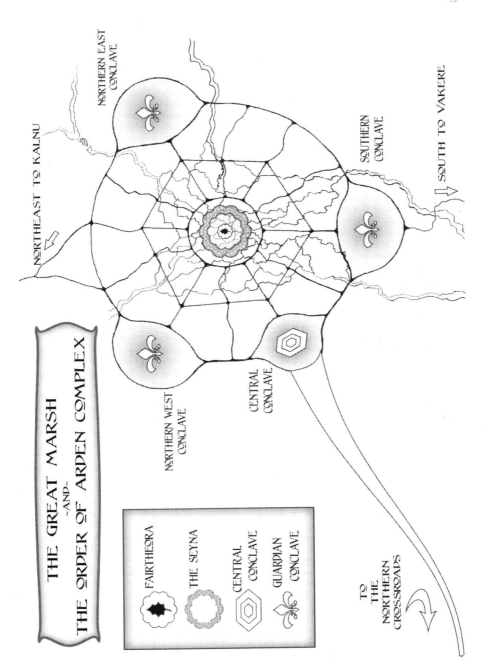

THE GREAT MARSH
~AND~
THE ORDER OF ARDEN COMPLEX

NORTHEAST TO KALNU

NORTHERN EAST CONCLAVE

SOUTHERN CONCLAVE

SOUTH TO VAKERE

NORTHERN WEST CONCLAVE

CENTRAL CONCLAVE

FAIRTHEORA

THE SEYNA

CENTRAL CONCLAVE

GUARDIAN CONCLAVE

TO THE NORTHERN CROSSROADS

Chapter One

Quinlan tried not to be short-tempered. His six-year-old legs barely reached the stirrups cinched to the shortest length. The horse was too big for him. Every stride the horse took meant another collision between tailbone and saddle leather. His backside hurt because he had been on the too-big horse all day, but he would not complain, not one bit, nor would he ride sidesaddle to ease the discomfort.

He wanted to live down *Tenderfoot*, his older brother's nickname for him. Once Quinlan tried to outrace his older brother, Lanry, but had to stop because his feet hurt. Lanry had called him Tenderfoot ever since. He didn't want to think about what Lanry would call him if he ever found out what was sore after this trip.

Most of his horsemanship training had been on much smaller breeds and limited to around his village of Calamere. He was surprised and excited when his papa announced Quinlan could come along to a *Gwylari* market more than three days' ride away. He had never been farther than the village limits before and he was determined to enjoy every minute of it no matter how much his backside hurt.

Riklan slowed his horse and brought him to a halt. He turned slightly in his saddle to look at him. His father had the typical olive-hued skin and dark features of the Vakerian people. Dark reddish-brown hair swept down past the collar of his tunic. Streaks of grey crept out from the temples. Black eyebrows shrouded deep brown eyes and fine black hair sprouted from cheek, lip, and chin.

"How are you, Quin?"

"I'm fine, Papa." He tried not to squirm in the saddle, but he was sore everywhere.

Riklan smiled at his son. "It's been a long day. There's a Gwylari inn amidst the farms right over the next rise. We can get a meal and a bed. Get an early start tomorrow."

Quinlan cleared his throat. "Well, if you need to, Papa..."

"Ha! Ha, ha! Then we ride through the night." Riklan turned his horse away from the road to the inn.

"We, um," Quinlan spoke quicker than he could think, "should consider the horses, Papa. They might like a bag of oats after such a long day."

Riklan slowly turned his horse back around. "Think so, do you? All right then, lead on."

The sun was low on the horizon as they crested the final ridge of the day's journey. Pockets of shifting soft colors stood out here and there across the fields below. The glow became brighter throughout the glade surrounding the inn.

"Papa, why does it glow?"

"Magic of the Gwylari."

"Uh-uh!"

Riklan put his hand over his chest. "Truth be told."

"Magic?" Quinlan looked out over the fields.

"And the inn is built from living trees bent and woven together by magic. Look there, where the glow is brightest."

Quinlan looked to the west end of the large valley. A structure in the distance gave off the same soft glow as the plants and trees surrounding it.

The form of the inn became clearer as they approached. Twenty-two hardwood trees stood around the exterior of the inn. Dozens of large branches reached out from each tree twisting and interlocking with the branches of the other trees to make the walls of the building. Oblong window openings that had grown into the branch infrastructure allowed sunlight and fresh air inside. Braced from underneath by intermediate limbs, layers of an over-lapping large-leafed canopy kept out the weather better than any thatch or clay roofing ever could. Plant-based oil torches burning with a smokeless flame illuminated the exterior of the building and the corral beside it.

A Gwylari man met them at the corral gate as they rode up. "Greetings, friends, hath thee traveled far?"

Quinlan thought the man talked more to their horses than he did to them.

Riklan answered, "We have come from the southern coast. They've done well today, so double the oats and throw in an apple or two if you would, please."

"'Twill be so," the man replied and swayed forward into a slight bow.

Quinlan watched a group of younger Gwylari greet their horses and lead them into the corral. He could not believe how fast they removed the saddle and reins. They spoke softly to the horses as they brushed them down and put feedbags on. Their mounts seemed quite content with the Gwylari's attention, but he felt they should not talk so strangely to his horse.

Riklan put his arm around Quinlan's shoulders and gave him a squeeze. "Nothing to worry about. With the Gwylari, our horses will most likely get a better room than we do."

His papa always seemed to know what he was thinking. "They talked strange to her."

"The Gwylari are friends of all animals, Quin. They'll be fine. Come on."

The inn's interior was even more awesome to Quinlan. He expected the inside of a tree house to be dirty and crawling with bugs. The Wayhouse of Rou Vale was far from the dirty hovel he had imagined.

Beautifully woven tapestries hung about the walls. The hallways were made of ivy vines grown together until the weave was too tight to see through. Smaller versions of the smokeless oil lamps lit the rooms and an area of tables in front of the reception desk. Eight patrons in two groups and one solo sat among the tables in quiet conversation while they ate.

A Gwylari woman greeted them as they entered the inn. Her long blond hair hung straight past the sides of her head like twin waterfalls of liquid gold. She had tan, weathered skin; calloused hands; and the greenest eyes Quinlan had ever seen. He gazed into those deep emerald eyes and completely forgot his soreness from the day's long ride.

"Pleasant night, travelers, thou art welcome at the Wayhouse of Rou Vale. I am Mare."

Riklan nodded in response. "Gratitude, Mare. I am Riklan and this is my son, Quinlan."

"*Shin Lahqui,*" Quinlan blurted out the Gwylari formal greeting for good day, which was the only one he knew.

Mare and Riklan shared a smile.

She kindly corrected him. "Shin Lah*quen*, young one, for the sun hast fallen below the world."

"Oh..." Quin replied and whispered the new phrase a few times over.

"We seek a meal and a room for the night," Riklan said.

"Of course. This way to thy room."

Quin thought back to when he sat around the cooking fire listening to his mother, Quella, and her sister, Cheari, talk about the Gwylari.

He heard his mama's voice in his mind. "The Gwylari are more akin to the land in many ways than they are to the other folk of Arden. They're the last of all folk to follow the teachings of Na'veyja and the living energy of the deep woods. They're masterful weavers of a magic they call the *flaura*. The Gwylari are taller and slimmer than most of Arden's folk, but they're bodies are strong and wiry, made so by their way of life."

His auntie was a great storyteller and loved to play to the crowd, which included Quinlan and the other children of his town. "Their slim graceful bodies and large deep-colored eyes weave a magic and take hold of your mind. Peer at them and they stand perfectly still, yet out of the corner of the eye, they gently weave back and forth as if they bend to a slight breeze or drift in the waters."

"Cheari, don't frighten the children," his mama said with a touch of scolding to her voice. "The Gwylari way is to be peaceful and quiet, patient and watchful. They are Arden's perfect shepherds and farmers."

"Oh, just a bit of fun, Quella." Cheari smiled a scoundrel's smile. "She's right, children, the Gwylari are a wondrous people. Do you know, from a young age, they weave and braid living plants in their hair and clothing?" She stopped to place her hand on her chest. "Truth be told! The clothing sustains the plants woven into them and the plants give off a soft glow. They can add or change plants whenever they wish when they want different colors or smells. And they can blend in with the plant life around them when they desire, too."

"The strange look of their clothing does have a practical aspect as well, children," Quella said. "Specific woven designs and colors indicate status, such as the individual's trade and skill level within Gwylari society. The tribes of the Gwylari live in complete harmony with the land they tend and in turn, they are nurtured by it. Once, long ago before the wars, it's said, all folks of Arden could blend with the flaura, but now only the Gwylari still follow the ancient beliefs. They are a peaceful folk and do not partake in the eating of animals. The Gwylari are farmers, weavers, and craft masters of unique skill and renown. Pay them respect should you ever meet any."

Quella's words echoed in Quinlan's mind as they followed Mare down a hallway. Small yellow, blue, and white flowers lined the stitching of Mare's earth-toned robes. The same blossom train circled her head with blossom streamers flowing down throughout her golden hair.

"Papa, how does she put the flowers on her clothes?"

"She wove them in with magic, I expect."

Quinlan's mind raced with images of powerful wizards fighting monsters and shooting beams of power from their fingers. "Does she fight monsters?"

"Ha ha, no, Quin, we're far from any danger here."

Mare led them to a room upstairs and slid open a thick curtain of ivy vines. She whispered to an oil lamp, which began to burn and light the room. An oblong window gave view to the woods beyond. Two cots lined one wall and a larger bed sat in a far corner opposite a washbasin.

"My papa says you made this with your magic," Quinlan said to Mare.

"With the grace of Na'veyja, Master Quinlan, the Gwylari serve and Na'veyja provides."

Quinlan turned to Riklan. "Is that who we're going to see?"

"No, Quin, Na'veyja is, ah—a goddess, of sorts." He turned to Mare. "We travel to the druid gathering to meet an old friend and to hear of the Order of Arden."

"A worthy cause. Time hath clouded keen eyes and shadows doth grow."

"What d—" Riklan began to ask.

"You mean like Seathia, Goddess of the Waters?"

"Not really, Quin," Riklan answered. "Mare, what did you mean?"

"All Gwylari hath seen how Na'veyja weakens. Rou Vale once shone bright with her flaura. Now, it doth glimmer much less."

Quinlan tried to think of other gods and goddesses his mother told him about. "There's Penle, Goddess of the Storm Winds."

"We'll talk about it later, Quin."

A Gwylari man showed up carrying a tray with a pitcher, glasses, sprigs of mint, and hand towels. Mare gestured to the washbasin in the corner of the room. He bowed slightly, put down the tray, and left.

"Here is water and mint to refresh thee. Dine at thy leisure. The hearth is warm 'til midnight. The privies set right outside the back entry. Rest thee well."

"Gratitude, Mare. May I give you this?" He reached into his travel bundle.

"Payment is not required, Master Riklan," Mare said.

"Oh, I know. Not my first night in a Gwylari Wayhouse." He produced a walnut-sized seed and gave it to Mare.

"A palerin seed? A most generous gift, Master Riklan, thee hath mine gratitude. We shalt all share of its fruit with our morning meal." She placed her hand on her chest and leaned forward slightly. "Shin lahquen."

Quinlan watched everything she did and repeated it back to her. She smiled and the ivy curtain closed leaving him alone with his papa.

"Papa, she's..."

"Oddly beautiful, yes?"

"Yes, very." The long trek seemed like it was a year ago and Quinlan could not have been happier with day's events.

"The woodland way has a natural beauty to it." Riklan smiled down at him and ruffled his hair. "Go on, wash up for dinner. We have an early start in the morning."

~~~

The next morning Riklan and Quinlan prepared to leave.

A golden-haired Gwylari woman stood at the desk writing in a ledger.

"Shin Lahqui, Mare," Quinlan said, and this time he knew he had it right.

The woman turned around. "Shin Lahqui, young master, but Mare I am not. She is mine birth sister. I am Sairyn."

"Oh, I'm Quinlan and this is my papa."

"Riklan, *lah ahm*, Sairyn," he said, using the Gwylari casual version of good morning.

"Lah ahm, Master Riklan. Mare left thee a bundle."

Riklan took the gunnysack and looked inside. "Palerin?"

"Fruit of thyne own kindness," she said.

"Surely not?" Riklan seemed surprised.

She simply nodded. "We sang over it through the night."

"What, Papa?"

"Do you remember the seed I gave Mare?"

"Uh-huh."

"They've grown the seed to a flowering bush since then."

"I don't understand."

"We'll talk about it today while we ride," he said and turned to Sairyn. "Our gratitude, please pass it on to Mare."

"'Twill be so. Dost thee desire to break the night's fast?"

"Yes, indeed. We still have a good day's journey ahead."

She swept her arm toward the tables. "Please sit."

Sairyn brought out a small tray and two glasses of a deep red liquid by the time they settled in. "Fresh-squeezed palerin juice, bread, goat cheese, and hot kaurapuuro."

"Ahh, wonderful." Riklan tore pieces off the small bread loaf and sliced enough cheese for them both. Sairyn set two steaming bowls down in front of them.

Quinlan felt like he was starving to death and quickly took the kaurapuuro she offered him. He stopped when he saw what was in the bowl and looked up at her in disappointment. "What's in it?"

"Oats and apples, with walnuts, cinnamon, and honey," she replied.

Quinlan reluctantly began to eat. Once he tasted the oatmeal, however, the bowl was soon empty. Sairyn brought him another, which he finished off as well.

They ate their fill and bid farewell to Sairyn before heading to the corral. A Gwylari girl about Quinlan's age stood with the stableman where they already had their horses at the gate. The man handed Riklan a gunnysack smaller than the one Sairyn gave them. The girl handed Quinlan what looked like a small cookie.

Unsure what to do, he looked up at his papa, who nodded.

"What's th—" Quinlan started to ask.

"Bee biscuit!" she said loudly before she ran off in a flash. She came back a quick second later with a few of the golden-brown biscuits. She gave one to each horse and ate one herself. "Food for all!"

Quinlan cautiously took a bite of the biscuit. He knew the flavor immediately and finished off the rest. "It's honey, Papa."

"I know, Quin. I've seen bee biscuits before. Much like what we just had for breakfast."

The girl ran over to Quinlan, whispered to a flower on her blouse, which came free, and handed it to him.

Quinlan slowly took the flower from her and looked up at his papa again.

He cleared his throat and shrugged. "It's a good thing, Quin."

Quinlan could see his papa was trying not to smile. He looked back at the girl who grinned wildly, laughed twice, and ran off again, this time behind the inn. She did not return.

"What do I do with it?"

"Keep it for now—it's probably magic, you know."

"Magic? A flower?" Quinlan pressed the flower against his shirt and let go, but the flower fell to the ground. He picked it up again. "How does it work?"

"You'll have to go ask the one who gave it to you."

"Uh-uh!" he said and used the corral fence to get up on his horse. He tucked the flower into the folds of his travel bundle and looked at his papa.

"Okay, we're good to go then." Riklan turned his horse down the trail and urged him on.

A short way down the road they came upon a roadside market nestled in a group of Gwylari farm fields.

Quinlan couldn't count how many people were out tending the fields around them. A small crowd gathered in each of the fields working at what seemed to him as different stages of the same task.

"Greetin's, good Vakerians!" a stocky Raskan merchant with hair the color of dark red wine called out to them. His speech held the heavy burr of the Raskan Highlands.

"Greetings in return, friend," Riklan replied. "You're a long way from home."

"Home of ma childhood, aye, but I call Rou Vale home now. I came here many years ago and the vale cast its spell upon me. I'm Jarl. May I fill a need fer yer journey?"

"Thanks, Jarl, but we're fresh from the wayhouse. Well rested and well stocked."

"A place of warmth and comfort," Jarl said.

"See here, Quin?" Riklan swept his hand in the direction of the fields. "This is what I meant about Mare and Sairyn growing the seed we gave her into a fruit-filled bush while we slept. This is Gwylari magic."

"Aye, it amazes the mind," Jarl said. "I never tire of watchin' them work with the flaura."

The melody of the chanting drifted through the air as the Gwylari farmers walked along the planting rows.

"Jarl, can you tell us what they're doing?" Riklan asked.

"Certainly." He stepped around the corner of the market stand. "Do ye see the older Gwylari lads and lasses out front there? They're called *furows*. They walk out ahead of the others but still in rhythm with the chant. They work the soil with a two-prong tiller leavin' a small mound of soil in the middle of two troughs. The ones behind them, they place holes in the dirt mound in the right spots with those slim wooden rods."

"How do they know where to put them?" Quinlan asked.

"Taught by their kinsmen," Riklan said. "Just like anyone else."

"Now, watch there." Jarl pointed to the group behind the furows. "The *sowans* come afterward ta lay the seed. They're the master weavers of the flaura and incredible ta witness."

Gwylari adults carried seed bags and followed behind the furows, chanting and weaving their hands in intricate designs. The sowans called to the flaura to bring forth the living energy of the land. A wispy blue-green glow rose up from the ground, forming a small flat cloud with a stem trailing back to the dirt. The seeds were drawn from the seed bags by the magic of the chanting. They floated up and out of the bag, traveled the short distance, and landed on top of the small cloud. The flaura cloud collapsed in upon itself back into the dirt taking the seed along with it.

Quinlan watched in wonder while the wizard-farmers planted their seeds. "Is that magic?"

"'Tis ta me, laddie," Jarl said. "They've tried ta teach me, but I've nae the skill ta make it work. Now, the last group out there, they're called *loamin*. They go by and finish up."

Other Gwylari, mostly older children and young adults, followed after the sowans. They chanted a rhythm both different yet in harmony with the first one. They filled in the hole with water and smoothed over the planting row before moving down the field. The seed took to sprout as soon as their chant was done and the loamin moved on to the next one.

"Look Papa—élan," Quinlan said pointing to the groups of birds flying in and among the farmers.

Along the field rows behind the Gwylari was a small host of élan flying back and forth performing small tasks to aid the farmers. Larger élan or groups of smaller ones carried bodas of water to the Gwylari loamin, who used them to perform a chant of harmony, instantly growing the seed into a sprout.

"Aye, youn' master," Jarl answered. "The élans are close companions with the Gwylari and work with them in the fields, orchards, and markets. If there're Gwylari nearby, ye can be sure some élan are close ta hand."

The avian creatures were of various sizes, shapes, and plumage. The feathery semiplumes curled and bent to form intricate shapes as the intensity and hues of the colors shifted and changed. The more intricate and colorful the display, the more attractive the élan was to prospective mates.

"Incredible, isn't it, Quin?" Riklan asked.

"Uh-huh." He was too distracted by the magic occurring right before him to say any more.

Jarl held his arms out to the fields. "The Gwylari tend great fields and orchards like this from shore ta shore and grow enough food fer all people across the breadth of Arden."

The chants of the Gwylari, combined with the glow of the flaura and the shifting colors and patterns of the élan, was a beautiful magic to behold. Quin watched and listened, mesmerized, before Jarl's voice interrupted his thoughts. "The freshly tilled dirt will transform inta a green-frosted field of new sprouts in the space of a mornin's time."

Jarl moved back to the front of the market stand. "The colors, flavors, and textures of Gwylari foods are renowned fer their incredible variety and flavors. The ability of the Gwylari ta blend with the flaura allows them ta grow food fer any number of specific uses."

"Don't you just eat them?" Quinlan asked.

"Aye, lad, and sometimes too many." Jarl grinned and patted an ample belly. He walked along the front of his stand to show off different produce. "Colorful fruits and vegetables with exotic flavors such as this muskmelon, and this crookneck cucurbit here, are grown fer festivals and gatherin's."

"Cucurbit?"

"A strange name it has, but really 'tis a squash." Jarl moved down the market stand. "Some crops are fer makin' breads and puddin's, others fer tasty jams, spreads, and sauces." He handed both of them a small square of yellow cake from a basket of samples.

"Mmm, what is this?" Riklan asked around a full mouth.

"A favorite of mine, bread made from ground corn." Jarl ate a sample piece as well.

Quinlan found the corn bread tasty, but it needed a good deal of water to wash down.

"Still other crops produce foods fer dryin' and preservin' so they last many days on lon' travels or fer storin' through the winter. Grains, nuts, and seeds of every variety are harvested from all over Arden. Here, take one of these as well." He handed them each a small woven hemp drawstring bag. "Nuts and dried fruits fer the trail."

"Gratitude. What do I owe you?" Riklan asked.

"Naught. The pleasure of conversation this mornin' is enough fer these tidbits."

"Kind of you in turn to take the time to speak with us. Pleasant day, Jarl!"

He waved as they turned their horses down the road. "Gratitude, laddies, fair travels!"

Chapter Two

The sun sat just past its zenith overhead when they crested the final rise of their trip and stopped for a moment. Quinlan took the opportunity to check one more time for any last bits of the trail mix Jarl had given him. He upended the drawstring bag, but barely a crumble fell into his hand.

"Here!" Riklan called out a second before he tossed his bag of trail mix to his son.

Quinlan managed to grab the bag after a brief impromptu juggle. "Ha! I got it. Gratitude, Papa."

"There it is, Quin—Telovin," Riklan said, looking down at the Gwylari market.

Fields of crops filled hundreds of acres surrounding the market grounds. A wayhouse ten times larger than the one at Rou Vale sat in the center. Market tents stretched out from the wayhouse to the fields. Flags and banners waved in the wind and gleamed brightly in the noonday sun. To Quinlan, it looked like an island of rippling colors nestled in a sea of green.

"Look there, Quin—a *kolosye*." Riklan pointed to a creature wandering among the tents. The shoulders of the quadruped animal stood as tall as the tent tops. The head was well above the massive body at the end of a long and slender neck. The tan, black, and white fur blended into a mottled brown blur at this distance, but the largest land animal on Arden was an awesome sight nonetheless.

"It's as tall as the wayhouse!"

"Taller, I think, even." Riklan looked up and pointed toward the sky. "And there among the clouds. Do you see the *wyndrif*?"

Quinlan looked up to see the sky flyer soar among the puffy white clouds. Wyndrives were native to areas of strong winds like open plains, coastal cliffs, and mountain ranges. Reptilian bodies twice the size of a man hung from massive bellows of semitranslucent flesh connected by lightweight bone and muscle. The bellows caught, channeled, and propelled air through the creature in a highly effective method of natural flight. The vivid colors of the skin stood out even from this distance. The wyndrif was nearly as big as the kolosye when all of the bellows were filled with air.

"Will it come down?" Quinlan asked.

"Perhaps, we can ask when we get there."

"We're going to see a druid?"

"Yes, his name is Bertrynn."

"Why?"

"He may have work for me. And also, we need to find a place for our family and people to make a new home."

"Because of the blood water?"

Riklan looked over at him. "Who calls it such?"

"Lanry and Gwenna," he answered. His older siblings had spoken about it. "They told me it washes up into our beds when we're not there."

"It's not blood, Quin. They're only trying to scare you."

His brother and sister always did things to him they thought were funny. It made him mad. "I hate them," he said.

"I know you *don't* hate them, Quin, and it is wrong of you to say so."

"But, they—"

"I *will*"—his papa stopped him with a look—"speak with them both about lying when we get back, but their wrong does not pardon yours. If you let words flow from your mouth like a river, then you may end up with a flood you didn't intend. A wise person uses their mind to stem the sea of thoughts and uses reason to gauge the flow of their speech."

Quinlan was confused and looked uncertainly at his papa.

"Okay..." Riklan laughed lightly. "Just do as your mama tells you. If you don't have anything nice to say, don't say anything at all."

"Don't say anything at all," he said at the same time and nodded his head. "Okay, Papa."

"You're a good son, Quin, and I love you."

"Love you too, Papa."

"The stables aren't far off. We meet Bertrynn tomorrow, so we have the rest of the day to explore the market. Come on!"

Quinlan was in favor of any period of time when he wasn't sitting on the horse.

The marketplaces of the Gwylari were full of wonder and astonishment, especially for the young. Multicolored flags and streamers flew from huts and booths. Baked goods of all kinds filled the breezes with tantalizing smells and aromas. Toys, wind-spinners, puzzles, and games for all ages were on display. Craftsmen displayed tools for fine craftworking. Fabrics featuring a kaleidoscope of colors hung in rolls of many sizes. Merchant trading was open to all.

The farms and markets of the Gwylari were spread throughout Arden, forming a central system of commerce and trade. Perishable produce was stored in dirt-covered longhouses cooled by blocks of the rhew-caled crystal that perpetually radiated cold.

"Papa, look." Quin reached out toward an open cooling chest.

Riklan grabbed his hand before he touched it. "No, Quin! Rhew-caled is enchanted ever-frost crystal. Don't ever touch it. It may be colder than winter's breath, but it'll you burn worse than a firebrand."

"How can it burn me if it's cold?"

"It doesn't burn with flame, but it burns all the same, trust me. I've seen it peel the flesh from a man's hand."

Quinlan's stomach turned at the thought of peeled flesh.

The merchant noticed the exchange and apologized for leaving the crystal exposed as he replaced the cover of his cooling chest.

Riklan nodded to the man before he turned back to his son. "Don't you touch it, you hear?"

Quinlan quickly nodded. "Yes, Papa. Why is it so cold?"

"The Kalnuvian frost mages have a citadel near the capital of Niege, where they mine a crystal found only in Kalnu and enchant them with the frigid winds of the frozen White Sea."

Quinlan looked up to check if his father was hiding another smile.

Riklan looked down at him and put his arm around his shoulders. "Would I jest about such a thing?" he asked and they walked on.

A great many animals, of fur and feather both, busied themselves going from merchant to merchant, running errands, delivering messages, even hanging streamers and banners with a great flourish of color and motion. Flocks of *élan* and other birds sat upon the tents and huts or flew through the aisleways, dodging obstacles and people along the way.

An array of different plants and flowers filled the tent framework and tops. The myriad of plants and blossoms growing together around the market grounds shimmered with flaura of a thousand different colors.

Quinlan watched an élan land on a bush branch and immediately adopted the foliage colors and textures. The élan blended in so perfectly he could not tell if it was still there or not.

"Papa, the bird!" He pointed to the bush where the élan had set only a second ago.

"What bird?"

Just as he asked, the élan shed its adopted colors and flew off past the tents.

"Oh! Yes, look at that. You know, Quin, many of the animals and creatures of Arden can change the colors of their feathers, fur, or skin to match the nearby plants and camouflage themselves or to stand out against them when they want to attract mates."

A commotion caught Quinlan's attention. He looked to see several Gwylari leading a group of horses down the main aisleway.

"Step aside here, Quin," Riklan said as he moved over to give the group some room to pass.

"Where are they taking them?"

"Look at the bridle crown and browband. See the blue braiding and fringe? That means they're for the quest riders. They'll be qualifying tomorrow to participate in the next festival quest."

Quinlan had heard of the festival quests as had every other child in Arden. Hopeful participants would gather at the Gwylari markets to petition for a spot to compete in the upcoming year's events.

"What do they do with the horses?"

"A quest rider must show high skill in horsemanship and husbandry, among many other things, to win a place in a quest."

"Were you ever a quest rider, Papa?"

He smiled warm and wide at his son. "Nooo, I've always been more at home with a ship under my feet than with a horse under my butt!"

They both shared a good laugh and Riklan put his arm around his boy's shoulders as they continued through the market. Quinlan could not remember a happier day.

The hustle and bustle of business and trade was in full swing at every booth throughout the entire market from daybreak to nightfall. The markets were not only places of trade but also the sites of meetings and councils between the different peoples of Arden. The Gwylari markets were considered neutral territory by all the realms of Arden. Weaponry and hostilities were forbidden.

The markets served also as waypoints for travelers. There, merchants could post jobs and notices. Staging areas for expeditions were set up as well. And you could find training in the healing arts, herb lore, and many other crafts and skills.

The smell of simmering foods and fresh-baked goods wafted from somewhere to their left.

Riklan sniffed the air. "What do you think, should we go that way?"

"Yes, I think so!" Quinlan's stomach echoed his sentiment.

The source of the smell, a large pit of coals lined with hot boxes and bubbling pots, sat beside a large pavilion sheltering an area of chairs, rugs, and tables in a horseshoe shape. Performers played music and danced around the open area in the center. Quinlan watched until Riklan poked his shoulder.

"Here, take this"—he handed him a bowl of vegetable stew and pointed to an open table in the pavilion—"and go sit down over there."

Riklan brought his bowl and a plate of biscuits to the table. A Kalnuvian girl brought a tray with a pitcher and glasses. Quinlan couldn't pull his eyes away from the girl. He had never seen one of the northern people before. She had the typical all-white hair, pale skin, and ice-blue eyes of her race. When she smiled at him the blush of her cheeks stood out like red roses on a sunny winter's day snowfield.

"Quin, don't stare." Riklan tapped the table with the end of his spoon. "Eat up."

"Yes, Papa," he said and set to eating his stew and watching the show.

Bards and balladeers sang of events and deeds from faraway lands and musicians played a vast array of instruments. Stringed instruments with elaborate, curved wood structures and carved panels emitted lively sounds. Gourds of every size were used. Some with seeds left inside to rattle and slide around, others cut open and carved out with dried fruit skins stretched over the opening to drum on. Chambered wind instruments, such as flutes and recorders, as well as the reed-equipped chalumeaux and xaphoons were also employed. The musicians and singers voted the most popular at the markets earned performances at the upcoming festivals and gatherings.

They finished their lunch and continued to explore the wonders of the market. Quinlan's face lit up when he saw the kite vendor's tent. Dozens of toys beyond the reaches of his imagination flew, floated, and soared in the air.

"Whoa!" Quinlan said as he watched a boy crash his flying toy into the ground.

The boy picked it up and held the toy above his head then ran until the toy flew once again.

Flying toys of every description packed the vendor's tent. Quinlan lost track of time as he watched all the toys flying around the vendor's tent until Riklan laid a hand on his shoulder.

"You may have *one*."

The smile of delight nearly split Quinlan's face in two. "Wahoo! Thank you, Papa!"

The brief search for the perfect flying toy ended when Quinlan found an eagle kite almost as big as he was.

"That's the one?" Riklan asked.

Quinlan nodded.

"So be it."

Riklan spoke with the vendor and made the purchase. The vendor thanked them and pointed out his nephew in the field next to the tent for instructions. Not long after, Quinlan had the kite up and flying.

~~~

Riklan watched his son run around the field across from the kite vendor's tent, his eagle kite high in the air, when he heard someone call out his name.

"Rik! Riklan!" A stout red-haired man in druid's garb and raiment waved at him as he walked down the road.

"Bertrynn, well met, my friend." Riklan gripped the man's forearm in greeting. "We met a countryman of yours in Rou Vale."

"Jarl? Aye, I see him now and again. A good lad."

Bertrynn stood next to Riklan and watched the children play in the field. "That yer boy there?"

"Quinlan, my youngest."

"Ahh, the days of runnin' around a field with naught on yer mind but catchin' a fair wind."

"Those days are far behind us both now, Bert."

"Aye..." he heaved a sigh and peered seriously at Riklan. "I'm glad ta see ye here, laddie. I was hopin' ye'd come. There's a place fer ye here if ye want it."

"Still not quite sure about it, Bert, but I can't doubt what I've seen with my own eyes. Besides, there's nothing left of Calamere now."

"Been no change then?"

"Pbfff—Change? Yes, all for the worse. Four years ago, the coastal waters teemed with sea life. Vakerian markets supplied all of Arden with fish and seafood. Then clouds of that damned reddened water began to show up, drifting in from the southern current, killing any plant, animal,"—he paused to take a breath—

"or person it came in contact with. Now, fog banks carrying the same red hue have begun to kill off the woods along the coast."

Bertrynn looked at him with concern. "What about the rest of yer family?"

"Safe for now. They journey inland with several other families and carry what we could save of our goods. Quin and I rode ahead to attend the meeting."

"Thank Na'veyja ye got 'em out in time," he said.

"About that..." Riklan replied.

"Now, I know yer as stubborn as the day is lon', Rik, but all I'm askin' is ye keep an open mind."

"I don't know, Bert. The Gwylari and a goddess of the eternal *Vast* trapped something evil behind a hedge in the middle of a swamp. I don't think my mind can open that far."

"The *Seyna*'s nae hedge, Rik." Bertrynn stopped to reconsider his statement. "All right, 'tis a hedge, a sacred hedge, but like nae hedge ye've ever seen afore, and burstin' with Na'veyja's grace. And surrounded by the Seyna is *Fairtheora*, the oak tree prison of our nemesis. *Acimasiz*'ll never get free."

"Acimasiz..." Riklan laughed skeptically. "Sounds like something you get after you've ridden too far in wet clothes."

"Dinnae laugh too loud, laddie. If my brethren are right, 'twas his disciples who're responsible fer the reddened waters at Calamere."

The smile fell from Riklan's face at Bertrynn's news.

"Now, isn't that somethin' worth fightin' against?"

Riklan remained silent and turned back to watching Quinlan fly the bird-shaped kite around the field as the evening sun touched the horizon.

Bertrynn broke the silence. "Come, fetch yer lad. I know a place where dinner's always ready. The rest can wait 'til the morrow."

"That I can do," Riklan said. "And gratitude, my friend, for all you've done for us."

"Naught, but what was right ta do, laddie." Bertrynn slapped him on the arm.

"Quin!" Riklan waved to catch his attention. "Let's eat!"

"Coming!"

~~~

After a quick morning meal the next day, Riklan and Quinlan met up with Bertrynn.

"Top of the day, laddies!"

"And the rest of the day to you, my friend," Riklan replied.

"Shin Lahqui," Quin said.

"And Shin Lahqui ta ye, youn' Master Quinlan." Bertrynn gave him a short bow.

"Gratitude for this. I only got partway through." Riklan handed Bertrynn a tome about the Order of Arden he had borrowed.

"Aye, a lot there, and that's only one of many. Come, the meetin's right here." He led them to a nearby tent.

Druids from the Order of Arden converted a large tent into a conference chamber to bring awareness to the public and address the issue of the red pestilence along the coastline.

A group of druids sat off to one side of a podium with a small table in front of it. A druid at the podium signaled to two more by the entrance who announced the beginning of the meeting. A few minutes passed to allow stragglers to come in and find seats.

"Greetings friends. Gratitude to all for coming to this meeting. I am Tyrosi. I hold the rank of Adjutant *Tretjey* in the Order of Arden. This meeting is a call to action to my fellow druids and to any folk who fear for the safety of Arden and all creatures that live upon it."

A male and a female druid began to arrange a group of plaques on the table in front of Tyrosi's podium. Two ethereal beings of the Vast cosmos faced each other with the world bearing the land of Arden between them. The faces and bodies of both were vague, obscured by veils of mist and clouds. Hues of many colors illuminated one being, while dark greys and blacks set the other being in shadow. A mix of the two colorways swirled around the world below.

"Throughout time, our lore has been passed down by songs and tales. In so doing, the knowledge of our ancestors passes on to us in the present. Before the songs of memory and the writings of history, two immortals of the great Vast came to our world in conflict. Na'veyja, whose essence brings forth life and sustenance, and Acimasiz, whose presence withers life and gifts only turmoil. Their endless battle continues even to this day."

The two druids set up different plaques depicting a battle between the two beings of cosmic power. A host of Gwylari fought beside Na'veyja. A force of equal size gathered around Acimasiz.

Tyrosi continued to speak. "Ages ago, Na'veyja and the Gwylari fought against and eventually imprisoned Acimasiz within the numinous oak tree, Fairtheora. Lost without guidance, his forces faltered and disbanded, or so it was thought."

The druid assistants changed the plaques to ones showing men and women shrouded in shadows. Some stood out, resplendent in their darkness and holding a strange allure. The others huddled, nondescript and anonymous around the first like mobs on a street corner.

"Acimasiz's overlords and their henchmen, the *dreyg*, have not been heard of in recent decades even though their black clouds of poisoned mist have never truly vanished from the far reaches.

We now know his overlords have not been destroyed and we fear they may return."

The druids changed the plaques to ones showing red waters and mists of red drifting through now-dead shorelines. A river of red was pictured down the coast from Vakere. The red river water washed out to sea where it caught a main current up the coast and back onto the mainland.

"A new menace has reared up along the Vakerian coastlines. A plague of red has come up the southern currents killing all in its path. The red water rises into a mist wherever it contacts land and continues its deadly advance. Our scouts have tracked the red plague to its source. What was found disturbs heart and mind. A foul-smelling estuary spills into the Cealjin Delta, which in turn delivers the red plague to the sea. Abandoned camps up current of the delta carry a stench too powerful to approach. The land around them was left white as bone and burns to the touch. We must do what we can to counter its effects and restore the delta to its natural state."

New plaques were put out showing how important the circle of life is to the creatures and humans of Arden.

"The woods, the animals that live within, the plants they glean nourishment from, and the humans who call Arden home are all cogs in the wheel of life. If even one cog breaks from the wheel, then all suffer the consequences. The Order of Arden exists to protect the land, which is vital to all."

The final plaques showed Gwylari people and the druids of Arden standing in the Great Marsh surrounded by glowing green energy.

"The Gwylari and the druids, aided by the grace of Na'veyja, fight to heal the damage done by Acimasiz and his dreaded forces and ensure that all the folk and creatures of Arden are alive and well from shore to shore. I invite all to attend the day's curricula and I implore you to join our cause. My gratitude for listening."

A round of applause came from the gathering as Tyrosi stepped down. The other druids joined him and they began to greet the attendees.

"Tretjey Tyrosi!" Bertrynn called out.

"Cinquey Bertrynn, greetings to you."

"Greetin's in return, Tretjey. I'd like ye ta meet Riklan and his lad, Quin."

"Ah, the ship captain from Calamere?" he asked. "A pleasure, Captain, and greetings to you, young one."

"It would please me if I could say the same, Tretjey," Riklan said.

"Yes, I heard of the destruction of your town by the red plague, condolences."

"Gratitude, Tretjey."

"Tyrosi, please, I've never been too comfortable with formality. Bertrynn tells me your people have been displaced."

Riklan put his arm around Quinlan's shoulders. "Yes, we have nearly ten score following behind us. We seek work and shelter, and perhaps a place for a new beginning."

"You and your people are most welcome. We have no seas to sail, but work is in no short supply and there are lands right outside the conclave farms open to homestead. Any who wish to join the Order may bring family to live within the conclave borders."

"The red plague will soon stretch along the entire Vakerian coastline and into Shaan," Riklan replied. "My heart weeps to think I may never again return to the sea."

"Never's a lon' time, ma friend," Bertrynn said.

"Agreed, and I have family and friends in need that must take priority," Riklan said. "I'm not too old to enter?"

"Never too old, Rik!" Bertrynn said.

Riklan looked down at his son. "Sound all right to you? We could move to the conclave, live there, learn to be druids."

"I could be a druid?" Quinlan asked.

"Why, of course ye can, laddie!" Bertrynn smiled so wide, a rare glimpse of teeth appeared through the overgrowth of red beard and moustache. "Usually a lad or lass has ta be ten or older ta enter the Order, but with ye livin' right at the conclave, I expect ye'll get in a might sooner."

"What do you think, Quin?" Riklan asked.

The look on Quinlan's face was all the answer Riklan needed.

Chapter Three

"*Toir salan magnor rotan.*" The druid's chant flowed through the air like smoke drifting in a lazy breeze. The enchantment called forth a wispy essence from the ground pulsing with a soft glow. The glowing pulse moved up from the soil forming a wispy cloud above that took on the shape of an ivy plant. The soft glow of the flaura moved through the ethereal plant's roots, stems, and leaves causing the immediate growth of an actual living plant. The druid's hands danced smoothly through the air as he controlled the plant's energy to stimulate its growth. The plant wove its way into and throughout the surrounding brush. The stems interlocked with other bushes while the leaves grew in to fill any gap or opening.

The task now finished, the druid stepped back from the Seyna, which stretched out in both directions until it curved out of sight and stood tall above him. A variety of plants linked together to form the Seyna into a solid barrier of flaura. The massive barrier of living energy had stood for more than a thousand years.

A hood pulled to the eyebrows swept down into a cowl forming a garment the druids called their *raiment*. The raiment fastened below the collar of his jerkin in the front, spanning the upper chest to cover both shoulders, then tapered to a rounded point midway down his back. The sigil of the Order of Arden, an "O" formed by a wreath of dried rynn grass under an "A" of green ivy, was embroidered into the back. Colored symbols woven into the fabric edges indicated the druid's rank and affiliation within the Order of Arden.

The raiment, as with the rest of his clothing, was made of various plant fibers that had been beaten, cured, stonewashed, and woven into strong fabrics of many different textures and styles.

The forest-green tunic underneath the raiment was soft and pliable yet offered protection equivalent to a lightweight animal skin. The tan trousers were made from a heavier fabric with reinforced knees and seat panels. The black hard-soled and well-worn boots rose up to the knee where they were laced and secured around the top of the calf with small braids of woven cord.

The fabric had a strange pattern. At first, it appeared random like ashes spattered in the rain and smeared over a darker color underneath. Upon closer inspection, a hint of tree bark and leaf shapes could be seen among the spots and streaks. The longer you looked at it, the more varieties of plant life you could see. One blink and it all shifted back to a faint and faded odd-patterned fabric with no discernable images whatsoever.

The brown of the raiment was darker than his trousers and rimmed with three-tiered crisscrossed embroidery bearing the forest, mahogany, and black color pattern of the *Northern West Conclave.*

Quinlan drew back his hood, revealing the olive skin and dark features of the Vakere. Dark brown hair swept down over his ears to brush the collar of his tunic. Black eyebrows, moustache, and chin beard matched his bushy black sideburns. Deep brown eyes scanned for any weak points or dilutions in the energy of the Seyna.

Satisfied, he continued on with his inspection. Quinlan caught up with his walking staff, which seemed to have been off "walking" around by itself as it did quite often.

"There you are—'bout time. I cannot waste the day waiting around for the rascally likes of you. What manner of mischief have you been into now?" Quinlan scolded the supposedly inanimate piece of wood.

If ever an inanimate stick of wood could look offended, it was Quinlan's druidic familiar, which he called *Askue.* The hop hornbeam walking staff rolled along the branch it leaned on and settled to one side as if to say, *Who—me?*

Quinlan was not certain if it reacted on purpose or if it was the sudden breeze just then, which happened to blow it over at the right time.

"May as well stick you up a wyndrif's flutter and leave you there for all the good you are. Come along, then. Quit dawdling!" He took up his staff before he turned and walked down the trail. Askue did not complain about traveling in the hands of the Vakerian for now.

Together, the two of them made their way along the Seyna and made sure all was well. Why wouldn't it be? The sun shone brightly through the fresh spring leaves. The sunlight and the breeze made lights and shadows chase each other across the canopy of the woods. The glowing flaura of the deep woods was exceptionally rich and bright during this *Cetria* of Green Rising. The Cetria of White Fall had recently passed, the snows were gone, and it was truly a beautiful day.

Darkness, however, never seemed to be too far away. Like pine pitch in your hair, you can't seem to ever get it all.

Quinlan knew what was on the other side of the Seyna. The brooding essence of Acimasiz was confined within Fairtheora. The demi-god had been withdrawn from Arden by Na'veyja and the Gwylari and contained behind the Seyna many generations ago. Even a minor disturbance in the flaura was a chink in the Seyna's armor against the escape of Acimasiz. A trivial thing could grow into a great danger if left unattended. The living energy of the Seyna had to be kept in place at all costs. The Druidic Order of Arden had been formed and tasked with the maintenance of the Seyna and its barrier of flaura.

The position of *Siestrey*, Druid of the Sixth Circle, took Quinlan fifteen years of study to achieve, which now was six years in the past. Any Third Circle Osmey could quickly grow a seed to full plant, but to form the plant from the flaura itself without a seed was a rare talent.

Quinlan's ability to blend with the flaura went deep into both the spirit of the land and into his own spirit. He could blend his energies with that of the plants and commune with the animals and creatures, explain things to them, and even ask them for help. He could immerse into the brush, disappearing completely, and had the ability to heal wounds and cure simple sicknesses. This degree of skill did not come so easily to everyone, and to some, it never came at all.

Quinlan's ability in blending made joining the *Dayne Kinship* a natural choice. The Kinship was an offshoot from the main order and there was no circle of rank to rise up through. Each member was simply referred to as brother or sister. Their only insignia was a solid green braid running down the shoulders of their raiments.

All brothers and sisters trained with and learned from each other in peer groups instead of a structured training program. Training with the Kinship taught the druid to move from being able to blend with the energy of the land into being able to call it forth from the world around them. The only requirement for the Dayne Kinship was to have the ability to call the flaura and form a plant from the energy itself with no seed to start from.

The development of this skill required a different focus than that of the Order, which was the maintenance of the Seyna and vigilance against the dark essence trapped behind it. The Dayne Kinship was formed to train those who showed talent in the skill of calling. The Kinship was still a part of the Order of Arden, so a brother or sister had druidic duties to perform as well as honing their calling skills.

In Quinlan's case, he could be referred to as either *Siestrey Quinlan*, a Druid of the Sixth Circle in the Order of Arden, or as *brother Quinlan*, a member of the Dayne Kinship. The Order sends out groups of druids called *groves* to monitor and maintain the Seyna and the lands surrounding it. It was typical that at least one member of each druid grove was a brother or sister of the Dayne.

Just shy of an hour later, Quinlan came up over a rise and looked down into the vale below. He saw some members of his grove had already gathered at the West Galion trailsmeet.

He could see Swela and Kian, a newly joined *Raskanish* couple. Kian's deep red hair was visible even from this distance, but it may as well have been a shadow compared to the bright gold of Swela's locks.

Kian was a lean man and stood an even six foot tall. His features were sharp and his eyes were as green as the southern seas. The angles of his face were so severe they gave Kian a perpetual scowl that belied his normally open manner.

Swela's shoulder fit perfectly under Kian's arm when they stood side by side. Her sky-blue eyes were set above slightly chubby cheeks that were always drawn up in a smile. The tip of a scar from a childhood animal attack started right below her left ear and ran down to disappear under the collar of her tunic.

Kian sat cross-legged atop a small boulder off the intersection of the trailsmeet. Swela leaned against the same boulder in front of him with her arms crossed over her chest. She smiled peacefully, face turned up, eyes closed, and basked in the early morning sunlight. She swatted away an occasional tickle that was really Kian teasing her with a long stem of rynn grass. Swela finally caught on to him and half smiled, half sneered at him. She pretended to be outraged at him for ruining her tranquility. A third person smiled and laughed at their behavior.

Cassae, a *Shaanlander* woman, sat nearby on the ground and rested against a tree with her hands folded in her lap. Her appearance, even though from different peoples, was so similar to Swela's one would swear the two were mother and daughter.

Cassae stood taller by less than a hand above Swela and was a shade or two darker in hair color, but the same sky-blue eyes peered out from nearly the same face except for the scar and Swela was a little heavier. The Raskanish and the Shaanlanders were once of one people before the Kindred Wars generations ago and the evidence of it could still be seen today in the two women's appearance.

Despite the difference in age, Cassae had a close relationship with Kian and Swela. The relationship with the young couple had helped ease the pain over the loss of her own family in recent years. Cassae's husband and two children died of the wasting sickness, a disease contracted from contact with the black cloud of Acimasiz, which slowly drained the life from its victims over many weeks of agonizing pain. The wasting sickness had taken her family's lives and two years of her own life. She spent a year after their deaths in special study at the Central Conclave to mend the shreds of her spirit. Now, she had been back on patrol with the grove for the last year. Even though the sadness sat over her like a curtain of black veil, the strength of her spirit kept the shadow from darkening her heart.

Quinlan could hear and see Ticca and Ticari, Vakerian siblings, as they walked up the lower trail a short ways down the vale. The brother and sister were from Quinlan's home province of Yarin in Vakere not far from Calamere, but not linked to him by blood or family. They were both topped with curly black hair so dark the ambient light gleamed off the curls in bright bursts. Ticari, the brother, had tighter curls due to the shorter length of his hair.

Ticari, mature for his age of seventeen, was the elder brother by three years over his younger sister and was close to his trials to enter the fourth circle of *Settey*. Ticca had just passed the trials of *Novey* and she was now *Osmey*, a Druid of the Third Circle, the point at which a druid can be assigned to their first grove. The upcoming rotation was Ticca's first time out with a grove on patrol.

Quinlan's thoughts went over the members of his grove and their duties for the day when a plant jumped into the path in front of him. "Yaa!" the plant yelled.

Quinlan stepped back in surprise.

"Ha ha ha, I got thee, Quinlan!" said the plant "Ha ha!"

Quinlan relaxed and laughed as the plant's leaves twisted and shrunk away until only Chyne, another member of his grove, stood there. Chyne was Gwylari and the Gwylari *loved* to play hide-and-seek in the woodlands.

The Gwylari stood apart from the normal rank and file of the Order of Arden's command structure. The Gwylari people, with the guidance of Na'veyja's energy, formed the druidic order generations ago after the imprisonment of Acimasiz. Chyne wore no uniform or raiment except for that which all Gwylari wore, clothing that bore living plants. The Gwylari people loved the *druidae* as they called their druid brothers and sisters. Frequently a Gwylari chose to support a particular grove of druidae simply because they liked to be around them.

"Lah ahm, brother Quinlan!" sang out Chyne, which was Gwylari for good morning, as she bounded down the path, no doubt to tell the others of her great victory.

"Lah ahm, Chyne," he called after her and laughed.

"Lah ahm to thee as well, Askue!" she called back to the walking stick. "I shall see thee below!" Her voice diminished as she got farther away. All the Gwylari seemed amused at Quinlan's unique companion and talked to it quite frequently. The stranger thing was they seemed to listen as if the staff talked back to them.

The Gwylari's love for fun, games, and surprises made sure being around them was never dull. That being said, a Gwylari as a member of your grove was still a great benefit. They were the ones who first formed the Druidic Order of Arden, then later the Dayne Kinship. The Gwylari were instrumental in the capture of Acimasiz and the raising of the Seyna. His grove's duty was maintaining the Seyna's integrity, so having Chyne along was both a pleasure and good sense.

Quinlan laughed to himself at Chyne's "positude" as she called her outlook on life.

"Askue, my friend, a great day looms ahead," he said as he continued down the path leading into the vale. "Yes, a great day indeed."

Two élan flew up to him through the woods, one small sized, one medium. All of the avian breed, regardless of size and color, could alter their feathers to blend into surrounding vegetation. Élan were covered with small semiplume feathers layered in between the other feathers that enabled them to change into different colors and shapes. A dozen longer semiplumes extended from the birds' heads, six on each side. He recognized Flit and Singer by their markings as the druidic familiars of two of his grove members, Sovia and Therin.

Sovia's familiar, Flit, was small enough to land in the palm of your hand. She was bright yellow with black wings, mask, and feet. Six fringes of the curled semiplumes matching the yellow of her beak and body sat above each eye extending back and slightly up over her head.

Singer was bigger than three of Flit put together. His belly was a reddish brown at the neck changing to white near the tail. His, back, wings, and head cap were blue with a thin black streak at eye level from his beak to the back of his head. Singer's twelve semiplumes were black and started behind the eyes running down along the back of the ear coverts to sweep out over his shoulders.

"Greetings, my friends," Quinlan said to the avian creatures.

In a series of chips and whistles, chirps and cheeps, Flit told Quinlan that Sovia and Therin would meet them farther down the trail.

"Very good, thank you," Quinlan responded.

The élans both chirped at him and flew back through the trees the way they had come.

Quinlan smiled as he watched the pair of élan disappear into the deep woods and he continued on his way to the trailsmeet. He was confused and somewhat irritated three years ago when his own familiar quest rewarded him with Askue instead of an animal like every other druid he had known. In the time since, however, he had become quite fond of the hop hornbeam staff despite its mysterious and troublesome penchant for mischievous behavior.

The vale below was a mix of forested glens and moss-covered woods. The deep green of the woods glimmered with the shifting glow of the flaura. The crisp airs of the winter season still drifted in over the night hours only to be chased back again by the bright spring sun. The morning sun shone brightly through the trees as Quinlan came around the last bend and saw most his grove waiting at the trailsmeet.

"Shin Lahqui!" Quinlan hoisted Askue into the air and called out the traditional greeting of the Gwylari.

The group called greetings back to him.

Quinlan's grove returned from their off-duty rotation for their first day back on patrol. Each grove went on patrol for three rotation periods of nine days, totaling twenty-seven days. They had nine days patrolling in each of the three zones, with one nine-day rotation period off. Every druid was required to spend three days of their off period in study at the central hall of their conclave, three days in the growing fields, and they were free the other three days to do whatever they chose.

Quinlan could hear Chyne's singsong voice as he approached. She told them of her great prowess at ambush, one of the Gwylari's favorite hide-and-seek games.

"Greetings all, greetings!" Quinlan said.

Cassae stood and smiled as he walked up. "Lah ahm, Quin.

"Lah ahm, Cass."

"We hear ya've already had a blendin' lesson from Chyne this mornin'."

Quinlan cocked his head in mock irritation and raised an eyebrow. "Yes, it seems my skills at blending are not even up to that of a Gwylari maiden." He engulfed Cassae in a warm and strong bear hug, which was a self-proclaimed specialty of his. "How are you?"

"I'm better." She warmly returned his embrace. "I've learned when the voices of the past yell in me mind, ta silence them with whispers of the future."

"A sound practice and sage advice all folk could benefit from."

Cassae separated from him and moved to his side. "And how was your time off?"

He slipped his hand around her waist. "Ehhh, you know me, you'll find me in the shade of a loom tree, feet up and eyes closed, still as a stone."

"Hah! The day Quinlan of Calamere is still as a stone is the day Arden will cease ta spin amon' the stars!" They both laughed.

It's good to be back in her company again, thought Quinlan. The bond between them had grown stronger since she had recovered from the loss of her family, and their feelings for each other were no secret, but Cassae had to walk her own path for a while longer yet. Quinlan knew, in the time ahead, their paths would come together.

They overheard Chyne as she told the others about her trip to visit a nearby Gwylari market and the latest news on the Festival of Na'veyja's Grace, which was held at the end of the Cetria of Green Rising.

"'Twas said Balas the Bard shall attend to sing the 'Ballad of the Drawing', and Alders the Elder shall be there as well. 'Tis rumored Alders hath the names of druids chosen for the Trials of the Circles," Chyne said to the other members of the grove with a special glance at Ticari as Quinlan and Cassae joined them. She turned to look at Kian and Swela. "And thee twain—wast thy journey to Raskan long?"

"Eck! Lon', ye ask?" Kian huffed in exasperation. "We rode all week and managed—by Na'veyja's grace—ta get there as the shadow of night closed over us on the day afore the gatherin'. We had one solid day of family, feastin', and fables. Then *another* week of travelin' just ta get back fer this rotation."

Kian and Swela chose to have their vowing ceremony in the Primerey's Garden on the grounds of the Central Conclave on the first day of the Cetria of Green Rising. *Primerey* Joseah, to their great honor, performed the ceremony herself. Some of the family couldn't make the trip from Raskan to the conclave, so they traveled home during a special leave for a clan gathering after the ceremony in the garden.

"It was a beautiful ceremony," Ticca said wistfully.

Swela gave her a hug. "Gratitude, Ticca, 'twas the happiest day of ma life."

"Our lives," Kian added.

Swela peered at Kian. "Aye, the trip was lon', but at least ye rode out all that blood sausage ye managed ta stuff in yer face in one day."

"Eck, dinnae remind me," Kian muttered and patted his stomach to try to ease some of the gaseous rumblings.

"Bowel gas comest only from the eating of animal flesh, didst thou know?" piped in Chyne, joking matter-of-factly. The Gwylari's disdain of eating animals was well known.

"It dinnae, Chyne!" said Kian.

"Ha ha, with my brother, bowel gas comes from everything!" said Ticca.

"Hey! That's not true!" cried Ticari in protest. "Better behave yourself—*Osmey*!"

"You're Osmey, too." Ticca couldn't help but tease her brother, even though Quinlan knew how much she did appreciate all the help Ticari had given over the last year. First was the preparation for the trials, which was tough enough, but then she had to complete them before she could achieve her goal to become a guardian druid on patrol. She had passed her second circle trials and advanced to Osmey. There was a small celebration in the conclave hall with friends and family, then two days of preparation for her first day out with a patrol grove. Ticari had helped her every step of the way. She told Quinlan once, "He was the best brother a sister could have."

"I'm not Osmey for long," he replied. "My trials are at the end of this Cetria and I will pass them and ascend to the fourth circle of *Settey*." He folded his arms. "A druid of *great power* I will be!"

"Ahem." Quinlan cleared his throat loudly.

"...and of great humility as well, of course," Ticari added with much less grandeur.

"Pride and humility don't often travel together, Osmey Ticari," Cassae said, glancing sideways at him and arching a brow.

"Yes, of course, *Cinquey* Cassae, 'the smaller self leaves room for the greater spirit,'" Ticari quoted from the *Book of Arden*. "Forgive me. It was only in jest."

"Ahh, it's nice to have the grove back together, eh?" asked Quinlan. "Come, let's get moving. We need to get to the conclave for the rotation meeting."

"Where's Sovia and Therin?" asked Ticari.

"There." Kian pointed down the trail.

A woman of the Kalnuvian people walked into view and waved joyfully when she saw them. The northerner was joined by a Shaanlander man of great height, next to whom Sovia seemed only as tall as a child. Sovia and Therin had each received an élan from their quests to find a familiar. Quinlan's case was the only time in the history of the Order that the familiar had not turned out to be an animal.

The two not only had élans as familiars, but their affection for the avian creatures was reciprocated by the élan in general as well. Groups of élan would come down to travel with the pair as they wandered the different woodland paths and shared with them the happenings of the local woods. No other druids had such a strong connection to the élan as Sovia and Therin.

"Lah ahm, everyone!" Sovia called out as the group moved closer to them. Therin smiled warmly and stretched out his hand in a motionless wave that was the standard greeting from the reserved and quiet man.

Sovia's came from a Kalnuvian city in the farthest northern reaches of Arden. She was a fair example of her people except for being shorter than most in height. Along with her pale skin and light blue eyes, however, she bore a mess of white hair well known for its ability to overwhelm any hair tie.

The one area where Sovia was respectively unique, however, was her short and stout legs. She had to walk three times as fast as Therin to cover the same distance. She won Quinlan's respect the day he saw Sovia's energy more than compensated for the length of her strides, and not only did she manage to keep up with the grove, she was often the last one needing to stop for the day.

Therin was much the opposite of Sovia in some ways, but their spirits bonded the moment they first met during their studies at the Central Conclave. Therin was tall and stood a head taller than even Quinlan and Kian. Thin black hair, braided as a rule, usually snaked around to hang over his right shoulder. Sparse facial hair grew from several scraggly patches like someone carelessly scattered beard seeds over the field of his face. The slim torso and much of his arms and legs were covered with many tattoos of his travels, which was the custom of the seafaring Shaanlander people. The sea still called to Therin, but his duty to the Order was stronger, and the tattoos beneath his tunic were not of endless waves and distant shores, but of the Great Marsh, the Seyna, and Fairtheora within.

"Shin Lahqui, Sovia! Greetings, Therin!" Quinlan called back to them. "Stay there—we'll come to you!"

Sovia and Cassae shared the long embrace of sisters when the two groups came together. The two had met when they entered the Order on the same day and traveled together ever since. When Cassae took time off to deal with the loss of her family Sovia stepped up to the second-command position. The rest of the grove welcomed the new arrivals and made sure they were both caught up with current events.

The small talk continued as they gathered themselves up and made their way down to the conclave hall. Quinlan again reflected on his concerns about where he really had been during his time off. The changes in the land around the Seyna and the increasing number of weak spots in the flaura indicated something was affecting the energy in the land itself.

The key to keeping Acimasiz confined was the continual flow of energy through the Great Marsh. If the flaura had truly weakened, then the other conclaves must be told and steps must be taken to discover the cause. A shadow began to grow in Quinlan's mind—a shadow he hoped Bertrynn, his friend and immediate superior, could shed some light on. His thoughts returned to the present as *Grove Seven* emerged from the forest and onto the grounds of the Northern West Conclave.

"Shin Lahqui," hailed the gateman as they approached. "Come up and name yourselves."

"Shin Lahqui! Siestrey Quinlan and Northern West Grove Seven, all members reporting for rotation."

"Welcome Siestrey." The gateman cleared them in. "Tretjey Sayon is here and requests a gathering of all grove leaders in the conclave hall before the rotation meeting."

"Very well—gratitude," said Quinlan as he and the others passed into the conclave. He wondered at the special meeting and if there was a connection to his own discoveries in the Great Marsh.

"Why the furrowed brow?" Cassae asked him.

"Tretjey Sayon wanting to speak to the grove leaders, that's odd," he said to them all and after a thoughtful moment turned to Sovia. "Take the grove, gather supplies and what news you can. I will talk with the Tretjey and catch up with you after the meeting."

"It'll be done, brother," replied Sovia.

She and the others moved off to collect patrol supplies and mingle among the ranks to gather the latest news and gossip. Quinlan had a foreboding sense the Tretjey's presence here and the weakening he had found in the Seyna was no coincidence. A million thoughts raced through his head as he entered the hall for a meeting with the leader of the Northern West Conclave of the Order of Arden.

~~*

Chapter Four

Primerey Joseah prepared for her day at the Central Conclave. She often thought the reason to have a leader was to have someone to throw stones at when you're unhappy. Her daily schedule was already planned down to the last minute. She rarely had time anymore to walk the marsh trails she loved so much.

A pregnant young woman waited for her outside of the bedchamber. "Lah ahm, Bekka."

"Lah ahm, Primerey. Did ye sleep well?"

"Wonderfully," she answered. "And you?"

"Only just, ma'am."

"Joseah, Bekka, you can call me Joseah."

"I know I *can*, ma'am, and gratitude, yet it brin's me comfort, if ye dinnae mind."

"Not at all, Bekka," Joseah said. "Are you still having a hard time sleeping?"

"Aye, but nae too bad." Bekka said. "Ma love built a cot and one end sits upright against the wall, so I dinnae have ta sleep lyin' flat."

"Oh, how brilliantly creative. It sounds like he will be a wonderful father. I am so happy for you, Bekka."

"Gratitude, ma'am, I cannae imagine bein' happier. The conclave 'tis a beautiful place ta be raisin' a family."

"I couldn't agree more."

"Little Taryl do be in a rush, truth be told. He be runnin' the marsh trails already and he's nae even out of ma womb."

"Ha ha! You are a blessing of joy from Na'veyja, my dear," Joseah said. "What does our day look like today?"

"A full day again, ma'am," she replied.

"Yes, of course it is. Well, I am famished. Shall we head for the meal hall?"

"Indeed, ma'am, even though I've had a breakfast already"—Bekka patted her swollen belly—"I could do with a second."

"Well, of course," Joseah replied. "Who doesn't appreciate a second breakfast?"

The two women left the private chambers of the Primerey, heading to the meal hall before they started their day of conferences, inquiries, and discussions with various leaders of the Order of Arden.

Later, after Joseah's long day was done, she sat in an open-air pavilion filled with low seats, where druids often came to meditate. A Raskanish man entered the pavilion and sat down beside her.

"Shin Lahqui, Silari," she said.

"Shin Lahqui, Joseah," he replied.

"I remember my time serving as *Segoney*," she said. "The Primerey is the only rank above, yet to this day, I believe the office of Segoney is the most unappreciated position in the Order. The three of you must deal with me here in the Central Conclave, then go and deal with the Tretjeys of each of the three guardian conclaves. And on a regular basis at that. It was maddeningly enjoyable."

"I agree with ye," he replied. "'Tis a pain and pleasure both, and I'd have it nae other way. 'Tis also why, at times, I must disrupt the peaceful afternoon of ma superior."

"Dung," she said.

Silari looked around to see if anyone heard. "Primerey…"

"Oh, pbfff, dung, dung, dung. When you've reached my age you can curse in the meditation pavilion or anywhere else. Cursing is what gets old people out of bed in the morning. Come then, share your dung."

"The *Wardens of the Woods* have sent a message."

"Ech, the War-*dungs*," she said.

Silari broke out in laughter.

"Apologies, my friend, I know of your affinity for them," she said.

"And I, in turn, know of the bad blood between ye, so I dinnae brin' this ta ye lightly."

"Proceed."

"They say *Fairtheora* is in danger."

"From?"

"They dinnae rightly know."

"Unsurprising."

"They warn of more attacks from the dreyg like the one at Cealjin years ago. The druid outposts in the south and southeast have reported foreigners in Shaan. They say the dreyg are in Driftin' Leaf Watershed."

"Nonsense."

"Are ye gonna answer with anythin' but a single word?"

"Perhaps."

"Joseah."

"All right," she said, "The southern outposts, have they sent in groves to investigate?"

"Aye, they were attacked by Shaanlander troops and soldiers in strange grey light armor."

"The dreyg."

"Aye, but why would Shaanlanders attack us?"

"Something ill is at work here, Silari. What news of the Cealjin Delta?"

"A renewed stench comes down from upstream."

Joseah closed her eyes a few minutes. "Send out two groves, one to the Cealjin Delta and one to Drifting Leaf Watershed. I will perform an ethereal separation and inspect the Seyna and Fairtheora. If anything is amiss there, or in the Great Marsh, it should stand visible to my spirit's eye."

"I will send word ta have the groves sent out immediately," he said. "Lah quen, Primerey."

"Gratitude, Silari, lah quen to you."

Joseah sighed, resettled herself, and relaxed. She blended her inner self with the world around her. She cleared a space for her spirit in the ethereal plane between the two realms. She often felt a lifting sensation during the ethereal separation. Her spirit rose from her body until it floated free in the ethereal plane like a spider riding the wind on the end of a silk string.

Joseah's spirit drifted out past the conclave and into the Great Marsh. She tuned in to every aspect of each animal and bird and even the plants themselves. Druids on rotation moved along trails that ran throughout the wetlands and the valley containing them. The reed-filled lowlands gave way to stands of trees filtering the sunlight and farther on to thick forests covered by canopies that almost blocked the sun completely.

Joseah moved her spirit deeper into the Great Marsh. Stands of large trees grew so closely, the deer of the forest could barely run straight. From the ground, one could not see more than two or three layers away in any direction.

A mist hung in the air seeping and flowing over roots and around tree trunks. It pooled in low places obscuring the ground and hiding mud pits. Tributaries and streams housed the aquatic and amphibian life living among the tree roots. The glow of flaura came from everywhere coloring the mist in a myriad of blended colors.

Joseah's spirit eye saw the Seyna rising from the root-covered ground of the Great Marsh. The sacred circular hedge stood tall and curved slightly inward at the top. The glimmer of the flaura was bright and all seemed well. Life nested in the Seyna, life walked around it, life crawled through it, and life called it home.

The area around the base of the hedge was lined by twisted brambles and pits of quick mud. The area within the Seyna was filled with vine-covered trees, thick snarly brush, and massive roots intertwined and covered with moss like a pit of giant green pythons.

Joseah let her spirit drift in place to admire the scene before her. An oak tree larger than any ever to exist on Arden grew in the middle of the sacred circular hedge.

Fairtheora, the living oak prison of Acimasiz, stood in the geographical center of the Seyna and the conclave grounds surrounding it as well. Na'veyja cast most of her ethereal essence into the wood of the tree when she and the Gwylari trapped Acimasiz within. The flaura of Na'veyja's grace ran bright all the way into the upper branches and out into the leaves. Layers of stout vines encased Fairtheora's trunk to protect it from cutting. Not a thing had changed since she did her last ethereal inspection of the Order of Arden's confinement complex.

Acimasiz was still confined inside Fairtheora, shielded by the Seyna in the middle of the Great Marsh, encircled by the conclave grounds and an army of guardian druids.

Then why do these nagging visions of fire and smoke still plague my dreams and harass my meditations over the past month? her spirit wondered. *Should I tell Silari and the other council members? Should I heed the Warden's warning? Are they more than just rogue druids?*

Joseah spread her awareness out past the Seyna in all directions at once. No concern became visible to her spirit's eye as she held her focus for a while longer. She saw a druid with a staff traveling the trails of the Great Marsh alone. She wondered why his grove was not with him. He stopped and chanted by the Seyna and filled a spot where the plants had died. Such occurrences were not unheard of, but had been uncommon until the alarming increases of dead or dying plants in the Seyna over the recent months.

Is there a connection between my visions and what is happening to the plants of the Seyna? I must look further.

She focused on the plants of the Seyna, touching roots, stems, and leaves with her spirit. The druid's staff burst briefly with silvery-white light like sunlight glinting off milky quartz. A plant began to glow with the same light and then many dozens of plants around the Seyna pulsed once in succession and dimmed leading to where the druid with the staff stood now.

How many plants have withered unknown to me? Why have I not seen this before? Was it the staff? Did it show it to me? What else have I not seen?

Joseah concentrated her spirit's eye on Fairtheora. The glowing flaura flow shimmered as it moved in and around Fairtheora. The shifting movement was filled with ebbs and flows of colors and hues. Joseah always found it mesmerizing and calming.

A spark suddenly popped off the trunk and sailed through the flaura. The spark startled Joseah and chased away the peaceful moment. Another spark flew off the tree and then five more. Soon the sparks became constant, shooting away in sparkling showers.

No! she screamed in her mind, but her spirit could take no action.

The sparks on Fairtheora ignited into flames which quickly engulfed the tree. The flames roared and grew until they exploded from the tree in a globe of fire. The inferno passed through her spirit in a flash and was gone. Fairtheora stood before her whole, unharmed, and wrapped in Na'veyja's grace.

Joseah was stunned by what she had seen. Never before had the visions fire and smoke included Fairtheora. Hesitantly she tried to spread her awareness again. She reached out with her spirit and held it extended once more. Only the deep quiet of the Great Marsh remained as it had for generations.

She called her spirit back and closed the space between realms. Now that her body and spirit had been reunited, Joseah opened her eyes. She sat and thought about her ethereal journey. She was not sure how to interpret the vision she had of Fairtheora.

Is the fire symbolic and of what? Are these visions portents of things to come? Surely Fairtheora is protected well enough. Na'veyja herself stands guard within and the Order stands vigilant without. I should tell Silari and the druid council of my visions.

The sound of people moving around the pavilion drew her back to the present. Druids walked among the woods, conversed on druid matters, with peace and contentment everywhere.

No, no need to share my visions of fire and smoke yet, she thought. *It would cause a panic. I will keep my own council on this. I will tell them of the Seyna and the increasing deaths of plants there. We must investigate that much more closely.* Joseah left the pavilion feeling positive about the decision. *Yes, but we shall do so without those woodland heretics, the Wardens.*

Silari walked out of a building with a group of clerical staff as the day had ended and it was time for the evening meal.

"Joseah! Join us," he called to her.

She waved and caught up with them.

"How was yer journey?" he asked.

"Everything is as it should be, Sil," she replied. "All is well with Fairtheora and I see only a small issue where the Seyna is concerned. We should increase grove patrols of the inner trails along the Seyna's perimeter and council them to be vigilant of even the smallest changes."

"Very good then," he said. "I'll put the Warden's message down as the ramblin's of storm crows."

"Yes, all is well," she said again. "Tell me, who is the druid with the walking staff familiar?"

"He is called Quinlan, comes from Calamere in Vakere."

"The site of the red plague years ago?"

"Aye."

"What conclave?"

"Northern West."

"That's Tretjey Sayon. Send word to Sayon. I would like to speak with him."

"I'll set it up."

"Thank you, Sil. Now let's eat!"

~~*

Chapter Five

Quinlan made his way to the upper walkway which ran along the perimeter of the compound. The opposite side of the compound was far enough away, people who walked there were nothing more than vague shapes and colors even to his keen eyes. The meeting chamber of the Adjutant was across the compound from the entrance he and Grove Seven had used, and many of the grove leaders had already gathered. He identified himself to the attendant at the door and entered the chamber, which was filled with a number of grove leaders that was far beyond normal. Animal and bird familiars moved about the chamber tending to the various errands of the druids inside.

The fact that Tretjey Sayon would personally address a standard rotation meeting with the Northern West grove leaders was highly unusual. The normal protocol would be to channel news from the Central Conclave through the two Adjutant Tretjeys, which in this case were a man named Zendis and a woman named Clarin. Quinlan was surprised to see that both Adjutants were present as was Tretjey Sayon, which only increased his curiosity.

"Quin!" a familiar voice called out to him. He turned and saw a Raskanish man wave to him from a table not too far away. A full red beard sprouted from the man's face like a bed of fire moss gone haywire. Shoulder-length hair matched the color and scraggly nature of the beard, which combined, left nothing but a nose and a pair of deep green eyes to show through the mass. Occasionally a hole formed to allow food and drink in or to let words and laughter out. Quinlan waved back and headed to the table surrounded by nine chairs, five of which were already taken.

"Bertrynn, you old stump!" Quinlan grinned as he grasped the man's forearm and gave him a friendly shoulder slap. "I see you haven't trimmed that bird's nest under your nose."

"Where else would I keep last week's soup?" Bertrynn countered loud enough for half the chamber to hear him. Quinlan was always surprised when a voice that loud came through so much hair. "Well met, ma friend. Ye know everyone?" He indicated the rest of the druids at the table.

A Vakerian woman stood and held out her arms as he came to the table. "Greetings, Quin."

"Lissa," he said and wrapped her up in a warm embrace. "Ha ha, you are more radiant than ever."

"And *you* are a wonderful liar, Quinlan," she said with a smile. Lissa had the olive skin and dark hair of the Vakerian people, but had unusually light irises turning the typically brown eyes into hues of tan and gold.

"Brother Tomas, good to see you." Quinlan took the forearm of a fellow Dayne kinsman. Tomas was a Vakerian man of average build, with long dark brown hair worn loose to fall about his shoulders and brown eyes so dark one could barely tell iris from pupil.

"Lah ahm, brother Quin." Tomas smiled.

"And Sander, you should be off duty, yes?" Quinlan asked a Kalnuvian man who reached across the table to grasp forearms.

"Yah, I was, but they called in all grove leaders, whether they be on duty or not," Sander said.

"And they didn't want us making a lot of noise about it, either," a second Vakerian man added. The man stood to greet Quinlan as he spoke.

"Tarrick, compliments on getting the command of your own grove." Quinlan took the man's arm.

Tarrick seemed to be a scrawny young man at first glance, but his slender frame held the kind of speed and agility most people could only dream of. His hair was a shade or two lighter than that of a swarthy Vakerian and he had blue eyes telling of mixed blood somewhere in his lineage.

"My gratitude to you, Quin." He nodded. "I couldn't have done it without your help."

"Yes, you could've," Quinlan said with no room for doubt. "But I was glad to help."

"Oh, and I suppose that Quin here was the only one ta help ye out, laddie?" Bertrynn asked in mock dismay. "I am wounded ta ma very heart."

"My undying gratitude to you as well, Cetrey Bertrynn," Tarrick said graciously.

"I heard Tyrosi passed away right after gaining the office of *Segoney*." Quinlan took a seat at the table.

"Aye, 'twas a sad day," Bertrynn replied. "'Tis a horror ta see a person suffer through the wastin' sickness."

"Yes, it nearly destroyed Cassae watching it take her children."

"I'd forgotten 'bout that," Bertrynn said. "I cannae imagine her pain."

Quinlan thought of the day he met Tyrosi. He and his father had traveled to hear him speak. "I remember meeting Tyrosi and you as well at a market fair when I was young."

"Aye, lad, I remember. Back when the red plague threatened the southern coastlands."

"I thought I'd never return home and that Calamere was gone forever."

"That nasty red ooze of Acimasiz stood nary a chance against the healin' powers of Na'veyja," Bertrynn said proudly. "Two years it took us, though, ta heal that festerin' river delta and put an end ta its vileness."

"A little over two, yes," Quinlan answered, "but the game and sea life took twice as long to return. I had started my training by then. Dad and I decided I should stay at the conclave when they went back to Calamere."

"A choice I thank Na'veyja fer every day, even though I missed yer folks when they left."

"Yes, the first few months being separated from them were hard to bear, but I knew the sea called to my dad louder with every day he was not on a ship."

"We all must follow our own callin'," replied Bertrynn.

"Have any of you noticed the group of Gwylari over there?" Lissa asked the group.

"No." Sander peered around. "Where?"

"Front row, far left." She pointed to the front of the chamber. "They all bear the mark of leadership from different tribes."

"Perhaps they consult with the Central Conclave," Tomas wondered out loud.

"One more oddity among recent many," Quinlan said cryptically.

"How s—" Bertrynn stopped midquestion.

"May we join yer table?" asked one of two Raskanish women who emerged from the throng of druids. They both bore the forest, mahogany, and amber color pattern of the Northern East Conclave along the edge of their raiments.

"Aye, and welcome!" Bertrynn answered. "Come sit down."

"Gratitude. I am Wylla and here is Freyn," said the woman who had first spoken. Wylla was small in stature with grey eyes shrouded by straight light brown hair lightening to blond on the outer layers.

"Shin Lahqui," Freyn said to the group as she took a seat at the table. She was taller than Wylla by nearly a head, which brought her close to Quinlan's height. Dull blond hair was pulled back from a gaunt face. She looked like she could stand a meal or two in a row to be more than mere bones. Calm light brown eyes, however, held a healthy spirit that stood out in contrast to her lean features.

"Ye birds are far from home," Bertrynn said after he made the introductions around the table.

"Aye, we were midjourney with a supply caravan when we got the call ta gather. We never would've made the gatherin' at our own conclave in time," Wylla told them.

"A gatherin' at yer conclave as well?" Bertrynn asked.

"Aye, at all three," Wylla answered.

Bertrynn and Quinlan shared a look of mild surprise. Quinlan was about to speak when Adjutant Tretjey Zendis called the meeting to order.

"Druids, brothers, and sisters, please be paying attention to Tretjey Sayon," the second-in-command of the Northern West Conclave called out to the assembly before he stepped away from the lectern.

Sayon stepped up to address the gathering of druids. "As you all can see, we have a few more in number than usual today." His voice held an edge of sarcasm. "And there is much to discuss. Sadly, I fear there will be more questions at this gathering than answers, so let's begin. There have been disturbing rumors from both within the Seyna compound and outside of it. We believe there has been a disturbance in the Great Marsh and a withering of plant life along the Seyna boundary."

A surge of comments and questions went through the gathering.

"Is it the dreyg?" someone asked from the group.

"Surely not! The henchmen of Acimasiz were driven from Arden generations ago," said another.

"It is being discussed at the Central Conclave. One option is Acimasiz may have found a way to contact the dreyg from inside

Fairtheora." Sayon barely got the last part out before another stronger outburst from the group.

"How? We have been diligent in our duty!"

"*No!*"

"There is no way in!"

"The Seyna is secure!"

Any other comments were lost when the noise of outrage blended into chaos. Zendis and Clarin stepped up with Sayon to calm the commotion and finally regained order in the chamber.

"Focus, please! Let me speak," Sayon roared until it was quiet. "We must be aware of every aspect of our duty and not grow complacent. We need to refocus our vigilance. Put no action beyond Acimasiz to escape, for he most assuredly seeks to do so every day."

"How can Acimasiz influence the world outside when he is confined within Fairtheora?" someone in the gathering asked.

"That answer is unknown and one that must be discovered in great haste. Certain groves will be pulled from rotation and assigned special duties to this end. This is a time when all of us need to double our efforts to be prepared even when all is quiet."

"What signs have been seen?" another druid asked.

"Recall the red plague that swept along the Vakerian coastline not too long ago? We discovered it was not only an attack upon the fertility of the sea and the life within but an effort to poison the land as well. The dreyg meant to cripple the environmental food chain at the most basic level."

"But we stopped the red plague and cured the delta of its vile taint," Tomas said.

"Yes, that is correct, and since then the forces of Acimasiz have not been idle. They have not sat back to lick their wounds. They work tirelessly to free their lord. Records that have been kept since the Order's beginning show animals have recently abandoned ages-old territories and habitats. Our long-range scouts report migration patterns have changed in these areas as well. Communes with Na'veyja show us poisoned lands and waters beyond our awareness, of black mists gathering in desolate areas, and once-fertile lands now withering to dust."

"Tretjey Sayon!" Bertrynn requested to speak.

"Cetrey Bertrynn," Sayon recognized his question.

"How can the black clouds of Acimasiz form leagues away when he is confined right here in our compound?" Bertrynn asked, which was followed by murmurous agreement.

"That remains unknown, but we believe it is evidence the dreyg are at work. The Primerey has looked with her spirit's eye and assures us Acimasiz is still held within Fairtheora."

"What of the Overlords?" one man called out.

"Acimasiz's overlords and their mercenaries, the dreyg, have not been heard of in recent decades even though their black clouds of poisoned mist have never truly vanished from the far reaches. But now, we know his overlords continue to work diligently and have, truth be told, returned to Arden in a new guise. They hide in plain sight as Disciples of Nemilos, architects of renown from the southern continent. Their trickery runs deep and they have not shown their true nature to the lords of Arden."

"Architects? What benefit is that to them?" a grey-haired woman asked from across the chamber.

"We believe their goal is to worm their way into the realms of Arden with the purpose of destroying the deep woods and replacing them with wide roads and sprawling cities, thus weakening Na'veyja's power. Even as we speak today, areas of the deep woods are under attack on many fronts. We must inform the lords of Arden of the dire consequences and convince them to halt the destruction."

Lissa raised a hand and spoke out. "How can this be? Are not the lords of Arden still friends to the Order?"

A look of disappointment passed across Sayon's face before he replied. "Sadly, our influence has waned recently with the courts of Shaan and the minor houses of Raskan. Raskan now stands on the edge of civil war. I believe the disciples have orchestrated this. They sow the seeds of distrust and their crop grows strong. The Vakere and the Kalnu still support the Order's cause and hear Na'veyja's call." He pointed to a woman at a front table who raised a hand. "Yes?"

"But, both Raskan and Shaan standin' alone are far greater in number than Vakere, Kalnu, and the Order combined. If they choose ta destroy the deep woods within their own territories, how could we possibly stop them?"

"As I said at the beginning, this gathering will likely produce more questions than answers," Sayon said. "We need to work harder than ever to find the answers. If the plants and animals of our world are destroyed, we *will* soon follow."

"Tretjey Sayon." Quinlan raised his hand and was recognized. "Where do we begin?"

"Our main concern must be the integrity of the Seyna. Our diligence must not falter! Through our efforts in Na'veyja's name, the Seyna will remain strong. We will continue to investigate and monitor the matters in the south. Stay aware of this first and foremost as you go about your duties and lend a keen eye to even the smallest disruption in the flaura. Small clues will lead us to bigger answers. Those of you placed on special duty—it will be explained when you pick up your patrol orders and log books. Peace be with you all."

"Well," Bertrynn said as he turned to the group around the table, "a very big meetin' with very few answers."

"A whisper of early warnin' is better than a later shout of urgency," Freyn replied.

"Agreed—and well said Freyn." Quinlan nodded. "With my own eyes, I have seen plants withered almost to rot when the surrounding brush is alive and well. I fear we are missing something."

"Such as?" Sander asked.

"If I knew what it was, it wouldn't be missing." Quinlan smiled lightly. "I believe we are healing the symptoms, not the illness. We must look deeper."

"As long as the Seyna is healthy, there shouldn't be a problem," Tarrick said.

"That is the point exactly," Quinlan responded, but with a different meaning. "Perhaps the Seyna isn't as healthy as we think and we simply don't know it yet."

"I think the true nature of the gathering will be better known after we get our orders." Tomas stood. "May Na'veyja smile on you until we gather again."

"Shin Lahqui brother," Quinlan said with a wave as the others replied to Tomas.

"Aye, we too must be on our way," Wylla said as she and Freyn rose to leave. "We've a lon' path ta travel yet before our feet rest at home's hearth."

Bertrynn stood to bid them farewell. "Well met, then, Wylla and Freyn. May yer trails be clear and yer feet swift." His sentiments were echoed by all.

"Gratitude, friends. Na'veyja's grace light yer ways," she replied.

"Well, shall we go see what the Central Conclave has in mind for us?" Tarrick asked.

"Oh, I already know." Quinlan grinned and pretended to read imaginary patrol orders. "I'm to inspect the loom trees to make sure they are putting out an adequate amount of shade."

"Ha! Only in yer dreams, laddie," Bertrynn scoffed. "Listen, Quin, that new lass who made yer grove, maybe we ought ta swap her out fer someone more experienced fer this rotation."

Quinlan shook his head and countered fluidly. "I see a good opportunity to teach a young druid how to recognize and interact with Na'veyja's energy. The knowledge to call the flaura has to be—"

Bertrynn tossed a hand up to quiet him. "All right, Quin, all right! Stubborn as an oak, ye are. Guess I know where ye get that from."

"Truly, Bert, I can't imagine a better place for Ticca than with us," Quinlan said.

"Aye, ye're probably right. Usually are. So be it." Bertrynn grasped Quinlan's forearm and gave him a solid embrace. "Go carefully out there, Quin."

"And you." Quinlan clapped him on the shoulder before he turned away. "Tarrick, may your grove grow strong."

Tarrick took Quinlan's outstretched hand. "Blue skies and bright sun for yours, my friend."

Quinlan hugged Lissa and turned to those at the table. "Fair paths to all."

The group bid him farewell. He picked up his order packet and logbook on his way out to meet up with the rest of Grove Seven.

~~*

Chapter Six

The rags she had wrapped around her feet were soaked, mud-covered, and barely protected her at all, but they kept out some of the early season chill. Trousers of woven flax were tucked into the rags that were wrapped and tied around her calves. A jerkin of the same fabric hung in tatters past her waist. The ragged, unfinished sleeves fell just past her elbows. The remnant of the woven flax fabric covering some of her shoulders and most of her head was tied snuggly under her chin. The clothing was a loose weave and the cold morning wind seemed to blow clean through her body, chilling her to the bone.

The city she called home came into view. She wanted nothing more than to march straight up to the gate, identify herself, and go through, but it would blow a cover persona she took great pains to create. She had to stay in character as she moved through Cammachmoor or risk being compromised.

She reached the outer wall of Raskan's capital city and the guard post there. All citizens of Raskan were allowed inside the village minor, where mostly the barnyards, butchery, stables, and smithy were located. The area also included a *hiremen house* where one could find a free cot and meal if needed or work if one wanted. Every major city in Raskan had a hiremen house in the village minor to help avoid a stagnant population.

The village proper was through the next guard post. No livestock was allowed into the village proper. Anyone who wanted to pass the guardpost had to be a citizen of the city; have authorized entry from a citizen; or show permits to do business with the citizens. Dressed as she was and without her papers of residence, she would never be allowed to pass.

Dirty and disheveled, no one even looked her way as she walked down a path leading to where the city's garbage was mulched and turned to compost. Hunger pangs turned her stomach into knots. She was so hungry, even the stench of rotting garbage made her mouth water.

She went past the last garbage piles, slipped around a large boulder, and squeezed through a thin crack to end up in a narrow alley behind a building inside the village proper. She could not relax yet. Her journey through the capital had just begun and now she had to stay within the shadows, or be caught.

The village proper held a large population and covered much ground. Beyond was the keep and castle grounds, where the guard patrols tripled. Beyond still lay her goal of the castle *Torr Amhairc* and her rooms within. The way she saw it, getting into the castle unnoticed would be her greatest test yet.

The main part of the village, the keep and castle grounds and even the outer castle walls were no match for her prowess. She moved through the castle halls avoiding guard patrols and the occasional person wandering by. The room she needed was now right down the hall. After waiting for one more patrol to pass, she snuck up to the door and slid a couple of small metal wands into the door lock. Five seconds later, she was inside the room with the door closed and locked.

She smiled, sighed happily, and calmly walked over to a table stocked with a few food items.

"Bless yer heart, Marteen," she said to an absent woman whom she knew had left the food.

She picked up a fuzzy red round fruit and bit deeply into the plump flesh. The fruit's juice ran down her chin, neck, and hands at first bite. The taste was so overwhelming; it almost brought her to tears.

"Ohh..." she moaned and devoured the rest of the fruit. She took a knife from the table and cut through the protective wax layers of a cheese round. She filled both cheeks with cheese as she pulled a wicker lid off a basket to see what was inside.

"Bread!" She ripped off a chunk and tore into it.

She tilted a pitcher, pouring water into a glass. She filled the crevasses of her food-stuffed mouth with the water and mashed everything together trying not to choke in the process.

The hunger momentarily satisfied, she peeled the rags from her body and threw them into a corner. She drew a bath from the large cauldron housed behind the fireplace to warm the water. The cauldron was connected to a valve placed over the edge of the bathing tub. Soaking in the warm bath, she was glad she only had one homeless waif persona to maintain. The destitute lived a bleak existence.

Freshly fed and bathed, she put on her uniform and left her rooms. She would have loved to sleep for even an hour, but there wasn't time. A large man with deep red hair was walking down the hallway as she came out.

"Lady Ronirah, pleasant evenin' ta ye." The man bowed as she walked by.

"And ta ye as well, General Gilburl."

Ascending the upper levels, she entered the council chamber to find she was the first to arrive. She barely had time to fill a glass with wine before she was joined by a man dressed in a uniform matching hers.

"Well, well, well..." Saith Callan said as he walked into the chamber. The man apparently couldn't resist taunting her at every chance. "If 'tis nae wanderin' Ronni MacRory herself." His voice held as much contempt as the look on his face. "Takin' a break from yer slummin', lass?"

"Piss off, Saith," she said with matching contempt. "I'm in nae mood fer yer shite, moron."

"Ooh, 'scuse me, I've forgotten yer a—*milady.*" He clearly meant to insult her.

"Yer jealousy disgusts me." She turned her back on him. Knowing him, he was picturing some kind of harm being done to her. Yet, he could not openly move against her without risking his position and lands. She enjoyed toying with Saith, but she had similar limits on how far she could go without risking her own status. Even being of royal blood as she was, she was so far down the family tree, Ronirah knew she would never advance any closer to the throne than she had already.

The two officers were counterparts in the Raskan Foreign and Political Affairs Bureau and each had their own network of agents, but that's where the similarity ended.

Captain Ronirah MacRory knew Saith's method of operation was far different from hers. Her focus was on the kingdom of Shaan, enemies they were currently at peace with. She was well versed in the art of disguise and subterfuge. The agents under her command were trained in her methods. They infiltrated Shaan, monitored military operations, reported back to her, and she to the minister of foreign affairs.

Captain Saith Callan oversaw covert operations within the kingdom boundaries in order to protect it from domestic threats and covertly monitor the comings and goings of the minor houses of Raskan. The methods he preferred were bribery and coercion. She knew him to be a skilled interrogator as were the agents under his command.

The door opened and a guardsman swung it wide and stepped back to attention. King Renalth MacRory of Raskan entered the room followed by his foreign affairs minister, Modgrin Macreeth.

Ronirah and Saith both snapped to attention and bowed sharply as he entered. "Sire!"

"Captains," he said, "as ye were."

Renalth had been king for eight years now, but he still preferred the furs and leathers of Raskanish tradition over the silks and satins of most royal courts.

"Captain MacRory, yer report, if ye please."

Ronirah moved to a table topped with a map of the entire northern continent. "The Shaanlanders have cleared the woods up ta the border, here and here."

She pointed to two valleys on both sides of a mountain range crossing Raskan and extending into Shaan territory.

"Right up ta our very toes," Renalth said.

"They'll be steppin' on our very toes if they get much closer," Modgrin replied.

"Even though the cuttin' stopped when they reached Raskan land, their work camps grow daily as do the guard outposts."

"Did ye get a count?" Modgrin asked.

"Aye, Minister, six outposts now, a thousand men at each."

"Six thousand troops?" Renalth seemed mildly surprised.

"Stables goin' up at three outposts, Sire."

"That means cavalry," Modgrin said.

"Aye, but nae enough ta invade," Renalth replied. "We still outnumber them and have the high ground."

Ronirah wondered if she should tell them of what she saw or actually thought she saw. Modgrin was watching her when she looked up.

"Something else, Captain?"

"I'm unsure, Minister, but I believe one of the Tenneth royal family was in the Shaanlander capital of Trossachsmuir."

"Why would ye think that?"

"Do ye recall the crippled lad?"

"Garett fell from his horse when he was youn'," Saith said.

"Aye, and Lord Tenneth had a carriage built so it'd be easier fer him ta get in and out," she added.

"Right, I remember the carriage," Modgrin said.

"'Twas the carriage I saw go through the streets. Cannae say as ta who was inside. I tried ta follow but lost them."

"Now, what would the royal family of a Raskanish minor house be doin' in Shaan?" Renalth asked.

"Here's a curious thin', Sire. One of our men was found dead in the Grannagh capital of Glen Arwe," Saith said. "He was stationed there under the guise of a merchant. The word just came overnight. He appears ta've been robbed, but now with Captain MacRory's report, I think he may've found somethin' and was murdered fer it."

"Ye think they'll take up with Shaan?" Renalth asked.

"If they do, we'll be fightin' skirmishes on both sides: the Shaan outposts ta the southwest and the Raskan minor houses ta the east. The Shaanlander main forces'll come straight up the middle, ye can be sure." Modgrin tapped the map table for emphasis.

"'Tis nae secret they've been wantin' ta secede from Raskan. Shaan'll grant them their ancestral lands, nae doubt." Renalth studied the map. "Give me yer assessment, Captain MacRory"

Ronirah quickly scanned the map so she could give her best recommendation based on the intelligence she had recently gathered. The largest portion of Raskan held the capital city of Cammachmoor and the ancestral lands of the House MacRory. The rest of the kingdom included the three provinces belonging to the minor Houses of the Grannagh, Tenneth, and Bothain. Lastly, there were the five fiefdoms of Hest, Cromarty, Inverbehg, Aonghus, and Colquenagh.

Shaan held the capital city of Trossachsmuir and the ancestral lands of House Tavish, the two provinces of Cavall and Hevonen, and the three fiefdoms of Soen, MacAlaway, and Cambeul.

She realized all three of the Raskanish minor houses were on the east side of the kingdom and Shaan to the south.

"Sire, the potential threat from Shaan cannae be ignored if any *one* of the minor houses were ta join with them and turn against us, let alone two or all three houses."

Renalth's frown deepened. "What of House Bothain, Captain Callan?"

"My agents report the border outposts and outlyin' roads are bein' repaired. They say 'tis an effort ta beautify the province. I say that's a load of manure. They either see somethin' comin' or they're a part of it."

"Our position dinnae improve with this news, Sire," Modgrin said.

"There's somethin' else, Sire," Ronirah said.

"Tell of it."

"The Shaanlanders executed two men in the public square the day afore I left."

"Nothin' new there," Saith said and smiled.

Modgrin silenced him with a look.

"Continue, Captain," Renalth said.

"Black as shadows they were, Sire. One so dark I could nae see the lines of his face 'til he was brought inta the light ta face the block."

Renalth and Modgrin exchanged looks upon hearing her news.

"Ye're nae surprised, Minister. Ye know of them then?"

"By word only, but sounds ta me they're men from the southern continent," he replied.

"Southern continent, same as those disciples?" she asked.

"Aye."

"One of them was there. He was the one presidin' over it."

"An architect presidin' over an execution, Sire?" Modgrin looked at Renalth intently for a moment.

"It seems the disciples have a bit more than the king's ear these days," Renalth said. "They've taken his mind and his heart."

"Ye turned away the disciple who came here..." Ronirah's voice trailed off as a memory surfaced. "Sire," she quickly finished.

"Aye, I dinnae care fer the smell of him." Renalth grinned. "Besides, any man who talks of clear-cuttin' my highlands is nae friend of mine, lassie! I mean—Captain."

"Kenri'll be glad ta hear that, Sire." She meant it to be an informal comment about the druid.

"Kenri's the one who told me ta expect him," Renalth replied.

"The druid told ye ta expect an architect?" she asked. "Ha, I think the old mystic has overcooked his noodles."

Renalth turned his countenance upon her. "Tread lightly, Captain. Regardless of the growin' disdain fer the Order across the rest of Arden, Kenri and the druids are still friends of Raskan—and of mine."

"Yer pardon, Sire, I dinnae mean ta show disrespect."

"Interestin' 'twas though"—Modgrin crossed his arms and eased a butt cheek up to lean on the map table, which groaned in protest of the man's weight—"ta see the flicker of surprise run across the disciple's face when he saw Kenri standin' alongside us."

"Surprise that let his hatred fer the druid ta show through a moment," Renalth said. "Lends credence ta what Kenri tells us."

"That the disciples are overlords of an ancient and evil god, disguised as architects who're out ta cut down all our woods?" Saith took a turn at being skeptical. "Sire, that's—"

"Very difficult ta believe, aye, I know, lad," he replied. "Regardless of what we believe, though, the disciples do all but sit on the throne in Shaan."

"The deep woods in Shaan are nearly gone," Ronirah said, "and the disciples've been there barely a year now."

Renalth repeated Kenri's favorite saying. "Ye kill the trees and ye'll kill the world and all who sit upon it."

"I fear King Traelin Tavish has become a puppet of the Disciples of Nemilos," Modgrin said.

"And I'll nae be their next fool," Renalth said. "Did that disciple leave Raskan, Captain Callan?"

"No, Sire, he's still in Glen Arwe."

"Is he now?" Renalth seemed pleased by that news. "Minister Macreeth, inform General Gilburl and ask him ta extend an invitation ta the man."

"Aye, we could do that, Sire"—Modgrin nodded—"but if the disciple says nae?"

"Ask him again at sword point."

"We take him out in the open then the people of Glen Arwe'll be askin' questions. Questions we should avoid fer the time bein', Sire."

"Minister, I could have ma men grab him with no one the wiser we're lookin' fer him," Saith said.

Modgrin looked to Renalth.

The king nodded. "All right, do it. I've questions of my own ta ask the man. There're grim days ahead, I think. We best nae get caught with our hands under our arses when they come."

Ronirah thought about that a moment before she pointed to several areas on the southern border of Raskan. "Sire, we could post scouts at these positions ta watch fer troop movements alon' the border with Shaan. That should give us some advance warnin'."

Saith Callen nodded as he leaned over the map table. "I'll send men, Sire."

"Nae Captain," Renalth replied, "Yer task is ta apprehend the disciple in Glen Arwe. Captain MacRory'll handle the scouts."

Ronirah straightened up and bowed sharply. "Gratitude Sire, I'll get ma agents afield at once. If any forces approach, we'll know well ahead of time."

Chapter Seven

The orders in Quinlan's packet were not what he was expecting and he wasn't pleased with them at all. Once he read them he doubled back to the conclave hall. He waited outside Tretjey Sayon's audience chamber for his chance to speak with his superior, Adjutant Tretjey Clarin, who was currently inside.

The doors opened after what seemed to Quinlan as nothing short of an hour, yet in truth, barely a quarter of that had passed since he arrived. Zendis, Clarin, and the Gwylari leaders from the meeting emerged from the office.

"Siestrey Quinlan?"

"Lah ahm, Adjutant Clarin, I was told you'd be here. May I speak with you?"

"Your timing is terrible, Siestrey. I have only the briefest of moments."

"I feel the Seyna is weakening."

The entire group stopped at his words and even Tretjey Sayon, who was at the door, came out to hear. He motioned the group and Quinlan to step inside and closed the doors.

"Continue," Clarin said to Quinlan.

"More and more plants are dying among the Seyna when none should even be in ill health. I have found unusual patterns in where and when the plants die. There is a strange feel to the flaura when I mend these plants—as if some force works against me."

"Yes, and of course he does, doesn't he?" Sayon asked him. "As an eternal being of the Vast, Acimasiz will never stop trying to escape."

"My orders are to travel, Tretjey. May I ask they be changed so I can continue my watch over these areas?"

"There are more than enough druids here to take over your watch, Siestrey," Sayon said. "There are important matters afar we need adept brethren to lay eyes on and report back what they find or be able to take any necessary action. This is critical to our ongoing plans."

"I agree indeed, but I feel I could be of greater benefit here. To continue to watch over areas I have—"

"And it is vital, *Siestrey Quinlan*, that we gather knowledge from afar. Would it be prudent of us to focus only on the Seyna and see not what goes on around us?"

Quinlan found wisdom in his statement even though Order of Arden teachings stated Fairtheora and the Seyna were of the greatest priority. "No, it wouldn't be."

Sayon answered in a calm but firm voice. "The druids who wander the land tell of distant disasters they believe have been created by the dreyg. We need groves to investigate, report back, and where possible, begin to heal the land. The health of the land is of primary importance to all who dwell upon it. Some days, I fear we druids and the Gwylari are the only ones who remember the ancient threat."

Clarin moved in and placed a hand on his shoulder. "Quin, your grove and the other groves with the same assignment were chosen for important reasons. We need to send capable groves of druids out to these threatened areas to identify the threats and be able to confront them. The same method was used to confront and destroy the red plague that attacked your childhood city of Calamere years ago. Now, it is your turn to provide much-needed aid to others."

The thought of aiding people who'd been run out of their homes by the poisoned mists of Acimasiz struck a chord with Quinlan. The druids were the only ones to respond to Calamere's need. They drove back the red plague and eliminated the source, healing the land in hope it would never return.

Sayon walked to a mural of Fairtheora on the wall. "Centuries ago, we imprisoned Acimasiz to protect the people of Arden. Even though many of them now shun us and no longer believe in the ancient threat, we cannot turn our backs on them now."

"Of course not," Quinlan said. "Please, forgive my arrogance, Tretjey, and gratitude for your council. I am honored to give aid to any who need it."

Clarin patted his shoulder and moved off. "I have much confidence in you and Grove Seven, Quinlan. I sense there is great potential within." She walked with Quinlan to the door. "Send élan with reports as frequently as you can. Go carefully, my friend."

"Gratitude, we shall. Fair paths to you."

Quinlan left the chamber and made his way down from the upper levels before he let his disappointment show. He stopped at ground level to collect his thoughts.

"Dung!" was the first thing that came to mind and out of his mouth.

"Can't be as bad as all that."

Quinlan turned to see Lissa coming down the same stairway right behind him.

"Heard that, eh?"

"Yep—ha ha." She stopped one step up from him so they were eye to eye. "What turns your mind to cursing this early in the day, Quin?"

"I have orders to travel southwest and seek a fen where the plants have gone fatal to the touch."

"And this shadows your heart? For what reason? A worthy quest in the eyes of most. You have a chance to leave routine behind and challenge the blight of Acimasiz directly."

"Yet, such is what I feel I do"—he emphatically pointed at the ground—"right here." He regretted the words even as he spoke them.

"Ah, ah, ah," she teased him. "The smaller self..."

"Leaves room for the greater spirit," he finished. "Yes, I know. It is not out of arrogance I grumble, Lissa, but from concern, there is danger that none other seems vexed by."

"The Seyna has stood for an age, Quin. It will still be here when you return. Complete your quest swiftly and come back to continue your vigilance all the quicker."

"Positive as usual, Lissa. What of your grove, travel or home?"

"Grove Twelve and I travel south to Hearth's Port, then northeast up past Cealjin Delta." She glanced at him as she spoke. "Rumors of strange sightings in the delta have been heard and black mists have been seen farther upriver. We go to find the cause."

"Oh, I see," he said. "They send you to our homeland and send me to the far end of Shaan."

"Sorry, Quin."

"Ehh, worry not, Lissa. I need to remember the battle against the ancient threat has to be fought on many fronts. Perhaps the answers we seek for questions here are to be found elsewhere."

"You may have the right of it there. Well, I have to go. Twelve waits upon my return. This is for you, Quin"—she kissed him—"and this is for Cassae." She hugged him. "Give her my love."

"I will, and I know she returns it. May you have clear skies and fair paths all the way to Vakere."

"The same for you to the southwest. See you in a month or so." She waved and was soon gone from view.

A short walk and brief thoughts brought Quinlan to the commissary staging area where groves going on duty could gather supplies. He found the rest of Grove Seven preparing for the trails when he got there.

He gave Cassae a hug. "That was from Lissa."

"Oh, that's sweet of the girl. How's she fairin' these days?"

"She's well—she heads to Vakere and beyond in search of rumored black mists past the Cealjin."

"Ugh! That poor place may never be free of its curse and taint. And what of Grove Seven?"

"We travel." He clapped his hands twice. "All right, druids, change of plans," he said as they came together. "Pick out your mounts and pack for a long journey."

"Horses? Where we be off to?" asked Sovia.

"Northern Shaan."

"Shaan?" Cassae asked.

"Yes, the council has ordered us to reconnoiter and evaluate Drifting Leaf Watershed."

"Driftin' Leaf? That's a fortnight's ride from here," Kian said.

Ticca couldn't hold back her excitement. "Two weeks on horseback? How wonderful!"

Quinlan smiled at her enthusiasm and felt slightly embarrassed at his own misgivings about their assignment.

"Are we ta survey and report only?" Therin asked.

"No, we are to take action if warranted and possible," Quinlan replied. "Sovia—"

"Right!" Sovia got the grove moving. "Kian, take Ticari and Ticca. Go to the commissary and get seeds and sprouts to be growing our vittles with. Enough for nine for a moon's time, mind you."

"Aye, Sovia," Kian said. "All right, ye twain, let's get goin'."

"A moon? But it's only a fortnight's ride," Ticca said.

"There, yah—we'll be needing to get back as well," Sovia replied. "Chyne, love, go have a word with our horses and let them know what be in the works."

"It shalt be so, Cinquey Sovia," Chyne said and danced away toward the stables.

"Leave me Therin, if you would, please," Quinlan said to Sovia.

"You got him, for all the good he be." She laughed and landed a loving yet swift and hard smack on Therin's behind before darting away on her short legs. "Cassae, Swela, let's be getting the travel gear together." Sovia quickly led them down the way to the quartermaster lodge. The laughter of the women drifted back as they disappeared around the bend.

"Bed a wildcat, ya best expect ta get bit now and then." Therin winked.

The pleased look on the normally stoic man's face made Quinlan laugh as he laid out the maps contained within his order packet. Together they began to plot their route to the Drifting Leaf Watershed. Even on this small travel map, the distance seemed great.

"You're familiar with this area of Shaan if I remember, right?" Quinlan asked.

"Yi, Quin. I grew up in Goldenfield a day's ride west of the watershed."

"Tell me of Drifting Leaf."

"An area so beautiful, brother, it was surely a gift of the old gods. Woods thick enough ta stop an arrow before its left the bow. It holds uncountable small lakes, fens, and rivers flowin' eventually inta the sea down here near Trossachsmuir."

"All the way to the capital?"

"Yi, the river from the watershed crosses Shaan from north ta south."

"Any old tales ever tell of it being a danger?"

"Ni, Quin, none at all. It's been huntin' grounds since ancient times before the Kindred War."

"Hunting grounds, you say?" A new suspicion began to form in his mind. "The Cealjin Delta is also an ages-old hunting ground."

"Ya think it's a quirk of happenstance or ni?"

"What do all people need, Therin? Food and water—shelter matters not if one cannot eat and drink. If you weaken the food chain in an area, then strife and famine will surely follow."

"Driftin' Leaf Watershed covers more ground than the eye can see. If it were ta become tainted…" Therin studied the map. Sadness passed over his face as he apparently realized how much land would be devastated.

"We won't let that happen, Therin," Quinlan said. "I believe the dreyg are at work here turning key habitats into toxic wastelands, hoping the poison sinks deep into the heart of the land before time runs out to stop it."

"Why do my people turn a blind eye?" Therin asked. "The Gwylari and the druids've managed ta live with the land, yet the rest of Arden is usin' up resources faster than ever before."

"Yes, well asked, indeed." Quinlan nodded and looked over the map again. "If the dreyg destroy the resources people depend on, the kingdoms will crumble to ruin from the inside out."

"Can we not send word?"

"The Primerey sent an envoy to Shaan, but they were turned away at the border and nearly set upon by Shaanlander guardsmen."

Therin shook his head. "Then the rumors are true. A Disciple of Nemilos resides in Trossachsmuir."

"I fear our appearance may not be welcome," Quinlan said.

"Ease your fear, brother, I know of trails where few tread, far from pryin' eyes."

"I'll count on your navigation through Shaan then."

"Yi, Quin. We should head here." He pointed to a small range of mountains between Raskan and Shaan. "We can drop into Driftin' Leaf through this pass with no one knowin'."

"Good. My gratitude. Now, we'd better go and help pack or we'll never hear the end of it."

Therin smirked and put his hand over his heart. "Truth be told, brother!"

~~*

Chapter Eight

A man stood in the province chamber of Castle Teivas Keihas, located in the central tower of the keep. He kept his body lean and wiry through the efforts of strict physical discipline. The pockmarked skin of his face and hands was tanned to a mottled bronze. Deep wrinkles around the mouth and eyes told of a life in harsh sun and dry air. Sharp facial features and dark eyes gave him the deadly calm look of a predator in waiting.

A long, narrow, lightweight cloth was wrapped and tied around his head with a small remnant hanging to the left shoulder. Triple-layered linen robes of white, grey, and then brown on the outside were tied at the waist with a sash of the same light grey cloth of his head wrap. Loose-fitting white pants of slightly heavier fabric than the robes were secured at the ankles above the sandals he wore.

The province chamber was high in the main tower of Teivas Keihas ringed by overlooks offering a 360-degree view of Trossachsmuir below. Nearby was a large table with a diorama of the Shaanlander capital city spread out across its surface. The attention to detail of the miniature city was enthralling. Every color was correct, every aspect included. One could even look inside the buildings to see miniature room settings.

The diorama, as wondrous as it was, did not hold the man's attention this morning. Today he studied a different tabletop that held a map of Shaan and the surrounding territories.

The ornate double doors of the province chamber were opened by two footmen stationed outside, granting passage to a man dressed in black leather armor. Black hair and beard speckled with white surrounded a face of the same bronze hue. Two long curved dirks sat in well-oiled crossed sheaths at the small of his back.

The studded armor was covered with streaks of ghostly pale white and splotches of grey, which was the standard patterning of dreyg armor. The random pattern made it easy for dreyg agents to blend into the shadows of the world and go about unnoticed. Only a black-and-grey herringbone-weave aiguillette running from left shoulder to left breast distinguished this man from other dreyg personnel as the commandant of the dreyg on the northern continent.

The man placed his right fist over his left breast and bowed slightly. "My Lord Praven."

"Do you have the new reports, Commandant Kwyett?"

"Yes, my lord. In the north, Prince Kazim was turned away by the Raskan king, but dreyg agents have infiltrated three Raskan fiefs and begun tainting the wells there. Our forces—the king's forces, I should say—have taken up positions along the Raskan border. In the east, Disciple Onidra and dreyg forces have ventured upriver of the Cealjin Delta and have buried the barrels of the shadow parasite infusion along the headwaters. They have already started to leach into the groundwater. In the south, the waters of Drifting Leaf Watershed now carry the infusion. The plants are toxic and animals there begin to show disease and madness. Estimates predict the infusion-laced waters will reach Trossachsmuir's reservoirs within the month."

"Good. We will have that fool, Traelin, proclaim great festivals to deplete the stores they have on hand and when it comes time to replenish, they will find only sickness and death to reap. Their ignorance is of great benefit to us. They have no clue their affluence is helping to destroy the only being protecting them from their own extinction."

Kwyett looked away for the briefest of moments.

Praven did not miss it. "They continue to be ignorant of our plans, yes?"

"There was—an incident—my lord."

"Speak," Praven nearly hissed the word out.

"We discovered and killed a spy in Drifting Leaf." Kwyett looked at Praven. "A druid."

Praven instantly considered and dismissed several initial responses before he allowed himself to reply. He let the anger flow from his eyes instead of his voice or actions.

"Why wasn't I informed immediately?"

The effect was not lost on his subordinate and Kwyett swallowed visibly before replying. "I, ah—forgive me, Lord Praven, I thought the matter concluded with his death."

"If there is one druid, Commandant, does it not make sense to assume there may be more?"

"Yes, my lor—"

"They do travel in groves, do they not, Commandant?"

"Yes, my—"

"Did you conduct a search for any others, Commandant?"

"No, m—"

"Did the druid send off one of their *forest friends* with a message of warning, Commandant?"

"I don't know, my lord."

"Such things, Commandant, would be discovered through interrogation, would they not?"

Kwyett no longer met his gaze. "Yes, my lord. I apologize for my lack of forethought."

Praven turned away for several minutes before speaking again. "We must consider the possibility that at least some portion of our plan may have been compromised. Increase the border troops along every inroad from Raskan and Vakere and fill the woods around the entire watershed with dreyg agents."

"I will see it done, my lord."

"And have the war masters maim several of the larger predatory beasts and set them loose in the watershed to wreak havoc."

"Yes, my lord."

"Gather your men and go back into Drifting Leaf. Perform the search you should have done when what could be gleaned was fresh."

"At once, my lord," Kwyett replied and turned to leave.

"Commandant—"

"My lord?"

"Another misstep from you would be an enormous disappointment to me."

"Understood, my lord."

The double doors opened again, but this time, the footmen stepped inside and came to attention.

"The king!" they announced.

King Traelin Tavish entered his provincial chamber followed by three chancellors, a sea captain of powerful stature, and four of the royal bodyguards. A scribe followed them in and took a seat at a small desk along a far wall.

Praven and Kwyett both placed a right foot forward, swept their hands out palm up, and bowed at the waist.

"Your Majesty," they both said.

Praven put on a friendly and benevolent face before he straightened to face the king. "Good day, Sire."

"Praven! Good day, honored architect. How goes the progress on the second capital city ta the north?"

"The land has been cleared, Sire, and the foundations are being laid. Its spires will soon reflect the sun's light all the way to the windows of Torr Amhairc and into the eyes of Renalth himself."

"Ha ha! I love it! Let my cousin behold the magnificence of Shaan every day upon wakin'."

"Indeed, Sire, all citizens should revel in our progress to show all of Arden how mighty and prosperous we have become. Let there be great feasts and festivals, Sire. Let the populace rejoice in your generosity."

"Show my cousin and the rest of Arden that Shaan has no fear of them either on the battlefield or in the marketplace. We'll crush them with the heels of our boots or the weight of our coffers!"

Praven had to play King Traelin with great care. No king would respond well if they discovered they had been made a fool of, especially at an opponent's benefit. The king's weakness was his desire to build an empire strong enough to unite Shaan and Raskan into one kingdom as it had been in ancient times but under his rule.

Once a tan-skinned, battle-tested sea captain and explorer of far shores, King Traelin Tavish developed desires for finer things in his later years as his generous amounts of rounded body showed. The body tattoos of his early adventures had to be altered in order to hide how much they had stretched. It was often said the amount of silk and satin it took to outfit His Majesty for a week would fill a merchant ship.

The king may have been soft of body, but his mind and eye were still sharp and he had no qualms about using force to rule his kingdom. Praven knew the times when he should push the king and when to back off. All he had to do was find a way to align his goals with those of the king and let the king's desires do the rest.

"Come and look over the new street plans, Sire, while I send Commandant Kwyett off with the day's orders."

"Yes, of course." The king turned and nodded to Kwyett. "Commandant."

Kwyett bowed again. "Good day to you, Sire."

"You may go, Commandant," Praven said.

"Yes, my lord," Kwyett replied, turned to Traelin, and bowed. "By your leave, Sire." He nodded to the chancellors. "My lords."

Commandant Kwyett turned and came face-to-face with the sea captain, who made no effort to move out of the way. The tradition of Shaanlander sailors was to tattoo images on their bodies of the destinations they had reached. The tattooist filled the torso first before extending to the extremities. The man standing before Kwyett had tattoos down his forearms and on the backs of his hands, as well as up his neck and onto his clean-shaven head.

Kwyett stepped to one side and bowed. "Good day, Prince Travell." He waited a second for the reply he knew was not forthcoming before continuing on his way.

~~~

"My son doesn't think much of your agents, Praven."

"A clueless lot, Sire, but one must work with what one has."

Kwyett heard no more of the conversation as he left the province chamber and walked down several flights of stairs until he was no longer on the royal levels. He stopped and thought of how many places he could stick a dirk into the prince's body without killing him right off.

"I hate that f—" Kwyett cut himself off as he heard people around the corner. He pulled a dirk from its sheath and sliced a nearby plant in half before quickly moving on.

Kwyett found solace in the fact that the blood of the prince would be on his blade once the approval was given to bring Shaan to its knees.

Not many knew his face, but all recognized his armor and insignia and did their best to avoid engagement. The dreyg did not have an instantly violent reputation, but those who drew too much attention from the grim mercenary group soon suffered strange accidents or disappeared entirely.

The stable hand brought his horse when he arrived. He checked over the strap adjustments before mounting the animal and riding out the main gate of Teivas Keihas. The ride down the castle's entry ramp at a trot took him a quarter of an hour and thirty or so minutes more beyond that to get through the crowded city streets of Trossachsmuir. Another forty minutes at a gallop along the coast brought Kwyett to the dreyg encampment of Cradle Cove.

A stableman took his horse when he arrived and his aide came up to meet him.

"Welcome back, Commandant."

"Olam." Kwyett nodded to the man. "Tell the captains I've returned and await them in the lodge."

"At once, Commandant," Olam replied and turned to fulfill his task.

Kwyett walked the short distance up a central hill overlooking the rest of the encampment. The barracks, drill areas, and training halls bustled with activity. The ranks of the dreyg were at an all-time high and the coffers were full. His heart raced at the thought of having even more, yet he reminded himself to be patient awhile longer.

The command and confer lodge sat atop the central hill. Pikemen guarding the entrance came to attention and brought right fists to left chests as he approached.

Kwyett returned the salute and passed through into the lodge. An elderly man with the lower portion of his right leg missing acknowledged his entrance.

"Greetings, Commandant."

"Calen, how fares the leg?"

"Better every day, sir." He patted the crutch he leaned on. "Croaker made me a new support and wrapped it so I wouldn't get sores in my pit."

Kwyett blinked a couple of times in hopes of avoiding the visual. "That's more than I wanted to know, old man. Consider yourself lucky, Calen, to have lost only a leg. The snake is called a death adder for good reason."

"At my age, I consider myself lucky for every day I wake up and draw breath."

"I should do the same. What is there to eat?"

"There's roasted pig, peppered whitefish, and stewed roots and bulbs on the hearth, sir."

"Very good. Have the servants lay out a table." Kwyett moved to an array of bottles on a small stand and poured a glass of spiced rum. "The commanders will be joining me shortly."

"I'll see to it, sir."

The captains gathered later around a table after eating and hearing their leader's orders. A man leaned forward grabbing the edge of the table like he was about to throw it across the room. "I don't like this. I am a dreyg mercenary. I fight against men. This sneakin' around and mutilatin' animals in their cages brings no satisfaction to me or glory to my name. Why are we workin' for these disciples?"

Kwyett turned to him. "Because they make us rich, Strand, or do you dislike the weight of their gold in your hand?"

They held eyes for a moment before Strand grumbled, sat back, and looked away.

Kwyett regarded the group. "Do you not see great rewards wait for us at the end? All of Shaan, Raskan, and Vakere will be ours to rule!"

A man with a pleasant demeanor spoke up. "If there is anything left at the end."

"What is this resistance, Cairs? Was there a council while I was gone?"

"No council, Kwyett, only questions. We are told we will rule over all of Northern Arden, yet we destroy that which we are promised to gain. If we clear the woods, destroy the crops, and poison the waters, what will be left for us but desolation?"

"Lord Praven has assured me they hold the magic to undo all that we have done and have yet to do." Even as Kwyett said the words he wasn't sure if he believed them, but he best not show it.

"As the reports go, only one of these disciples has been accepted," a third man said. "Raskan, Vakere, and Kalnu have shown no interest or turned them away completely. Perhaps we are overestimating Praven and his plans."

"I agree with Aydgar," a fourth man said. "I think the disciples have their own agenda and they keep it secret from us."

"If you feel that way, Reeve, then you and Aydgar can go ask Lord Praven what his plans are—*in person*."

The idea of personally voicing their concerns brought a halt to any more questions. The image of what happened to Kwyett's predecessor was still fresh in their minds.

Kwyett didn't like bowing to Praven any more than they did, but at least he was still alive and he meant to stay that way.

"Your orders, Commandant?" Reeve asked.

"We are mercenaries and have been paid well. Form three search squads and scour Drifting Leaf for signs of any druid activity. If there are any druids out there, we will hunt them down and take them captive. Understood?"

A unanimous affirmative ended the meeting and they went to carry out Lord Praven's orders.

~~*

Chapter Nine

"The full moon'll be up, Quin. Will we dance tonight?" Sovia asked as they set up the first night's camp.

"I see no reason not to." Quinlan pulled Askue from its sheath on the horse. "We're still in kindly territory."

"Yah, I do be loving a good *moon dance*," she said.

"Truth be told?" Quinlan asked with well-meant sarcasm. Sovia's love of music and dancing was known far and wide.

"Och, be on with you now—ha ha!" She smiled without a hint of shyness. "I'll out-dance you, and I'll be singing, too."

"Ha! Don't I know it! We are many years from our first sharing of the moon dance, Sovia. I know your energy."

"As I do yours, Quin." She hugged him tightly and pulled him down to speak quietly in his ear. "I think Cassae be ready, yet she still be reluctant to reach out, you know, after what she's been through and all. She's grieved enough in the last two years to be filling two women's lifetimes. Maybe she needs a little help, you know, being happy again."

He straightened up and hugged her this time. "Gratitude, Sovia, for looking after us both, and agreed, she and I have spoken of it. The time is near."

"Moon dance, you know—all I'm saying, love." Sovia's eyes twinkled. "I do be finding myself a bit aroused after a moon dance. Much to Therin's delight—on most occasions that is."

"Ha ha, no need to elaborate." Even for a druid, Sovia's openness about intimacy brought color to most people's faces. The moon dance was performed solo and the movements covered three to four steps of space in any given direction, so there was no physical interaction, yet the blending of one's spirit with the natural energy of the world normally left the druid participant with an abundance of vigor. Druids were far more comfortable and open-minded about physical sex than most, but sharing that openness was optional.

A shriek of surprise and a soft thud came from where the rest of the grove was unpacking the night's gear and supplies.

"Ticari!" Ticca exclaimed in irritation.

Quinlan and Sovia both turned to see an angry Ticca sitting on the ground with her feet tangled in *tievines*. Someone had fast grown the vines around her feet and she hadn't noticed until she tried to walk away. It was a popular joke among the younger druids as it had been since the beginning of the Order. Her brother laughed and seemed pleased.

"Here now!" Sovia yelled. "You don't be using the grace of Na'veyja for your self-serving shenanigans! You're not a child no more, you ninny! Now mind your duties afore I dust your backside with the sole of my moccasin!"

Ticari stopped laughing. "But Chyne plays jokes on us all the time."

Chyne laughed lightly and nodded her head with glee.

Quinlan walked over. "Chyne is not a druid in the Order of Arden, you are," he said. "And you will abide by the Order's code of conduct."

"Yes, Quin," Ticari said.

"Besides, my brothers and sisters weren't druids and they found plenty of things to get my goat without using *druid magic*." Quinlan wiggled his fingers at the end. "And you, Ticca, a druid should always be aware of what is around them at all times. It is a skill you must hone to perfection if you—" He stopped when he saw Cassae try to hide a smile. "What are you smiling at?"

She pointed at his shoulder.

Quinlan turned his head and watched a small green and white ivy vine creep over his shoulder and down his chest. He looked down to see it had already wound around his leg and up his back.

Chyne smiled playfully and laughed as she effortlessly controlled the vine's growth.

Quinlan gripped Askue with both hands and murmured a chant. "*Graleth ma na zeezee.*"

Purple and yellow blossoms grew instantly at Quinlan's end and followed the vine back to Chyne where they burst open leaving her face covered with purple and yellow splotches of pollen.

The grove laughed together including Chyne, who was always a good sport when it came to jokes and games. Only Sovia scowled at them.

"A grove full of children, I say!" she said sternly, before she grinned and joined in on the laughter. "All right now, that be enough chicanery! Kian, Swela, Therin, you trey bring in wood for a fire and remember only be taking what's down and dead! Cassae and Ticari, fetch water from the river. Chyne, you'll be helping me grow dinner. Ticca-love, it be your turn on the *tinder boat.*"

The grove broke up to set about their individual tasks. Most were out of sight, but occasional noises indicated they were still nearby. Quinlan pretended to go over the map while in secret, he watched how well Ticca did at the task she was given.

She chose a large spot of bare rocky ground to place the kindling pile. She built a square hut of long twigs, eventually placing thicker twigs followed by small sticks on top of those. She stacked larger sticks around the kindling hut in a pyramid being careful to leave a hole at the bottom of one side.

She quickly braided some of the tall grasses surrounding the camp and used them to tie five sticks together. Next she placed two sticks on top of the other three, tying them so there was a V-shape between the top two sticks forming a tinder boat. At last, she built a pile of dried grasses and tiny twigs in the middle of the tinder boat.

Quinlan took a wrapped package containing the fire striker from a saddlebag and walked it over to where she was building the fire.

"Here you are, Ticca."

"Gratitude, brother, I was about to come after that. Which is your favorite striker?"

"I prefer the chert or the quartz. They knap easier yielding bigger sparks but wear the quicker because of it. The ironstone will outlast time itself and give forth a shower of smaller sparks, but they are short-lived and you must be quick to ignite them or lose their heat."

"Ugh! This is heavy," she said when she lifted the handstone from the bundle. The chunk of granite was narrow enough to hold and twice as long as her hand was wide. A groove ran down the length of the handstone worn in from years of service. Ticca dug through the bag of small striker stones and chose a milky-white stone with many sharp-angled edges.

"Now, you have to—" Quinlan stopped when Ticca already went into action.

She struck hard and fast at the handstone with the quartz until red-hot flakes of stone ran down the groove and landed on the grass pile. The flakes shot off tiny sparks for a brief moment before they died off. Ticca gently blew on the embers while she pushed more of the tinder around them. The pile of dried grass and twigs ignited quickly. She carefully placed the entire tinder boat with the burning pile into the spot she had left open at the bottom of the kindling hut.

"Very well done, Osmey Ticca," Quinlan said.

"Gratitude, Siestrey Quinlan," she said as she kept working on the fire. "Ticari taught me. He will tell a tale it took him days, yet in truth, it took him only the space of a single noon to night."

Quinlan laughed lightly at the thought of the two of them working together. "He's a stalwart young man and a good brother."

"The best." She looked up at him and smiled.

The flames jumped from the tinder boat up into the kindling which flared up into the main pile of sticks. The small fire was catching on nicely when the wood gatherers returned to camp with larger limbs and logs. They stoked the fire as Sovia and Chyne finished preparing the fast-grown vegetables for dinner.

Sovia said, "Chyne, give the horses some bee biscuits and let them be grazing. Be sure to tell them to stay close by."

"I wilst do so, Cinquey," she replied.

"Can I help?" Ticca asked Sovia, who looked at Chyne.

"Certainly, thy company is most welcome," Chyne said, and the two went off to care for the horses.

Sovia brought a pot of vegetable stew over to where Kian had set up a nice place to sit around the fire. She held the pot out to him. "Slow boil then be simmering it for half an hour, love."

Kian held his hands out to the sides without committing to taking the pot. "Oh nae, Sov, come on now. Cookin'? I'll gather more wood. How 'bout that? Ye know I'm a terrible cook."

"I know you be terrible at *wanting* to do it, you louseabout," Sovia replied. "You take a turn like everyone else."

Kian grabbed the pot and sighed. "It shall be done, Cinquey."

"Good! Simmer until the carrots be tender—but not mushy, mind you," she said. "And don't you be nibbling, either."

"Aye, ma'am," he said with the shadow of a wolf's grin. "Nae nibblin'."

"Swela, be keeping an eye on that husband of yours and make sure he's not eating dinner afore it's cooked."

"Aye, Sov, I will." Swela plopped down on the spot Kian had made for himself before he was put on kitchen duty. "Ahh—this's nice," she said. "Gratitude, hubs."

"Glad ye like it, Swayz-hon. Does ma heart good knowin' yer fanny's pleased."

"'Tis—ye can rest assured." She settled back folding her arms behind her head.

"Oh, a fine wife ye are—tauntin' poor I as I toil ma fingers ta the very bone," he said yet did nothing but squat near the fire watching the pot slowly bubble and stirring it occasionally.

"Ha!" Quinlan laughed at his make-believe tale of woe.

The rest of the grove had gathered by then and joined in poking fun at Kian's misery. Idle chat occupied the time until dinner was ready and filled the spaces between mouthfuls of bread, cheese, and vegetable ciambotta.

One sip of Swela's favorite light wine turned Kian's face sour.

"Eck! Therin, please tell me ye brought a jug of yer wheat berry brew alon'?" he asked.

"Yi, brother, I'll grab it."

Therin returned and poured a bit of the deep violet alcohol for himself and Therin as the others quickly declined.

"Yaaah!" Kian exclaimed after he downed the drink. "Now, that's more like it, laddie. A proper drink has ta have a proper bite ta it."

"One hath not danced in delight, if one hath not drank of aged persimmon sujeon," Chyne said with a sigh of remembered pleasure.

"Ni, ni, ni, Chyne." Therin waved a hand in playful distaste. "Sujeon is fit only for children cryin' from the fire throat. Coats your tongue for days with its thickness."

"'Tis divine nectar for the enlightened spirit," she said with the certainty of a temple sage.

Singer and Flit flew in at that moment. Flit landed on Sovia's shoulder, chittering up a storm.

"Quin, riders be coming," Sovia said.

Several minutes later, a Raskanish woman called out, "Hail in the camp! May we approach?"

"Come ahead!" Quinlan called back. "Is that Wylla and Freyn?" he asked as they drew closer.

"Aye, 'tis," Wylla answered. "Who's askin'?"

"'Tis Quinlan," Freyn replied, but Wylla gave her a blank look, "from the gatherin' we attended two days back."

"Oh! Aye, aye, right," Wylla said. "Apologies, Quinlan, good ta see ye again."

"None needed. Please join us." Quinlan motioned to Ticari. "Come care for their mounts." He walked the women to the fire. "There's ciambotta, bread, and cheese, if you've not eaten. Wylla and Freyn, this is Grove Seven: Kian and Swela here, and then Cassae, Chyne, Ticca, Sovia, and Therin. Ticari tends the horses."

"Lah quen ta ye all," Freyn said.

"Gratitude fer the meal," Wylla said. "A much warmer camp than we were expectin'."

Cassae prepared two more bowls of ciambotta. Wylla spooned most of the vegetables into one bowl and poured the broth from that bowl into the first, then took the broth and some bread to Freyn where she had settled around the fire.

"Wylla dinnae fret. I'm fine," Freyn said.

"Ye're nae fine. Ye have nae eaten all day. Now, it's mostly broth, but I've left a few carrots and zucchini. Ye need ta eat them." Wylla stood there and did not look like she was going to accept any negative answer.

"Gratitude..." Freyn said but did not act overly enthused as she took the food.

Cassae took Chyne and they sat next to Freyn where they had a quiet conversation among themselves, after which Chyne disappeared into the woods.

"Wylla, what brings you this far south?" Ticca asked.

"Now, Ticca, don't you go being a nosy Rosy," Sovia said in a scolding tone.

"Nae bother," Wylla said as she waved off any concern. "We travel ta ma home city of Cammachmoor, child, in search of a druid there."

Quinlan saw Ticca stiffen the tiniest bit at the word "child" but only for a second before she smiled.

Wylla apparently had noticed the same slight reaction. "Apologies—Ticca, is it? Only a phrase. I've nae doubt ye've earned yer place here."

"My first patrol," Ticca said and smiled even wider. "I thought we'd be on the first leg of our rotation through the Great Marsh by now, but our orders send us to"—she stopped and looked quickly at Quinlan, who nodded—"a place called Drifting Leaf, a week's ride on horseback."

"Aye, I know the place. 'Tis beautiful country, or once was leastways. Ye should keep yer wits about ye down there now, I hear."

"Befouled, or ni, it'll be beautiful once again," Therin said. He held his fist to his chest. "This I swear. The beauty of Driftin' Leaf will be inked inta my flesh!"

"Ha! There not be enough room left for a blade of grass tattoo, let alone an entire watershed, Therin-love," Sovia replied.

Therin smiled and winked before he mimicked her Kalnuvian accent the best he could. "You're the one who'd be knowing, Sov-love."

"Yi, thet ah yam." Sovia slathered on the Shaanlander and returned his wink, which got a laugh from the group.

Chyne returned from the woods with small mushrooms, yellow seedpods, and several herbs and gave them over to Cassae, who prepared a coulis from selected bits.

"Here," Cassae said to Freyn, "you can mix it in with the broth and eat it with bread or by itself."

Freyn showed only a little discomfort at being the center of attention as she scooped some of the coulis with bread. She gave it a quick sniff before she ate it, after which she nodded in satisfaction. Cassae left her to eat in peace.

Wylla brought her dishes up to the washbasin after she was done.

"Here, let me get that for ya," Cassae said as she washed what she used making the coulis.

"Nae gratitude, I'll get mine and let me get those, too," Wylla said, "in return fer the meal and the kindness ye've shown Freyn."

Cassae gave wash duty over to Wylla and playfully swiped the drying cloth from Quinlan's hand. She smiled at him as she handed him a dried bowl to store away.

"What ails her so?" Quinlan asked Wylla.

"She was touched by *the shadow*," she said.

Quinlan could hear slight discomfort in her voice. Cassae held his eyes for a moment and went back to drying dishes.

"The black cloud of Acimasiz?" he asked. "But how—"

"A cost fer ma arrogance," Freyn said as she walked up with her bowl.

"Apologies, Freyn, I do not mean to stir dark memories."

"'Tis naught ta worry about, Quinlan. Dark memories left in the shadows only become darker still. I believed my powers as a druid stron' enough ta drive back the black scourge. 'Twas that day I learned the powers were never mine ta claim, but a gift from Na'veyja. I broke my vows ta Na'veyja and my body bore the cost, yet by her grace, I still draw breath. A lesson I've taken ta heart."

"You're truly blessed to have survived."

"Aye, the pain is gone, yet the flaura dinnae answer ma call anymore."

"Is there nothing you can do? Some time at the Central Conclave, perhaps? It was of great ease to Cassae's pain of heart."

"'Tis different fer me, brother. The sickness has taken the brightness of the flaura from ma eyes."

"Surely, you can still call upon Na'veyja's grace?"

"She speaks to me still, but instead of a son' in my heart, I now hear a whisper in ma mind. It dinnae bring me as much cheer as it once did, but in ways, I find it more insightful."

"Your answers bring more questions, Freyn," he said.

"I see by yer raiment, Quinlan, ye're a brother of the Dayne Kinship."

"That is so."

"Then I've questions fer ye as well," she said. "May I have yer arm and ear fer a time? If I can break ye from yer duties, that is."

He cleared his throat as if to state a matter of importance. "It may be a hardship, but I think these women can—"

Cassae snapped the drying cloth at him. "Oh, take your arse out of here, before I snap it with this cloth!"

Quinlan danced out of her range before he offered Freyn his arm and they walked off toward the horses.

"Ye've a very diverse grove here, brother," Freyn said. "Gwylari, Vakerian, Kalnuvian, Shaanlander, Raskanish…"

"A wonderful blend of energies," he replied. "Speaking of that, you should dance with us tonight."

"A moon dance? That'd be welcome. Gratitude, Quin. Pardon the askin', but have ye lain some kind of spell on yer walkin' staff?"

"Askue? No, Askue came to me during a companion quest."

"'Tis a familiar?" she asked in surprise before she nodded. "Aye, that follows."

"What does?"

"The feelin' I get. It has an energy of its own about it. What does it do?"

"Do? Ha! Mostly it disappears when wanted and is under foot when not. Why do you ask?"

"When I was stricken with the sickness, ma death was certain. One day Primerey Joseah herself came ta ma bedside. She said a possible cure had been brought ta light. It had nae yet been tested and the risk ta the body was great."

"You chose to do it, obviously."

"Aye, the sickness was banished and as I said afore, I was mended in some ways yet left broken in others."

"A fair trade, some would say. Cassae lost a son, a daughter, and a husband to the wasting sickness. I'm sure she'd rather have them back, frail or not."

"'Tis a sad thing ta hear," she replied, "and a terrible loss ta endure."

"What does the curing of your sickness have to do with Askue?"

"The druid who performed the ritual used a staff to channel the energy. I'll nae ever forget the feel of it coursin' through ma spirit. I feel somethin' close ta that from yer friend there."

Quinlan picked up Askue and wondered at Freyn's story. "Who was the druid?"

"I know not. He bore no insignia of rank or conclave. His clothes were well worn and he smelled of the woodlands. Whatever was done to me has changed somethin' inside, brother. Sadly, I cannae longer call the flaura, but I can enhance Wylla's druid abilities tenfold by channelin' Na'veyja's grace through me and inta her."

Quinlan looked at her sharply. "What's this you say?"

"Truth be told! People such as me, and items too, are called conduits," she replied. "I think yer staff is such."

"Askue—a conduit of Na'veyja's grace?"

"Aye, Quin, I believe so."

Freyn's story brought him still more questions than answers. "How do you know there are others?"

She took a moment to size him up before she spoke. "The only reason I'm tellin' ye is I think ye're fated ta be involved somehow. I'm part of a contingency group on the fringe of the Order makin' preparations quietly fer the day when the dreyg forces make their attempt ta free Acimasiz."

Quinlan was partly stunned by the news. "Is there new concern of attack? Why the need for secrecy?"

"Nae, but for every dreyg incursion we stamp out, another comes ta life. The druid influence is dwindlin' throughout the country. The disciples never stop tryin' ta position forces around Arden and once they do, Quin, they'll have the advantage. The Order needs ta be ready fer that day when it comes."

Quinlan wanted to argue, but in his heart, he felt the same thing. He wanted to be outraged no one had told him, but now he saw the signs had been there all along.

"And the secrecy? Does the council know?"

"'Twas the Tretjey Sayon of yer conclave who recruited me," she said. "And it's nae that we hide what we do. We simply weave it inta the everyday, so in case the Order is infiltrated..."

"It's business as usual," Quinlan finished, "with nothing out of the ordinary."

"Exactly."

"So, is that all this group does? Makes plans and gathers supplies?"

"Nae, brother, we work on special defenses and strategies, as well. There're others like me, other conduits. We're teamed up with a partner and trained ta work together." She pointed a thumb in Wylla's general direction. "Like Wylla and me. There're regular druid forces, too, who're trained in craftiness and sent on missions across Arden. We're called the *Wardens of the Woods*—unofficially that is."

"So, you and Wylla are on such a mission right now?"

"Aye, we need ta contact Kenri in Cammachmoor and speak with him in private."

"And he's part of the—"

"Wardens, aye. One of the founders actually."

"Why do you tell me all of this?" he asked. "Did you approach us with purpose?"

"Nae, brother, our meetin' is of chance, yet fated in my eyes. At nae other time have I seen a staff as a conduit except for the day I was cured. I'm surprised that ye don't know of the Wardens afore now. Ye've nae been approached by anyone?"

"Indeed not. It feels more that I'm held at arm's length when it comes to the conclave and the Tretjey's plans."

"Ah, well," she said, "I think ye should come ta Cammachmoor and have a word with Kenri before ye continue on ta Driftin' Leaf. 'Tis the opposite direction, I know, but it could be a great benefit ta ye."

"Perhaps we could. I'll discuss it with the grove. It wouldn't hurt to resupply before we enter Shaan. I'm uncertain as to what exactly awaits us there."

"If ye've a mind ta, then we can travel together ta Cammachmoor. It'd give me the chance ta speak with Cassae more. Her knowledge of herb lore is extensive. The coulis she made helped more than I thought it would."

"She's gone through hell and high water for the knowledge," he said.

"Agreed. I personally know the agony of the black cloud's touch. Ta lose a child ta it would be beyond bearin'."

"The esbat rises!" Sovia's voice boomed from the group by the fire.

"Coming," Quinlan answered.

The glowing face of the full moon illuminated the night sky as it crested above the horizon. Silvery light began to pour through the woods in loving contrast to the shadows of night. Wylla waited for them to return before she and Freyn disrobed and took their places around the fire.

Quinlan chose an area wide enough for movement, disrobed, and took a look around to make sure all were ready to begin. He drew in a breath centering his spirit into the *root circle* deep in his lower abdomen where all human life begins. He brought his hands up past his belly, palms up, passing through the gathered energy before raising his hands to the moon.

He called out, "Sister of the stars, we bathe in thy beams."

The group followed his lead and recited, "*Esbat nom krayla nom talsa.*"

Quinlan brought his hands down in front of him and moved his left foot forward. He placed his right knee and hands palm down onto the ground.

"Mother Arden, we live from thy bounty," he said taking the lead.

They followed in Gwylari. "*Arden nom krayla nom talsa.*"

Quinlan stood, keeping his spirit centered. He held both arms out in front of his chest, palms to each other. He moved his torso sideways undulating like he was a banner waving in the wind.

"Great winds bear our spirits aloft."

"*Rynn nom krayla nom talsa.*"

He brought arms and legs together crossing his arms over his chest.

"Na'veyja we rest in thy embrace."

"*Na'veyja nom krayla nom talsa.*"

The group stood quickly as one and raised their arms to the full moon, calling out in unison, "*Esbat nom krayla nom talsa!*"

The opening of the moon dance was complete and each druid was free to dance as they wished until the moon reached its zenith.

Quinlan reached out with his spirit. He felt the trees breathing in the woods and the grass bending in the soft breeze. He touched the spirits of animals living in the nearby woods and moved in rhythm with the energy of the natural world until only energy remained. His spirit rose from his body and hovered above in ethereal separation. The usual calm, peaceful meditation of the moon dance did not take place.

A curious-looking green-and-white-striped gemstone appeared before his spirit's eye this time. He took the gemstone and could hear the stone whisper to him. He obeyed the instructions and placed it into the ground. A globe of white and green energy burst from the ground shooting a beam to the esbat.

Askue suddenly took off on its own, riding the energy beam to the moon. Quinlan was pulled along in its wake as he reached out to grab his staff before it flew away. He soared through the woods, pulled along by the draw of the moonlight. When he caught up with Askue, he felt the pull of both woods and moon. He reached a spot where the two were equal and his spirit floated for a time in peaceful balance.

Quinlan's body began to tire and the rhythm of the movements began to falter. His spirit heard the body's call and returned home. He brought his moon dance to an end being careful not to shut down the energy flow completely but letting it ebb through his being. He was covered with sweat and the rest of the group was already done. Noticing the moon was well past its zenith, he dressed and grabbed Askue from the ground.

"Askue—*moonbeam rider*," he said to the staff. "How faired your travels, my friend?"

The question was playful and rhetorical, yet an unexpected vision flashed across his mind. He caught his breath as the images of a sharp-featured, dark-skinned woman, a block of ever-frost crystal, and an ancient moss-covered cave entrance, repeated three times and faded away to memory.

"What...?" he said and looked at his staff. "Do you hear me? Does she speak the truth? Are you a conduit?"

No answer this time.

"Be as you will, then, spiteful twig! Your riddles trouble me not," he lied.

"Oh, listen there, Chyne," he heard Cassae from the fire, which had died down considerably. "Is that Quin?"

"Yes," he said as he made his way to her side and plopped down. "The others?"

"Ticca and Ticari are fast asleep. The rest have gone ta the cover of the woods ta be frisky."

"Wylla and Freyn?" he asked.

"Oh, aye..." Cassae nodded her head slowly. "Lovin' creatures, those two—barely reached the woods before they're in each other's arms. Port?" She held out a cup.

"Yes, gratitude." He took the cup and raised it. "Well, good for them. To each their own heart." The women echoed the toast and they drank.

"We thought thee wouldst dance the night gone," Chyne said. "I've not known one to dance for such a time."

"Nor I," Cassae said. "Is all well, Quin?"

"I have not the answer," he replied. "It was at once the most enlightening and yet most vexing." He told them of the experience with Askue and the moon dance as well as of the vision at the end.

"Askue—and moonbeams?" Cassae started to smile. "Did you eat another *greengrin*?"

"I've eaten no mushrooms." He scowled at her. "It was only the once anyway. And gratitude for your helpfulness!"

"Apologies, Quin." She smiled in a way that always charmed him.

"I have no idea who the woman is, nor have I seen any such cave," Quinlan said.

"Perhaps the next moon dance will show ya more of the vision," Cassae said.

"Perhaps," he replied.

Chyne grabbed Quinlan's staff. "Askue and I will dream upon the matter. Lah quen to thee both."

They bid Chyne good night and watched as a layer of leaves sprouted forth covering her body like a leafy green cocoon.

"The Gwylari are a wondrous people," he said.

"Agreed, and let us dream upon the matter as well, me love," she said. "The dawn will brin' a new day and a fresh light will be shed on dark questions."

"Yes, fresh light," was about all he had time to say as they nestled down together and sleep quickly washed over him.

Chapter Ten

"Mmm..." the reclined man hummed in pleasure. "Exquisite! Now, one of the red ones."

"Aye, ma prince." A pretty young girl from Glen Arwe was more than happy to comply.

Long ink-black curls of the man's hair hung over the back of a silk-covered lounging couch. Sweet oil made from the malla tree blossoms ensured the curls were tight and reflecting the sunlight in a million sparkling highlights. A thin line of finely trimmed beard ran along the man's jaw meeting up with an equally immaculate moustache. The desert-tanned skin of his ancestors was moisturized daily in an effort to keep his arid homeland a distant memory.

"Ma prince," the girl said and held an oblong red berry up.

He leaned his head back and opened his mouth and the girl dropped the fruit in. Red juice ran from the corners of his mouth as he bit down on the berry.

"Oh—get it, get it!" he said.

The girl moved with speed in order to catch the juice before it stained her prince or his clothing. "There, ma handsome Prince Kazim, all is well."

"Thank the gods for you—what was your name again, girl?"

"Gwen, ma Prince."

"Thank the gods for you, Gwen." Kazim rose from the lounger and walked to a full-length mirror. He looked himself over. His looks were renowned: deep dark brown eyes, long curly black hair, and tan-colored skin. A slim and muscular body belied his voracious appetite for exotic food, drink, and company. All who saw him thought he was a handsome man, yet none thought it more often than himself.

"Exquisite," he murmured to his reflection.

"Tell the prince I'm here." He inwardly cringed as he heard the commanding voice from the other room even through the closed heavy doors.

"Gwen, it appears that it is time for you to go, my dear."

"Yes, ma Prince."

She reached the doors as the dreyg guards opened them from the other side.

"Commander Malent to see you, Prince Fhadlam," one of the guards said.

"Yes, I'll see her, thank you."

A black-skinned woman dressed in a dreyg commander's uniform strode through the door. Streaks of premature grey nearly filled her head of tightly curled black hair, giving her the look of wearing a storm cloud about her head. She looked at Gwen with such disdain, Kazim expected the woman to bare her teeth and snarl at the girl as she went by. Gwen looked only at the floor and edged up against the door to stay as far as possible from the mercenary.

The woman began to speak in an angry tone once the doors were closed again. "Kazim, we need—"

"Ah, ah, ah…"

"I will not call you *prince* when we are alone. You are as much a prince as my horse's ass. It should have been *me* chosen as disciple."

"It is truly baffling why you were not, Marza," Kazim's voice dripped with sarcasm. He let that sink in for a moment before he continued. "Make your report, Commander."

"De plans move ahead as scheduled, but we need to cut more timber."

"Not yet. There will be some kind of response from Cammachmoor after we recently eliminated the Raskan agent in the marketplace. We wait until after we deal with that to begin clear-cutting Glen Arwe."

"You are sure of dis?"

"Positive. They won't risk an open move in Grannagh Province. It will most assuredly be a secret attempt to capture one or both of us or an ambush of some kind to eliminate us. Have dreyg forces taken over the Grannagh military?"

"Yes, and de invasion force stands ready right across de Shaan border to take control of de province."

"Imagine the surprise when old Lord Grannagh discovers we've taken his province out from under his feet and he will be lord of nothing but the dirt of his own grave."

"De norderners breed dull minds."

"Don't let your contempt dull yours, Marza." Kazim turned to face her. "It is the northerners who have forced us into a secondary plan. Lord Nemilos has sent word. He sees the loss of the Raskan capital city as a failure—on our part."

A look of question and fear passed across Marza's face and her hand moved toward her sword grip. Her eyes darted around the room.

"Ease your mind, Commander. There is no bowman waiting in the shadows. We should be so fortunate. Death would be far easier to accept than the fate we have been given." Kazim filled a glass with wine and drained half. "Praven has been given command of the northern continent. We now answer to *him*."

"What are you going to do?"

"We all have our parts to play. I am going to continue to play mine."

A knock at the door interrupted their conversation. A dreyg messenger walked in and handed a message to Marza before he saluted, turned, and left.

"A band of MacRory hunters was found crossing de border nordwest of Glen Arwe. Dey tried to escape when de militia put dem under guard. Eight killed, two captured, and one evaded de militia and escaped."

"MacRory agents, to be sure. See, I told you they would try something. Have them hold the prisoners until I arrive. You, personally, are to track down the one who escaped. We cannot let word reach Cammachmoor. Fail in this, Commander, and you will not see the arrow that pierces your heart."

"Understood, *my Prince*." Kazim could see she held back a sneer as she spoke the last two words.

~~~

An hour short of sundown, Commander Malent arrived at the dreyg encampment accompanied by the prince, who was escorted by a dozen elite dreyg fighters. Two dreyg fighters and an officer from the camp approached and came to attention as they road in and dismounted.

Marza greeted him. "Captain Fen Rollen, dis is Prince Kazim Fhadlam."

The dreyg officer saluted and bowed at the waist. "An honor, Prince Fhadlam."

"You are to be congratulated, Captain Rollen. You have caught a great prize," Kazim said.

"Gratitude, my Prince. These men are no mere hunters if their fighting ability is to be held in judgment."

"No, surely not. Agents from Cammachmoor, if fortune smiles upon us. Have they spoken?"

"No, my Prince."

"Delightful, they shall before the night is out. It has been months since I drained the life force from anything, not even a dog."

Marza caught a flash of anger in Fen Rollen's eye before it could be hidden. Kazim must have caught the same thing.

"You don't approve, Captain."

Anger still tinted the man's visage as he answered carefully, "I live only to serve, my Prince."

"Good—then bring me a dog, so that I may torture and kill it."

The man seemed troubled by the request.

"*You* have a dog. Don't you, Captain?" Marza asked. "Bring *dat* one."

Anger twisted Fen Rollen's face as he cried out in rage and drew his sword. Faster than any could see, Kazim stepped forward to grab the wrist of Fen's sword arm with his left hand and Fen's neck with his right. Kazim's power instantly began sapping the man's life force from his body.

"Perhaps, Captain, your future is not so bright after all," Kazim said pleasantly to Fen as he struggled in vain.

The two remaining dreyg fighters glanced uneasily at their commander, but Marza took no action while Fen gasped and gurgled until he died at Kazim's hands. Kazim looked at one of the men left standing there.

"I'll fetch the beast at once, my Prince," the man said.

"Then you shall be named Captain for your efforts," Kazim replied before he turned to Marza. "Don't you have an escapee to track down, Commander?"

"Yes, my Prince." Marza returned to her horse, giving orders to the dreyg squad as she went. "You men—wid me! Gadder your gear and mount up! Be quick or be left behind."

The squad members hastened their departure as the man returned to Kazim with Fen's hound. Marza knew the dog was a friend to them all and rightly guessed none of them wanted to be anywhere near camp at the moment, nor their sadistic prince. *Sentimental fools*, she thought, *and they call themselves dreyg*.

The barking of Fen's hound could still be heard as they rode out of camp. Sounds of surprise and aggression coming from the hound changed to whimpering of fear and despair as Kazim undoubtedly drained the dog's life force.

The search for the MacRory agent did not take long. A blood trail marked the man's passage clearly through the thick brush.

"Fan out! Watch for any signs of doubling back!" Marza called out to the squad. "Ready! Forward!"

The line of horses scared up every small beast and bird in their path as the squad slowly moved ahead. Movement caught her eye when a man shot out from under a log pile and ran over a ridgeline away from them.

"Dere!" Marza shouted and spurred her horse to go as fast as it could in the thick woodland. The squad fell in behind her and they chased after the agent.

A clearing began to show through the branches of the woods. The squad rode over the ridge the man had disappeared behind. Ahead of them was the Wildron River Gorge, which had brought the flight of the MacRory agent to a dismal end. A jump from this height was surely a death sentence.

Marza and the dreyg squad moved in to capture the man. The agent's breathing was labored and shallow. He bled from a head wound, yet it was the stab wound in his belly, which was robbing him of his life's blood. He turned to face his opponents. He placed one fist in the crook of his other arm and gave a quick upward thrust before he turned his back on them and leapt from the cliff edge.

Marza looked down at her saddle horn and shook her head. "Shit."

She sat there mulling over her thoughts until one of the squad spoke up. "Should we search the gorge, Commander?"

"No, if de fall did not kill him, his wounds will take him before long. Return to camp."

Marza turned her horse and led the way back to the dreyg encampment. Kazim was waiting as they rode in. The same pleasant expression made it impossible for Marza to judge his mood.

"Failed once again, Commander?"

She did not really know why, but she chose to lie. "He was dead when we found him."

The dreyg squad members quickly found tasks far away from the two of them.

"You did not bring back the body?"

She felt oddly thrilled, so she lied more. "No, I drew him into de gorge."

Kazim's speed took her by surprise, even though she knew his powers. In an instant, his hand was around her throat. His touch stung painfully, like a necklace of burning embers. She struggled against the agony.

He sucked air in through clenched teeth. "I will drain you here and now if you are lying."

Marza glared at him and drew in a painful and raspy breath. "I would—if it were you in my grasp."

Kazim let her go and she dropped to the ground. She got to her feet as the pain subsided.

"You are still of some use to me, Marza. You might wish it to remain so."

"Yes, *my Prince*," she said, using little effort to hide her disdain.

"Have these burned." Kazim waved toward the bodies of Fen Rollen, his hound, and the MacRory agents. "And bring me the dead agent's corpse from the gorge. There is *a thing* I would like to try."

Marza motioned to her squad members. "You—lead a squad into de gorge and recover de body from de river. You—form a detail and build a pyre downwind of camp and burn dese." She calmed herself after they left and turned to Kazim. "Did dey speak?"

"The dog did not have much to say, but surprisingly, the goal of the MacRory agents was to abduct—me—of all people. Can you imagine? Thinking a band of commoners could overpower a Disciple of Nemilos. They have not a clue what gathers against them. The northerners will hit the ground before they know they have fallen."

"What of Lord Grannagh?"

"He and the royal family will suffer a mysterious and sudden illness. Such a horrible tragedy."

"Den, if dat it de case, do we begin?"

"Yes, Commander, you may give the order to begin clear-cutting the deep woods of Glen Arwe."

~~*

Chapter Eleven

Kian rode just out of sight ahead of Grove Seven to scout the trail to their new destination. He was content with his life as a druid. He was wed to the most beautiful woman in the world. He admired Quinlan and was honored to be one of his grove. The trip from the Northern West Conclave was halfway through its second week, yet he had enjoyed the travel so much it seemed they left only yesterday. He stopped at the edge of a river flowing with a current strong enough to carry his horse away. The Wildron River marked the boundary of Glen Arwe in Grannagh Province. They'd likely reach the Raskan capital city of Cammachmoor in another two days.

Siasta shifted uneasily as the wind changed direction, bringing smells from downriver to the horse's nose. She looked back at Kian and nickered. Kian focused his senses and picked up the scent of an open wound.

"Aye, ma sweet girl." He reached down and patted Siasta's neck. "I got hold of it now."

Kian dismounted and grabbed some gear from his saddlebags. He took Siasta's head in his hands and thought of what he wanted her to do. A nicker and a neigh let him know she understood. He patted her neck and she turned to head back in search of Grove Seven.

Kian continued to search the banks downriver on foot. A mass of grey fabric lying among the tall reeds was the source of the smell he tracked. He moved along until he was directly across the river from the mass. He could make out an arm stretched out toward the river, but there was no movement.

The druid took out a few seeds and piled them on the ground. He covered the seeds with his hand and chanted.

"Feen hass nasu vek navi."

Kian wove his hands over the seed pile. The seeds began to glow and produced tendrils of bright green and white flaura. The tendrils moved out over the river under Kian's control. Vines grew from the seed pile and followed the ethereal tendrils across the fast-flowing water. The tendrils of flaura reached the far riverbank and into the ground. The vines grew heavy and strong on Kian's side while the small creepers reached their destination and took root there. The vines grew thick forming a line across the strong current.

Kian secured his possessions and waded into the river. He let his legs hang in the current as he went hand over hand along the sturdy vine line. He made it to shallower water and waded to the opposite riverbank. Nearing the man's body, he saw he was still alive. Kian carefully rolled the man over. At first, the man was startled until it was apparent Kian was not a threat.

"Help..." the man's breathing was labored and words did not come easily.

"Hold fast, friend, I'll do what I can fer ye."

"Druid...?"

"Aye, name's Kian."

"Na'veyja's grace shines—on me."

"As it shines on us all. What're ye called, friend?"

"Wilam..."

"Let's have a look here, Wilam." Kian moved the man's tunic aside. A large chunk of flesh had been torn away exposing a portion of the man's innards. He cringed inside when he saw the severity of Wilam's wounds but did not let him see his shock.

Kian wound some grasses together to pack the tear in Wilam's abdomen. He sprinkled a fine dust over the grasses, chanting lightly as he did. *"Ren fonn stet hala."*

A line of flaura radiated out from the middle to the outer edge, sealing the grasses and dust into an instant poultice. "Hold still now, brother, ye lost a lot of blood."

"No—must warn—King Ren..."

"Warn King Renalth? What warnin'?"

"Disciple loose..."

"Disciple? A Disciple of Nemilos?"

"Aye, Glen Arwe..."

A nicker in the distance told Kian that Siasta had returned. A quick look revealed Grove Seven had arrived upriver. Kian whistled to let them know his location.

"Help is here, Wilam. Be stron' a moment more, lad."

Kian went to the edge of the water and called to the far side, "There's a wounded man here, Quin! Beyond ma skills!"

Quinlan and Ticari crossed as Kian had, hand over hand with their legs dangling downriver. Chyne stepped up to the riverbank. She performed a small dance with an accompanying chant almost out of Kian's hearing. Kian's vine line suddenly swelled in size and sprouted many uprising branches until a bridge was formed with handholds along the way. She crossed the vine bridge so smoothly she could have been dancing at a festival.

"Just here," Kian said and led the others to where Wilam lay.

Quinlan and Chyne exchanged concerned looks when they saw the open belly wound. The man's breathing had gone even shallower. He grimaced in pain whenever he tried to move. Quinlan turned to Kian and shook his head. Wilam was dying.

Quinlan placed a hand over Wilam's forehead, "*Na'veyja gon hem grev.*"

Wilam quieted immediately and his eyes opened. He locked eyes with Kian and reached out to him. Kian took his hand.

"Beware Glen Arwe," Wilam whispered. "Dreyg have taken over the military."

"Dreyg in Glen Arwe?" Kian asked.

"Aye…" he managed a nod of his head. "They mean ta invade MacRory lands and take the castle." A fit of coughing racked his body.

"Easy lad," Kian said.

"Ye must—warn—Cammachmo…" Wilam said as his eyes lost their focus and he breathed his last mortal breath.

"Rest easy, Wilam," Kian said. "Yer message will reach the king's ear. I swear ta ye." He laid Wilam's hand on his chest and closed the sightless eyes.

Most of the grove had crossed the river before Wilam passed and had gathered around to hear his last few words.

"This dinnae bode well," Wylla said.

"A disciple and dreyg forces here in Grannagh Province. Should we warn Lord Grannagh?" Ticari asked.

"I believe Lord Grannagh's ambition is behind them bein' here ta begin with," Freyn said.

"What goes on?" Kian heard Ticca call from where she, Sovia, and Therin waited with their horses across the river.

"The man has died, Teek," Ticari called back.

"Chyne, will you make the bridge strong to cross the horses here?" Quinlan asked.

"I shalt do so at once, brother," she answered.

"Do we confront the disciple, Quin?" Kian asked.

"Not at this time. If the dreyg have taken control of Glen Arwe, then we must warn the surrounding provinces. Sovia, send an élan to the conclave with word of what has come to light."

"We should be more wary travelin' through Grannagh Province," Kian said.

"Yi, take the northern trail," Therin replied, "through the mountain pass inta MacRory Province, then south down ta Cammachmoor."

Flit and Singer soared in and circled the group, both chittering excitedly.

"Flit says shadows be moving this way and almost be upon us," Sovia said.

"Dreyg!" Kian said.

Quinlan grabbed Askue from his horse as he instructed the grove. "Quickly, lone-traveler strategy. Chyne hide the horses, the rest scatter into the brush."

~~~

Quinlan alone stood next to Wilam's body when the first dreyg came into view.

"Ho there!" the first mercenary to see him called out.

A second dreyg advanced and seemed to recognize Quinlan's raiment. "Druid!" he said to alert the others.

Quinlan was circled by seven dreyg fighters in the space of two breaths.

"What's your business here, druid?" the second man asked.

The man's skin was a deep tan and his speech had an unfamiliar accent.

"You are not of Grannagh Province, friend," Quinlan said. "What is *your* business here?"

The man seemed surprised at being questioned in return but narrowed his eyes. "None of yours, *friend*."

"Indeed, we should go our separate ways, then." Quinlan smiled and leaned on Askue.

"Not likely." The man advanced on Quinlan followed by another.

"Grove Seven!" Quinlan gave the command to engage as he turned to face the closest man.

The dreyg moved in with his longsword forward at waist level with hilt to hip.

Quinlan took Askue up in both hands and stepped into a forward stance.

The dreyg lunged in.

Quinlan stepped offline and cracked the man's knuckles with Askue before tossing it in front of the second man's feet. Two steps, a spin, and a small poke in the neck from a spinose thorn left the first mercenary temporarily paralyzed. Quinlan had him trussed up like a goose before he could groan twice.

~~~

The second dreyg closing in on Quinlan stepped where Askue had landed. The walking stick rolled away under the man's weight and happened to take the man's foot with it.

The man staggered to catch his balance only to step on the rolling Askue once again. Both of the man's feet shot out from underneath him, landing him flat on his back, and flinging the hop-hornbeam staff high into the air.

Askue, being an admirer of gravity, came back down. Coincidently landing in the same spot the man had, specifically on his forehead.

The impact left the man out cold and with a growing lump over the center of his right eyebrow.

~~~

Ticari and his sister lay hidden in the bushes behind one of the dreyg fighters around Quinlan.

"Ticca, beddie-bye," Ticari whispered.

"Right," she replied and rummaged through her stuff.

Ticari threw seeds at the man's feet and worked the tievine spell, "*Sro man uut nataz.*"

The seeds sprouted instantly, growing into strong vines that ensnared the dreyg's feet.

"What trickery is this?" the mercenary said in surprise. He looked around and caught sight of Ticca and Ticari. The man slashed through the tievines with his sword and freed a foot.

"Ticca, hurry!"

"Found it!" Ticca took a dried fungus ball from her pouch and whispered "*Shushana,*" over it.

The dreyg grimaced at them as he yanked his other foot free. Ticca threw the puffball hard and landed it square in the man's face. The dreyg inhaled the spores, coughed twice, and fell face-first to the ground in a deep sleep.

"Well thrown, sis! Come on."

~~~

Chyne disguised herself as a bush and stood still as one of the dreyg fighters passed close by. She brushed his shoulder with a branch leaving a tiny vine behind. When Chyne focused her spirit on the little vine, it began to sprout rapidly.

The dreyg went to tear the nuisance from his body, but the ivy quickly latched onto his arm as well. The ivy wrapped up and around his torso and began to cover his face. Tiny vines quickly crept up his nostrils, down the inside of his nose, and back out through his mouth. He began to choke and gag as he tried to pull the plants from his nose and mouth, but the ivy continued to ensnare his hands and arms. The dreyg let out a muffled and panicked scream before he ran off in haste.

Chyne knew the vines would recede after a time. Giggling, she went to help the others.

~~~

Therin gathered handfuls of red berries growing nearby. *"Dun vas mah sikla,"* he said to the berries causing them to rot and smell badly.

"Flit, come here, love," Sovia said. She reached out to the élan with her spirit.

Flit chirped three times and flew to Therin's shoulder landing next to Singer where she let out a long string of chittering. Dozens of élan and other birds flew in and circled Therin. Each bird dropped in to grab a berry and take off again. The flock flew toward the dreyg and circled around Quinlan. The feathered dive-bombers dropped their load over two of the dreyg fighters.

The men were momentarily distracted by the unexpected appearance of berries from the sky and their horrible odor, but they were dreyg mercenaries and smells could be disregarded. The mercenaries ignored the smell, but not the hard-biting flies of the river lands that found the smell most attractive. Only a few flies buzzed around the men at first and then they were everywhere, crawling into their eyes, mouth, and ears, biting everything. Two swords hit the ground as their owners ran for the river.

~~~

Wylla and Freyn stood close together. Freyn wove invisible runes in the air. She stopped with her hands up, her palms out toward Wylla. Glowing strands of energy flowed between them. Wylla gathered the energy in a cloud swirling over her head and shoulders.

"Swarl en mar!" she called out.

A low buzzing noise grew louder as thousands of bees, wasps, and hornets converged around Wylla and set off after the last remaining dreyg fighter.

The man froze when we saw a swarm of bees heading his way. He looked around for help and seeing that it was not there, he turned and ran. Yelps of pain could be heard from a growing distance as the bees escorted him from the area.

~~~

Quinlan picked Askue up from the ground making sure the dreyg with the lump on his head was still unconscious.

"Gratitude, Seven—and Wylla and Freyn," he said to the group. "Well done, one and all."

"I like the bees, nice touch," Cassae said to Wylla and Freyn. "I can only call a dozen or so on a good day."

"I could nae call a one afore I teamed up with Freyn," Wylla replied. "Now, any zinger with a stinger answers ma call."

"Dreyg fighters and a disciple, here in Raskan," Kian said. "Why dinnae the Tretjey warn us? Surely he must somehow be aware there's an overlord of Acimasiz within a fortnight's ride of the conclave, right under our very noses."

"Should we return to the conclave?" Ticari asked.

"No, we'll send word by élan and continue on to Cammachmoor and Drifting Leaf as planned," Quinlan said. Kian's comment stuck in Quinlan's mind. How could such a powerful adversary be so close and the druid council not know it?

"More dreyg'll come fer these men," Kian said. "We must be a ways down the trail when they return."

"What about Wilam? We cannae just leave him," Swela said.

"Bringeth the body of Wilam hence," Chyne said, moving to a spot near a large bush.

Kian and Quinlan picked Wilam up, careful not to spill anything from the man. They laid him out where Chyne had indicated.

Chyne wove a design in with air over his body. Grass and small plants encased Wilam and several hooked-thorn briar bushes grew up around it.

"Thy rest shant be disturbed," she said when she was done.

"What of the dreyg?" Ticari asked.

"Leave them to free themselves," Kian answered.

"Agreed, better than they deserve," Quinlan said. "Mount up, Grove Seven. We ride for Cammachmoor."

~~*

Chapter Twelve

A man stood behind a podium in the audience chamber of castle Torr Amhairc in the city of Cammachmoor. The large group before him consisted of his friends and fellow citizens. He was an elderly man and slight of stature. The horseshoe of hair remaining on his head was white as snow. A wooden casket carved with a forest scene was close behind him. One lid panel was still propped open.

"Forty-two times the wheel of seasons has spun since I first met Eldret," Kenri said. His eyes shone with emotion and rimmed with tears. "My heart was his from the moment I saw him. We were young men in the Order of Arden and the world was under our feet. The happiest day in my life was the day he became my husband, and the saddest day was the day"—Kenri stopped to maintain his composure—"was the day I watched him take his last breath."

Kenri looked down and tears ran from his eyes. A man with dark brown hair and beard and clad in the traditional leather and furs of the Raskanish King approached the podium. He embraced the old druid briefly before wiping his own eye and returning to his seat.

"Eldret brightened the lives of all those around him and he touched so many. He would be pleased that you are all here. A gathering of remembrance will be held in the courtyard. Gratitude for coming."

Kenri took some time at Eldret's side and walked down the center aisle, taking his place at the door. The first rows emptied and the rest of the people rose to pay their respects to both Eldret in the casket and to Kenri on the way out.

Kenri saw a guardsman go to the king about an hour or so after the gathering had started. After a brief discussion, the king's minister, Modgrin Macreeth, walked over to Kenri.

Kenri smiled at the man as he approached. "Mod, what puzzles thee?"

'Tis not my puzzle, Tretjey Kenri, 'tis yers. A group of yer brethren are here and askin' ta speak with ye."

"Former Tretjey, Modgrin, former Tretjey," Kenri replied. "Now I am only a simple and solitary druid."

"In a pig's eye."

Their eyes met and they both laughed.

"Very well, Minister Macreeth, let us go see what is afoot."

~~~

Grove Seven and company waited on a covered balcony overlooking the city of Cammachmoor. Quinlan admired the bright flags of Torr Amhairc as they fluttered in the afternoon breeze. King Renalth, Modgrin Macreeth, and Kenri joined them not long after they arrived. All there rose to their feet.

Kian, Swela, Wylla, and Freyn placed their hands over their hearts and bowed their heads. "My King," they said.

"Ah, ma Raskan druids." Renalth grinned widely. "Does ma heart proud ta see my folk in the service of the Order." He turned to the others. "Greetin's ta ye all."

"Nin shi sha talla wathi," Kenri said to Chyne in Gwylari.

Chyne smiled and hugged Kenri. "Fensi nah sequa, Kenri."

"Always wonderful to see one of the Gwylari," Kenri said. "Shin Lahqui, Quinlan."

This took Quinlan by surprise. "Shin Lahqui—apologies, have we met?"

"No, I am Kenri."

"How do you—"

"Askue told me," Kenri said and stopped short. He turned and walked toward Freyn. He put his hand to her face. "Two conduits? Fascinating."

"I'm Freyn, Master Kenri."

"I am master of nothing, child," he said and sat, quietly thoughtful for a moment before he looked at Wylla. "And you are her catalyst. Wylla is it?"

"Aye. The Wardens sent us."

"Indeed. Eldret and I have been waiting, but Eldret had elsewhere to be."

"We heard when we arrived. You have our sympathies for your loss, Kenri," Quinlan said.

"Most kind." Kenri's hand went to a ring on a chain around his neck and the mist of memory clouded his eyes. "Well, Eldret could not wait, and neither can we. There is much to do if we are going to save Drifting Leaf and the rest of our world from the clutches of Acimasiz."

"You know of the trouble in Drifting Leaf?" Quinlan asked. "Have you been in contact with the Order?"

"Not exactly," he answered cryptically and looked at Cassae and Therin, the only Shaanlanders there. "The lands of your home are in terrible danger. The overlords—they call themselves disciples as if a word can hide their hideousness—they poison the hunting grounds and watersheds of Arden hoping to weaken the essence of Na'veyja enough to break Acimasiz from his oaken prison. The deep woods have been cut and burned from one end of Shaan to the other by that demon, Lord Praven. The ruining of Drifting Leaf Watershed would be a devastating blow to the Shaan eco-structure and it is only one of several areas under attack across Arden."

"The Cealjin Delta?" Quinlan asked.

"Yes, the Order foiled their plans in the Cealjin years ago, but they have returned." Kenri walked to an illustrated map of Arden painted on the balcony's inner wall. He dragged a finger from the Cealjin Delta in Vakere to the east, along the southern coast of Arden to Shaan, then up the west coast to the border of Raskan territory. "The dreyg have infiltrated the entire coastline. Once they have poisoned or clear-cut all of this area, they will begin to push inland until they reach the gates of the conclave itself. Stopping them at that point would be impossible, so we must stop them now."

"Brother Quinlan," Ticari said. Quinlan looked his way. "The man we found."

"Yes, thank you, Ticari." Quinlan told the king, the minister, and the druid about the events at the Wildron River.

King Renalth turned to one of the guardsmen. "Find General Gilburl and Captains Callan and MacRory and have them report ta me here at once."

"Aye, Sire."

"I thought as much when we got nae word from them," Modgrin said. "Gratitude fer seein' ta Wilam, 'twas a kindness."

"So, dreyg've taken Glen Arwe and probably all of Grannagh Province with it. First the Tenneths turned against us and now the Grannagh. The Bothains are the only house left. If they turn against us we'll have enemies on all sides." King Renalth leaned on the balcony rail and looked out over his city. "I'll remember this day— peaceful and quiet in the times to come."

The guard returned with the people requested. One was a man dressed in midweight armor that he wore as easily as if it were made of linen. A younger man was with him dressed in somber finery for Eldret's service and also a woman in similar attire yet quite a step up in quality over the younger man's. Quinlan and Modgrin made the introductions for their respective sides. The group informed the newcomers of what had transpired in the gorge.

"General Gilburl, I want ye ta close up the city, set watches in the towers, and begin regular patrols of the surroundin' woods. Post troops at the gates and muster the militia. Bolster and supply all the border outposts and prepare fer war."

"Aye, Sire, I'll have Cammachmoor secure by sundown," he replied. "I'll send dispatches out ta the commanders and quartermasters. Our forces will be on the way by midday on the morrow."

"Grand." Renalth turned to the younger man. "Captain Callan, get yer agents afield. I want ta know the second any troops threaten our borders."

"Aye, Sire," Saith Callen answered, a bit distracted at first but then focused on Renalth. "I'll send them out at once."

"Ma condolences ta ye and yer kin fer the loss of yer brother, Captain," Renalth said to him.

"Gratitude, Sire. Wilam knew the risks when he signed on."

"I'll see that the annals show he gave his life in service ta the city," Renalth said. "Captain MacRory, have yer people watch fer any sizable forces musterin' and marchin' toward Raskan."

"I'll send word immediately, Sire," she answered.

Kenri said to Renalth, "Sire, with your leave, I would like the blending pair, Wylla and Freyn, to join Grove Seven's quest to heal Drifting Leaf Watershed—and that they take the artifact with them."

"The artifact? What's in yer head, druid?" Renalth asked.

"I believe I understand the artifact's purpose now, Sire. I believe it must be buried in the heart of the watershed to neutralize the poison. The runes show two pairs of figures connected by some power to the artifact under the mionad esbat, which means the middle full moon of green rising. I believe the figures are Wylla and Freyn and Quinlan and Askue."

"Pardon me, druid Kenri, green risin'?" Ronirah MacRory asked.

"Yes, the Gwylari wheel of seasons consists of the Cetria of White Fall, the Cetria of Green Rising, the Cetria of Na'veyja's Bounty, and the Cetria of Forest Glow."

"So, their green risin' is equal ta our sprin'?" Saith asked.

"Roughly speaking, Captain." Kenri worked out something in the air. "The mionad esbat will occur two weeks and one day from now."

"Kenri, are ye sure about this?" Renalth asked. "Give them the artifact without an escort?"

"A grove of druids in the woods is far less conspicuous than a host of troops anywhere, Sire."

"Ye're sure?"

"The artifact and two blending pairs, here, and at almost the exact right time," Kenri said. "Yes, it was meant to be."

"I must confess bewilderment, Kenri," Quinlan said, "You know our names and mission, yet it seems you speak of others. I have no knowledge of any artifact necessary to our goal, nor was it our intent to seek you out or even to travel to Cammachmoor. I must send word to Tretjey Sayon at the Northern West Conclave."

"Sire, may I speak with my brethren privately?" Kenri asked.

"Certainly. We've our work cut out fer us preparin' the defense of the province," Renalth answered. "Inform me when ye've reached a decision. We'll let the gatherin' continue."

"Gratitude, Sire." Kenri waited until only the druids were left. He gestured to the table and chairs in the middle of the balcony.

"In the early days of the Order," Kenri said, "druids and Gwylari were everywhere across Arden. Old tales tell that the flaura was widespread and bright, like a blanket of glowing gossamer over the land. Over time, the druids began to focus only on the Great Marsh, the Seyna, and Fairtheora, which was their duty, yes, but not their only one. When their focus narrowed, other places were left untended. Now, the flaura only glows in the deep woods and the forces of Acimasiz work tirelessly to hew the deep woods and extinguish every last glimmer of flaura. Tell me, what good will the Order and its grand conclave be if the rest of Arden lies dead around it?"

"Yet we are here," Therin said angrily. "Here ta tend Driftin' Leaf and fight the forces of Acimasiz!"

"Yes, and why?" Kenri replied calmly. "Why take a grove off rotation at the Great Marsh and send them all the way to the far side of the northern continent? There are druid outposts in Vakere that are much closer. Word is they've already sent two groves into Drifting Leaf. They have not yet returned. You've heard none of this?"

"What's this dung you be shoveling?" Sovia asked. "The council just up and sent us, Grove Seven, away—why?"

"My guess is someone discovered something they shouldn't have or perhaps asked too many questions someone else did not want answered."

Cassae looked over at Quinlan when Kenri mentioned the last part. Quinlan looked back.

Kenri noticed. "Brother Quinlan, have you a tale to tell?"

"None that include Drifting Leaf, but I have expressed concerns regarding the Seyna."

"Indulge me."

Quinlan cleared his throat and thought how to begin. "I have noted changes in and around the Seyna, in both plant growth and the vibrancy of the flaura. I've mended more than fivescore holes in the Seyna in my last off period."

"Quin!" Cassae looked at him in shock, which quickly changed to irritation.

"Apologies, Cass, I intended to speak with you. I just..." he shrugged to finish.

"What? Not enough time in the last two weeks as we rode across Arden?" she replied. "Fivescore holes? Ya should'a told us."

"Cass has the right of it, Quin," Sovia said. "You need to be sharing with us matters of such importance."

"I was uncertain of my suspicions and my inquiries met with resistance," Quinlan said. "I was assured the Seyna was in no danger and I did not want to spread unnecessary concern."

"Have these dead spots appeared before?" Kenri asked.

"Only since this last white fall," Quinlan answered. "I mended twelve dead spots a moon ago."

"A dozen dead spots ta more than a hundred in a moon's time." Kian whistled.

"Yes, a fair amount of death to have in a hedge that should be imbued with everlasting life," Kenri replied.

"What does this all mean?" Ticari asked.

"Poisoned watersheds, barren hunting grounds, dwindling flaura, and now the Seyna falters." Kenri's face dropped. "It has already begun. Na'veyja is weakening."

"Surely Na'veyja cannot weaken?" Ticca asked. "She is an essence of the Vast."

"Aye, that's right," said Cassae. "The Primerey would know if the Seyna or Fairtheora were at risk."

"She does know," Quinlan said, coming to the same realization as Kenri.

"Yes, she knows Na'veyja's power has been drained away to heal the damage done by the dreyg over the centuries," Kenri said. "We must heal the watersheds and save as much of the deep woods as we can if Na'veyja is to regain her strength."

"A tall order for one grove and a couple of Wardens." Swela frowned.

"And an artifact," Kenri added.

Wylla turned to him. "Can we see this artifact?"

"Oh, indeed, you'll be taking it with you," Kenri replied.

"Where do we start?" Cassae asked.

"By restoring Drifting Leaf to its former glory," Kenri said, "and with recent news, your departure should be even swifter. If war breaks out, your journey will be much more difficult. I'll make some arrangements. For now, fill your bellies at the gathering and we'll reconvene at the stables."

~~~

Swela walked into the stables after refreshing herself at the privy. A conversation was already underway.

"Watershed rescue contingent," Ticca said.

"We're not a contingent," Ticari replied. "It should be a special rescue grove."

"The brotherhood of the woods."

"No, too much like Wardens of the Woods. Drifting Leaf quest—tarians."

"Questarians?" Ticca exclaimed, "Ha! That is dung."

"It is not dung!"

"Such a stimulatin' conversation the twain of ye are havin'," Swela said.

"We're standin' in a stable, Swayz," Kian replied. "Nae better place ta talk about dung. They're tryin' ta give a name ta our mission ta save Driftin' Leaf."

"Oh, and *dung* come inta it somehow? I do fear fer the outcome of our title."

A commotion outside the stable brought their attention to a cart drawn by a grey beast with long ears and a black-and-white nose. The creature seemed to disagree with everything in the world.

"A burro?" Kian asked. "Do ye have anythin' a little less stubborn—like an ogre?"

"Oh, poor dear, what manner of torture is upon thy face?" Chyne said to the burro and reached up to take the leather mask from its head.

"Nae miss, dinnae do that," the stable handler said. "She bites somethin' fierce."

"I blame her not." Chyne reached for the bridle this time.

"Miss, ye'll be needin' that. That's how ye control the beast."

"How thee controls *the beast*, mayhap," Chyne said and some of the leaves of her blouse turned red. "By what name is she called?"

"She dinnae really..." The man stopped when Chyne scowled at him.

She nuzzled the burro, which seemed much happier than a few moments ago and quite content to nuzzle back.

Swela had never seen Chyne get angry before. She was proud to be the Gwylari's friend.

"Thy name shalt be Blossom and thee shant ever returneth to this place," Chyne said to the burro.

"Now, han' on here," the handler said.

"That's all right, Rendice," Kenri cut him off. "A small price to pay for the service they do us."

The grove, which now officially included Wylla and Freyn, gathered around the cart as Kenri unfastened the heavy cloth cover. The artifact was bigger around than Quinlan's torso and nearly twice as long. The outer framework looked like snow-white plant flesh over some kind of endoskeleton. The entire artifact was covered by a network of green veins that throbbed like the vessels and capillaries of a living being.

The inner part of the artifact was connected to the framework with a membrane of the same fleshy material. A sack held in place by the membrane had various ports and orifices, with tubes coming out from various spots and disappearing into others.

"The resemblance to the gemstone from my vision is too great to be coincidence," Quinlan said.

"I thought there might be a connection when you first told me of your vision," Kenri replied, "but you said 'gemstone' so I was not sure until now."

"The shape is similar to the gemstone I saw and the coloring is the same," Quinlan said. "Are we to bury it?"

"It was half-buried and totally submerged when it was found," Kenri answered. "I believe it should be returned so. I had thought the damage we had done could never be undone, yet now I look upon you all with great hope."

"What does it do?" Swela asked.

"I believe it to be a purification device of some kind," he said, "but truth be told, I am not absolutely sure. Wylla and Freyn can wield Na'veyja's grace while Quinlan and Askue channel the power of the esbat. How I wish I could be there. Surely, it will be fascinating to behold. I have faith in all of you and may Na'veyja guide you on your journey."

"Grove Seven, mount up," Quinlan said. "Gratitude, Kenri, for resupplying our stores."

"My gratitude to you all for what you do. I will ask Na'veyja for good fortune. Farewell to all, Grove Seven."

The group waved as they urged their horses from the stables and out into the main road out of the city.

"Come, Blossom," Chyne said and the burro followed along without any complaint.

The grove of druids led Blossom and the ordinary-looking cart from the city of Cammachmoor and turned south heading for Shaan and Drifting Leaf Watershed.

Chapter Thirteen

Ronni MacRory finally caught up with the druids after leaving nearly ten days behind them. She needed to tend to her duties in the upcoming defense of MacRory lands, but once she had done that her curiosity got the better of her and off she went like a thief in the night.

Three days of hard riding left only two more days until the moon would be full again and the druids could bury the artifact. She had to be there to see for herself what it would do firsthand. The strange artifact had captivated her from the moment it was found and brought to Torr Amhairc.

Ronni tracked the grove to a campsite late in the evening and risked a few hours' sleep. The next day she used the hills to stay hidden while tailing the druid grove. She would let them get just out of sight before moving to the next ridge. The druids stopped at midday, so Ronni stopped as well. She tied up her horse and snuck up a hill to recon the group's activities.

Satisfied they were staying put for a meal break, she backed off a ways and found a fallen tree to hide behind, where she munched on trail snacks and dried meat. She was happy being back out sneaking around the country. Her skills had greatly improved and she was at home in the woods. She'd be able to watch what the druids did with the artifact and report back to King Renalth with what she had learned.

Ronni looked up to admire a bird that had landed in a tree above her. She almost screamed out when horrid smelling blobs began landing on her face and shoulders. The smell made her gag and she could not wipe whatever it was off fast enough to avoid retching her small lunch onto the ground.

Though she splashed what water she had in her bota on her face, it was not enough. She waved away some flies, but started for her horse when they got worse. Hordes of flies gathered around her, landing on her face and crawling into her nose and mouth. She couldn't see where she was going. When she tried to take a quick breath the flies were there to immediately crawl inside her mouth.

"Ah! Ah!" Ronni exclaimed in pain as the flies began to bite. She brushed her face and swatted the air, but the insects were relentless. She stumbled and fell to the ground. "Help!"

"*Maad jues kom tralee raza.*" She heard a woman's voice say and the flies were gone.

Ronni spit flies from her mouth and blew them from her nostrils before she lay back in exhausted relief.

"Who are you?" she heard a man's voice ask.

"It's Lady Ronirah!" she heard another male voice say before she had a chance to reply.

"It do be her," another woman's voice said.

Ronni opened her eyes to see the grove stood around and looked down at her.

"Do you be all right, love?" a Kalnuvian woman asked. "We thought you be a dreyg."

"Because dreyg skulk around and spy on folk," the red-haired male druid said pointedly.

Ronni rose to her elbows and accepted hands to help her up to her feet.

"Here." The youngest druid girl gave her a kerchief soaked with water.

"Gratitude." She dabbed at her face a couple of times, but then stopped. "And apologies. 'Tis a bit humblin' ta have rotten fruit, bird poo, and flies run yer arse off." Embarrassed, she felt her cheeks flush, yet she had to admit it worked well enough.

"Ye are Lady Ronirah?" asked a young woman with a scar on her neck.

"Aye, Ronirah MacRory, but it's Ronni, if ye will. Apologies, but I dinnae remember yer names."

Quinlan made the introductions as they retrieved Ronni's horse and walked back to where Wylla, Freyn, and Chyne waited with the horses and Blossom.

"Does King Renalth think us treacherous?" Quinlan asked.

"Nae, I'm here without his knowledge and I may pay fer that when I return, we'll see," she answered. "He trusts Kenri as do I, yet the artifact has captured ma curiosity. I must see what it does. I ask ye ta let me travel with ye. I'll be nae trouble." The last bit brought out a few smiles. "Well, from here on anyway." She smiled as well.

"Come, love, let's be getting you cleaned up," Sovia said.

Ronni pulled off her outer tunic to wash off the berry residue and bird poo. Her blouse underneath was by no means revealing, but the light fabric billowed in the breeze and at times outlined her figure. She noticed the druid, Ticari, nervously looked away whenever she turned in his direction. On one glance she smiled at him and he went still like he had been caught with a cookie from the cooling tray.

Sovia must have noticed the same thing. "One body do appear smitten," she said quietly to Ronni along with Cassae and Swela, who were nearby. Ronni nodded.

"I know, how sweet." Swela leaned in and said.

"Ugh, I remember when he joined the grove three years ago," Cassae said, "He was small for fourteen but now stands as tall as I."

"He is a handsome lad," Ronni said. "So, if ye dinnae mind me askin'—the artifact, how do ye know where ta bury the thing?"

"It do truly be a puzzlement," Sovia said. "First, we're off to Drifting Leaf to heal some ailing plants, and now we be on a mission to save Na'veyja. Strange as that—*carraig*, for a better term—may be, it still feels right being around it."

"Aye," Swela said. "I feel the same. 'Tis almost a gratitude comin' from the carraig. Like it knows we're takin' it where it needs to be."

"Carraig, dinnae that mean 'stone'?" Ronni asked.

Cassae nodded. "Quin had a vision durin' a moon dance. He stuck a gemstone inta the ground and he and Askue rode the light from it to the esbat."

Ronni understood only half of what Cassae said. "Apologies, I dinnae follow ye. What're a moon dance and an esbat?"

"The esbat be the full moon, love," Sovia answered, "and the moon dance is the dance we do under the esbat."

"Oh, and who's Askue? Is he here?"

"Yi, right next ta ya," Cassae said.

Ronni looked on both sides of her and saw no one. "Where?"

"There." Cassae pointed to where Askue leaned on the log next to Ronni.

"What, this stick?" she asked.

"Yi, Askue, Quin's familiar," Cassae said.

"He rode a magic walkin' stick ta the moon?" Ronni felt sure these women were having fun at her expense.

"In a vision, love, in a vision," Sovia said.

"Nae, Kenri said Askue told him who Quinlan was, it cannae be—" Ronni went to pick up Askue and there was nothing there. "What in the name...?" She looked around and saw the walking stick in the hands of the Vakerian druid on the other side of the road by the cart. "Ohhh, nae, nae, nae, 'twere right here a second ago!"

"Aye, Askue loves ta mingle," Swela said.

Ronni did not know whether to trust what had just happened. "Did—did ye just bewitch me?"

The women laughed.

"Do ye know naught of the world ye live on, Ronni?" Swela asked.

"Ye mean the tales of Na'veyja and Acimasiz?" she said. "Aye, I heard the tales when I was a lass. There're many tales of gods and goddesses though, and I cannae say I believe in any of them. Religious folk've always been a puzzlement. I believe in what I can wrap ma hand around."

"Ya feel nothin' when you're near the carraig?" Cassae asked.

Ronni looked down and absently scooted some dirt around with her foot. "Aye, truth be told, it do call ta me."

"Then mayhap Askue be more than a mere hunk of wood," Sovia said.

"Hmm..." Ronni said. "Is this what ye lot do, run around and heal ailin' lands?"

"Nae, we usually patrol the Seyna," Swela answered.

"The Seyna?"

"Perhaps a quick refresh on the tale of Na'veyja?" Cassae asked.

"Apparently." Ronni shrugged.

"Two eternal bein's of the Vast beyond Arden," Cassae said, "Na'veyja and Acimasiz we call them. Adversaries for ages they were. Weak from the eternal struggle, they fell ta Arden where they fought a great battle. Na'veyja and the Gwylari tricked Acimasiz and imprisoned him inside a massive oak tree called Fairtheora. The oaken prison stands in the center of a sacred circle hedge imbued with Na'veyja's grace, the Seyna, which is deep in the Great Marsh. The grounds of the four druid conclaves surround the Great Marsh, where the Order of Arden stands vigilant against Acimasiz's escape, and so, that's what we do, patrol the Great Marsh."

"Well said, sister," Swela said.

"We be Grove Seven of the Northern West Conclave," Sovia said.

"So, I can travel there, ta the marsh, and see this sacred hedge?" Ronni asked.

"Yi," Cassae said with a nod. "Come back with us, if ya will."

"Nae, I should nae be gone now. I can spare only 'til the full moon and then I must return ta Cammachmoor."

"How'd the carraig come ta be at Cammachmoor, if ye dinnae mind *me* askin'?" Swela asked.

"Kenri and his late husband—Eldret, a druid himself—went on a quest nigh on sixteen year ago with another druid, Tangetan, and his band of druids. A grove ye call it?"

Sovia nodded.

"Yet they dinnae dress as ye. Anyway, six months later, only five of them returned. They brought back the artifact and the sickness, which eventually killed them all years later, Eldret bein' the last one ta go. They spoke of travelin' through black clouds of mist and of misshapen creatures ta reach a glade of peace and beauty."

"Where be this glade?" Sovia asked.

"Gone now," Ronni said. "The glade withered and began ta die the moment they took the artifact from its restin' place. Try as they might, they could nae put it back. The glade turned as black as the mist surroundin' it. They did the only thin' they could and took the artifact. They were doomed ta live with what they had done fer the rest of their days, which ended up nae as lon' as they thought."

"Quin," Cassae called out, "all of ya—ya must come hear this. Ronni, would ya tell it again?"

Ronni told the story of Eldret's quest to find the ancient druid artifact they now called the carraig.

"Wee as I was, I thought them all wizards." She smiled.

"A curious tale indeed," Quinlan said. "I never heard the name of Tangetan before. Kenri, I had—he is one of the few druids to resign from the council. A former druid council member, his spouse, and a rogue grove of druids embarked upon a quest to unearth an ancient artifact in years past, and we are now burdened with its reinterment. This journey has awakened many peculiar insights."

"Ye think them yankin' the thin' is what started weakenin' Na'veyja?" Kian asked.

"I know not, but it did no good to the glade it slept in," Quinlan replied. "I know we have tarried here long enough. Let us return to our travels. We should reach the watershed by high sun on the morrow."

Ronni and the grove fell in behind Chyne, Blossom, and the cart hauling the carraig to resume their journey to Drifting Leaf Watershed.

~~*

Chapter Fourteen

The sun sat just past its zenith the next day with not a cloud around it. The group crested the last rise before Drifting Leaf and saw the watershed basin spread out for acres to a mountain range on the horizon. The roadway followed the edge of the forest a ways before it turned away from the watershed to run along its perimeter and continued on all the way to the southern crossroads between Shaan and Vakere.

Patches of tall trees grew here and there mixed with small glens and open fields of grasses. Ponds of standing water dotted the basin connected by streams and rivulets. A grey haze hung over a large area a half league to the west along a rocky escarpment. The bright sun should have penetrated the thin haze, yet the haze seemed to swallow the sun's light before it hit the ground underneath. A large majority of the trees and plants throughout the basin stood brown and on the verge of dying.

"An ill spirit hangs over this place," Quinlan said when he saw the terrible condition the watershed was in.

"It breaks the heart," Therin replied.

Quinlan turned to him and indicated the hazy area. "Let me guess, the heart of Drifting Leaf lies there."

"Yi, Quin, what gave it away?"

"Hmm, I believe it was the unwelcoming and evil black fog that caught my eye."

"Your wits are as sharp as ever, no matter what Cassae says."

Quinlan flashed his friend a quick smile. "We'll have to leave the roadway when it reaches the level of the basin and turns away to the east."

"A trail runs alon' the edge, which should brin' us ta the bottom of Goat's Fall Cliff. Afterward there's no easy way ta get the cart down through."

"We'll deal with that when the time comes," Quinlan said.

The group's horses came to an uneasy stop right before they reached the turnoff. They all began to shift in place and nicker.

"Easy there now, Sayhaa," Swela said to her horse.

"Whoa, Biscuit, what's the trouble, boy?" Quinlan asked his.

Biscuit turned his head to look at Quinlan and nickered a few times. Quinlan read the motions of Biscuit's eyes, ears, nose, and lips.

"He senses a predator nearby," Quinlan said to the grove. "Best be wary."

Blossom began to bray nervously when some beast let loose a terrible roar in the distance.

"That sounded big," Ticca said.

"Aye, it did," Kian said as he spun Siasta around in a circle so he could check the area around them.

A man and two children ran out of the woods and out onto the road ahead of the group. The young girl stumbled and fell to the dirt roadway. The man scrambled to pick her up and continue running. The boy stopped and began to half hop, half stomp in a panic while urging them to hurry. They must have noticed the group because they made a beeline straight for them.

A thunderous crashing came from behind the family as a tremendous beast burst onto the road, snapping the trees before it like twigs. The giant beast's momentum took it into the tree line on the opposite side of the roadway before it spotted the family again. Enraged, it charged at the man and his children.

"Torac!" Cassae yelled out in warning.

The Torac had grey skin with sparse black hair growing along the ears, spine ridge, and underbelly. The tapered tail, long enough to reach its head, ended in a hair-covered tip. Wide flat teeth lined the back of the gaping jaws. Four tusks, each the size of a man's arm jutted out to the sides of the top and bottom jaws. Jagged teeth filled the gaps at the end of the snout. The beast had two stout horns protruding from its forehead, one above each round black eye. Five times the size of the biggest horse, the creature's body was massive enough to fell full-size trees and rip them, roots and all, from the ground.

~~~

Swela urged her horse into a gallop, racing past the panicked family and toward the charging beast. She dismounted while she still had time.

"Cha Sayhaa!" she said and the horse immediately bolted away.

Swela turned and walked into the beast's path.

"Swela, nae!" she heard Kian yell, but she dared not break her focus on the beast.

The beast roared and lowered its tusks as it charged in on the new target and would reach her before any of her druid companions.

Swela held out her arms as she would to an old friend. The scar running up her neck began to pulse with a soft yellow-golden glow. "Ease yer anger," she said calmly and repeated it in Gwylari. "*Talath on hongna.*"

The beast ceased its roaring and slowed to a run.

"*Talath on hongna...*" she let her voice trail off slowly.

The beast slowed again, shook its head, and came to a stop within an arm's reach of Swela. The giant Torac dwarfed Swela standing in front of it and could have easily torn her apart.

"*Na tasu on grev*—I feel yer pain."

The beast moaned and warbled, pitifully turning a bit to one side.

Swela looked down the beast's flank and saw many wounds. Sharpened steel coils had been fastened around her feet cutting the flesh down to the bone with every step. Torn and bloody areas marked the spots where the beast's toenails had been ripped away. Septic puss oozed from gangrenous round holes in her head and neck. Her sides and belly had been slashed and torn open.

Silent tears fell from Swela's eyes as she closed them against the horror of what had been done to the beast. She set her will against her sorrow and focused on compassion.

"*Na'veyja gon sha grev*—Na'veyja please take her pain," she asked in prayer.

The beast quieted immediately and gazed into Swela's eyes as it slowly lowered its hindquarters to the ground. Swela held the beast's gaze until the entire massive body lay upon the ground. She knelt and gently stroked the beast's head.

"*Kip ri granis tala*—sleep in deserved peace," she whispered.

The beast rumbled softly, closed its eyes, and left its misery behind.

Swela sat back on the heels of her feet. Touching the spirit of any animal took energy, but this encounter left her exhausted. The Torac's misery was so strong she could barely stand it. Tears welled in her eyes and began to glide quietly down her cheeks.

The group, including the family, approached in time to see the glow of her scar slowly fade away.

"Swayz-hon, ye all right?" Kian asked as he knelt down next to her and took her into his arms.

"Aye." She rested her head on his shoulder for a breath or two. "Help me up."

"Do ya be wizards?" the man of the family asked. He had a look of caution on his face and kept his children behind him.

"No, friend, we are druids from the Order of Arden," Quinlan answered. "I am Quinlan and you can rest easy. We mean you no harm. How came you to be chased by this beast?"

"We live not far," the man said slowly and his wariness seemed to ease. "I be Delvin. We come here ta forage and hunt, but Driftin' Leaf has gone foul in recent days, so we must venture farther inta the woods ta find food. We were gatherin' roots and mushrooms when we came upon the beast."

"Who could do such a horrible thing?" Ticca asked when she saw the injuries.

"The grey soldiers," Delvin said. "It's their doin'. They hunt down all the wildlife and don't even strip it down. Leave it lay there ta rot. Better than what they do ta the ones they capture like this one here."

The sight of the tortured beast changed something in Swela. She felt the creature's spirit as she had with other encounters, but with this one came the agony of the pain compounded with what she could only comprehend as shock and disbelief. The injured creature could find no escape and with every movement came more pain.

"What do we do with her?" Swela asked and swooned slightly.

"Ye're gonna sit down a spell," Kian said to her.

"I'm—"

"Going to sit down a spell," Quinlan said. "Chyne and I will see to her."

"I'm—gonna sit down a spell," she replied and let Kian lead her away.

~~~

Quinlan watched the two walk away and turned back to the beast in the roadway.

"Chyne, Sovia, lend me your aid?" he asked. "Let's get the poor girl off the roadway."

The three druids began to chant which brought up massive brown vines from the ground under the body. The vines had rough bark and many fibers to provide great strength. Interwoven, the netlike vines wrapped around and lifted the giant body as though it weighed nothing. The group deposited the body a far distance from the roadway. Chyne finished the job by covering the body with grasses, moss, and wildflowers.

The family stared in stunned silence as the druids did their work.

Quinlan made a quick decision. "Sovia, cut out what supplies we can spare and give them as much as they can carry."

"It will be so, brother."

"Me gratitude ta y'all," Delvin said. "This is Dylen and Dylah, my cherubs." They stayed tucked behind their father until Sovia brought out a bag of apples. He gave them permission and they happily lightened the bag by two.

"There be more by the cart and a small bag of seed for your fields to boot," Sovia said.

"Blessin's be on ya, ma'am. We've not seen much kindness from folk since the grey soldiers have taken over Trossachsmuir."

"What do ya mean taken over Trossachsmuir?" Therin asked.

"Yi, and the military too, led by a sorcerer from the south, it's said."

"Calls himself a Disciple of Nemilos?" Quinlan asked.

"I know not what he's called."

"Lord Praven," Ronni said.

"Lord Praven? What do you know of him?"

Ronni told Quinlan and the others what she knew of the disciples who were sent to the capital cities of Raskan, Shaan, and Vakere.

"One in Vakere?" Quinlan asked.

"Aye, do ye get nae word from the outside?" Ronni asked. "These are nae exactly current events here, Quin. Renalth ordered Kazim Fadlam out of Raskan, but the Grannaghs secretly welcomed him inta Glen Arwe. A grove of druids captured a disciple in Vakere and Lord Ilywodre Dronjida, Khan of Vakere, burned him in the city square. The obese moron, King Tavish of Shaan, on the other hand, all but handed over the keys of Teivas Keihas to Lord Praven."

"Ni." Therin shook his head, his features downturned. "What of the druids posted there?"

"Hunted down and killed in Driftin' Leaf," Delvin said. "We seen it. Folks dressed such as y'all, they were fightin' the grey soldiers."

"The dreyg mercenary army," Ronni said.

Quinlan felt a deep dull anger build in the depths of his mind. Had this been kept from all druids? It troubled him, Tretjey Sayon saying to keep watch for the dreyg when all the rest of Arden knew they were already here.

Ronni must have guessed what was on his mind. "Feelin' a bit like a mushroom, Quin?"

"I have been a fool," he said. "Kenri once asked me, 'What good will the Order and its grand conclave be if the rest of Arden lies dead around it?' I do not know Kenri, yet what he said rang true and what my superiors have told me has not."

"What're ye gonna do?" she asked.

"I'm going to go shove this thing up Drifting Leaf's wellspring and see what happens," he said with a wink.

The group broke out in laughter.

"Now, let's send these folk on their way and be on ours," he said.

The grove said good-bye to the family and continued into the watershed.

Chapter Fifteen

The group stopped at a small clearing before the trail narrowed in width and thickened with trees. The sun dropped behind Goat's Fall Cliff casting a deep and growing shadow over the watershed. A cool damp breeze seeped down the trail from the heart of Drifting Leaf.

"We'll have to leave the cart behind," Quinlan said as he dismounted from Biscuit. The rest of the group dismounted as well.

The horses and Blossom all moved to the far side of the clearing from the trail, their ears twitching back and forth.

"Perhaps we should leave them, too," Cassae said.

"We must reach the wellspring by nightfall," Quinlan said. "We'd have to haul the carraig the rest of the way by foot. Therin, how much farther to the heart?"

"Two hours' walk," he answered. "And Cassae has the right of it, the woods're too thick ta ride much more."

"We cannae leave them here unguarded in this blackness," Kian said.

Quinlan needed no more than a breath to decide who stayed behind. He turned to the Vakerian siblings and they knew right away what was in store for them.

Ticari pleaded with him, "No, Siestrey, please."

"What decision would you make, Ticari, if you were grove leader?" Quinlan asked.

"But we'll have no part in what needs to be done," Ticari replied.

"Not so," Quinlan said and put his hand over his heart. "Truth be told, your value is as great as the sky in my eyes. I think you have shown true worthiness on this journey. I know our travels have caused you to postpone your trials for advancement. So, in recognition of your dedication to the Order of Arden, I advance you to the circle of Settey and grant you all the privileges of such."

The disappointment faded from Ticari's face but not quite completely.

"I am not doing this to get you to follow my orders. I know you'll do that no matter what. You deserve it, Ticari, and I fear we won't be back at the conclave in time for your trials."

Ticari smiled and nodded. "Gratitude, Siestrey, I will strive to make you proud."

"I am that already, kinsman." Quinlan turned to the group. "I give you, Settey Ticari, of the Order of Arden."

The grove each took turns congratulating the new Settey and he in turn conveyed gratitude to them all.

"I'm nae sure what that is, lad, but ma compliments," Ronni said and gave him a quick hug.

Ticari stood tall and complained no more.

Quinlan looked around for Ticca, but she already stood with her arm over Blossom. She simply smiled and waved. He nodded and smiled back.

"Therin, help me unload the carraig and we'll rig up a carry harness," Kian said.

"Yi, I'll grab the rope."

"We'll need the lanterns, too," Quinlan said.

The carraig was almost the size of Blossom, but nowhere near as heavy. Chyne unhitched Blossom and the men used the two tug shafts from the cart and a rope harness to construct a carry litter. Looped ropes tied to the ends of the shafts could be worn around the shoulders to take most of the strain off their arms.

The group bid farewell to the siblings and started down the trail toward the wellspring heart of the watershed.

"The dark is so heavy. There's nae even a glimmer of flaura in the entire countryside," Swela said. "Barely make out the trail."

"Well, we can do somethin' about that," Cassae replied. She brought out a small piece of citrine-encrusted quartz. Holding it in both hands, she chanted, "*Londa neath kalra hom ruhn.*"

Cassae's chant called a horde of fireflies to line both sides of the pathway in a large radius around them.

"Oh! Can ye teach me ta do that?" Ronni asked.

"Yi," Cassae said, "and it only takes about five years."

"Is that all?" She laughed. "I'd best get started."

When the group proceeded down the path, the fireflies in back took off and flew to a plant ahead of them to land again. They continued to do so all along the way. The effect was pleasing to see, but after another hour the dark around them grew even heavier. The fireflies pooled at one point and would go no farther as the grove neared the wellspring.

"What be that foul stench?" Sovia asked.

"Break out the lanterns," Quinlan said.

Swela brought up her carry bag and pulled out a small metal and glass lantern. She placed an oblong item into a holder inside the glass.

"*Tomm sa see naa,*" she chanted over the lantern.

The item she placed inside began to glow with a brilliant white light. The illumination of one was enough to light up the woods around them. The grove lit three more.

"'Tis like nae flame I've ever seen," Ronni said. "What do ye use ta burn?"

"A cured mixture of glow fungus and bog peat," Cassae told her.

"Bring your lights," Quinlan said. "Let us see what we have."

The search did not take the grove long. Just past the boundary of fireflies, a noxious-smelling black pod lay in the middle of a small rivulet. Streaks of black ooze were being carried down the slow current.

"*Cooth jath frey urula san hajime,*" Quinlan chanted over the pod.

The pod's output slowed momentarily but resumed after a few seconds.

"Chyne?" he looked at his Gwylari friend and she joined him. Together they repeated the chant in unison.

The black pod broke apart and disintegrated leaving only the clear water washing it away, yet the plants around it remained black and withered.

"Tough little bugger," Wylla said.

The fireflies lined the trail once again until they had traveled a ways where they once again pooled up in protest.

The grove found another black pod, which Sovia and Swela took charge of dispatching.

"Seems we can use the fireflies to hunt down these festering pods," Quinlan said.

The dark of night began to settle over Drifting Leaf Watershed. The shadows along the edge below Goat's Fall Cliff were as black as ten feet down. The grove worked their way along dispatching the toxic black pods wherever they found them. The breeze brought a stench to them worse than that of the black pods.

"We must be drawin' nigh ta the heart," Freyn said.

"Another twenty minutes," Therin replied.

"The esbat will rise soon," Cassae said. "We must hurry."

The grove rounded a turn and came upon the heart of Drifting Leaf, a large spring flowing out from the base of the escarpment. The streambed in front of the outlet was piled with the black pods. The edges of the stream were lined with oily black slime that was the origin of the hideous smell.

The grove worked as fast as they could to clear the toxic pods from the spring and the headwaters of the stream, which flowed through the watershed. Chyne, Swela, Sovia, and Therin used the fireflies as scouts and continued to neutralize the black pods strewn around the area.

Quinlan and rest of the group eliminated the pile of noxious pods from the headwaters before they placed the carraig in the spring flowing out from the base of the escarpment. The green veins over the white flesh swelled and throbbed as if some internal pressure began to ebb and flow. Ports on the bottom opened, pulling water and stream bottom into the carraig while other ports ejected the material back out over the top. The carraig buried itself like a tortoise in the sand until it was fully submerged in the water.

"Oh..." Ronni said. She gasped and seemed at a loss to say more.

"Never have I seen the like," Quinlan said. He stood back and waited, but nothing else happened.

"The esbat be rising," Sovia said as they returned from the search-and-dispatch mission.

Quinlan looked at Wylla and Freyn. "What do we do now?"

"Ye?" Wylla asked. "Nae a clue. Us on the other hand, Freyn, bein' a conduit, will channel Na'veyja's grace ta me, and 'tis my job ta brin' the carraig ta life as I would a seed ta saplin'."

The comment brought memories of a trip he and his father had taken in his youth. Riklan, his father, had given a Gwylari maiden a palerin seed and by the next morning, the Gwylari had grown the seed into a fruit-bearing tree.

"Quin?" Cassae brought him out of his reverie.

"Right, apologies," he said. "I am certain now my vision came from Na'veyja. Whatever comes of this night, it has been my honor to tread life's trails with you all."

"What, are ye retirin', brother?" Swela asked, with a sly smile on her face.

"Never!" he replied and gave a short laugh. "There will forever be a plant or animal in the world and those who would do them harm. I will always be there to rise against them and do what I can to protect the world I live in."

"Well said, brother," Sovia said, and the rest of the grove sounded off in agreement.

The moon's course took it past a heart-shaped hole high up in the canopy of an oak tree. Moonlight beamed down through and temporarily brightened the area around the wellspring.

"That be a sign for sure," Sovia said.

"Aye, now's the time," Wylla said.

Quinlan trusted in his vision and focused his spirit. He lifted Askue high, pointed it at the full moon, and began to chant repeatedly, "*Esbat nom krayla nom talsa.*"

The moonlight pouring through the heart-shaped hole was drawn to Quinlan and Askue. A shimmering silver glow built up around the staff, sparkling with bright white lights followed by shimmering tails like thousands of tiny shooting stars. The silvery-white starfield traveled down Quinlan's raised arm, flowed across his body, and continued down his other arm toward the carraig.

Freyn began to weave back and forth as if dancing slowly to music only she heard. She drew intricate designs in the air with her hands. An emerald-green mist formed around her body. The mist grew to a cloud swirling around her and flowed toward the invisible runes in the air.

Wylla stepped in front of Freyn, facing away from her. She chanted, "*Toir salan magnor rotan.*" She repeated the phrase seven times while working ethereal runes in the air around the carraig. The glowing runes flowed from Freyn drawn in by Wylla's chant of calling. The emerald energy gathered around Wylla pulsing with every word she spoke. Glowing green vapors formed around her hands and drifted down to cover the carraig in a bright green mist.

The green vapors from Wylla and Freyn mixed with the slivery-white starfield flowing from Quinlan's arm. The tiny bright stars whirled through the glowing green cloud, and together they pierced the waters of the wellspring without a trace, pooling around the carraig.

The blended energy was drawn in through the fleshy exterior and a strange thrumming began, deep and low pitched. *Whoosh-woom, whoosh-woom, whoosh-woom.* The thrumming became a vibration right before a deep boom resounded and a micro shock wave passed through the ground under their feet.

The esbat moved past the heart-shaped hole in the trees and the tiny white star field faded away. Wylla ceased the rune dance and Freyn brought a stop to the energy flow. Quinlan relaxed and leaned upon Askue, pleasantly exhausted. The vibration had faded and the watershed was quiet.

"Do it be working?" Sovia asked.

The grove gathered around and brought their lanterns in close. The carraig quietly drew in and expelled water. The outflow shimmered with glowing green particles that drifted downstream and caught on the bottom and sides of the stream. The particles pulsed briefly before they disintegrated and healed the injuries inflicted by the black pods.

"Yi!" Therin exclaimed. "Yi, my brothers and sisters, the healin' of Driftin' Leaf begins!" He lifted his arms to the sky. "Gratitude Na'veyja, my goddess!"

The grove, and Ronni as well, joined him both in celebration and in a show of gratitude.

Freyn borrowed a lantern and held it over the carraig. "'Tis a wonder ta behold."

Wylla joined her to watch the carraig pump out the glowing particles. Quinlan wondered if the two might consider relocating to the Northern West Conclave when they returned.

Flit and Singer chittered excitedly and sent out warning calls.

A low whistle turned Freyn's smile into a look of shock as an arrow plunged into her back, ripping completely through and sticking out of her chest. She dropped to her knees, letting go of the lantern, and fell forward. She was dead before she hit the ground.

Wylla screamed, "Nae! Freyn!"

Quinlan screamed, "Take cover!"

The lanterns went out and more arrows whistled through the darkness around them.

"Ah!" Quinlan heard Kian cry out and Swela call to him.

Quinlan snuck forward and risked standing up to throw a handful of seeds out in front of him. "*Toir salan magnor rotan.*"

The seeds instantly grew into a hedge of thick twisted branches forming a wall between them and the attackers.

The glow of several small fires could be seen a short distance away. Flaming arrows filled the night around them. Many struck the water-fat hedge and succeeded in starting a smolder only. Only three flew over the top and landed behind them where there was brush or trees. The rest sputtered out in the water. Another volley sailed in, striking more targets. The flames around the arrows behind them began to spread.

Quinlan let loose a series of quiet whistles and animal noises. Grove members closed in on his position.

"Kian?" he asked.

"Arrow ta the leg, but okay," Swela answered.

"Good," he said. "Okay, I'm assuming they're dreyg. We need two groups to flank each side, and one up the center to distract them. Use flash fungus and gympie gympie plants. That'll change things up. Sound off with a night bird call when ready. Go when you hear a northern owl screech."

The grove split up and used woodcraftiness to move around the attackers without being seen or heard. Quinlan heard the birdcalls soon afterward. He took out a chunk of the lantern fuel and dropped it into a small drawstring bag of powdered tree bark. He called out a northern owl screech.

"*Tomm sa see naa,*" he chanted over it, waited five seconds, and threw it toward their opponents' position.

Three loud bangs went off in close succession each one accompanied by a bright flash of light. Shouts of surprise came from the attacking party.

Chyne was next to him and began to chant over a spiked seedpod, "*Sul olo gavel gympie gympie notso.*" She lobbed the seedpod into one of the groups while the attackers were still stunned by the flash fungus.

Screams of pain and agony came from the attackers as the silica-tipped hairs on the twigs and leaves of the gympie gympie plants penetrated any exposed skin releasing a neurotoxin into the blood. The neurotoxin set the skin aflame with a terrible stinging pain wherever the hairs penetrated.

Quinlan let loose another northern owl screech and the grove repeated the attack. The sounds and yells of men diminished as they scrambled to get away from the scene of their brethren's misery. Only moans of pain could be heard from where their attackers were.

"Close in," Quinlan called out. He retrieved a lantern and chanted it into brightness. Others in the grove did the same and they circled the men who remained. A man was on his knees, gympie gympie hairs glistening on his hands and face. He held his hands out in front of him like he was afraid to touch anything. A black-and-grey herringbone-weave aiguillette ran from his left shoulder to the left breast of his uniform.

"What did you do to me?" he asked in a voice quivering from the pain he was in.

Wylla strode forward and threw vine seeds and an oak nut at the man's knees. "*Toir salan magnor rotan.*"

"Wylla, no!" Quinlan yelled in an attempt to stop her.

Tievines grew and wrapped tightly around the man's ankles. The oak nut sprouted into a sapling and quickly into a tree. The tree pushed into the soft flesh between the man's legs. He screamed in terror and pain as the tree grew up through his torso, lifting him from the ground. The branches erupted from his rib cage, wrists, and neck and continued to grow. Gurgles and squelching sounds of flesh ripping came from the man as the growth of the oak tree tore his body limb from limb.

So passed Kwyett, Commandant of the Dreyg, from the realm of the living.

"Oh, Wylla..." Quinlan said. He could only guess at the turmoil her spirit was in at the moment.

"Just desserts, if ye ask me," Ronni said.

"As druids, we've vowed never ta take a life," Swela said.

"The rest have run off, Quin," Therin said.

"Come, we must gather Freyn and go," Quinlan replied.

"Nae—she would want to stay here," Wylla said. "She'd not have us makin' a fuss."

"How great thy pain must be," Chyne said. She moved up and laid her head on Wylla's shoulder. "A loom tree doth stand nearby. Freyn shall rest peacefully under great beauty."

"Aye," she replied. "Gratitude, Chyne."

The group returned to the wellspring where Kian waited and Freyn's body lay upon the ground. Quinlan knelt beside her, snapped off the nock end of the arrow, and slid the shaft from her chest.

"So?" Kian asked.

"We routed them," Therin answered.

Kian scowled and nodded at the news. "Blasted cowards, hope they meet an end they deserve."

"One has already," Ronni replied.

"A man be dead," Sovia said, "and not upon accident either."

"Oh?" he asked, but then took one look at Wylla. "Oh..."

"Can ye walk?" Swela asked.

"Aye, the arrow's out and I've packed and wrapped the wounds. Managed ta put the fires out, too."

"Well, ye dinnae need me, then," she teased him. "Come on, up ye go." Swela tucked her shoulder under his arm and helped him to his feet.

Quinlan checked the carraig before they left to make sure nothing had changed. The druid artifact continued to draw water in and pump glowing green particles out. The areas of healing could already be seen in the light of the lantern. The edges of the stream were beginning to turn green again.

"Okay, then," he said, "Therin, lend me a hand. We'll carry her to the tree."

"I got her, Quin," he said and the tall man easily picked Freyn's body up from the ground.

They sat Freyn upon a rock outcropping under a broad-leafed tree halfway back to the horses. Wylla folded her hands in her lap and laid her head gently to the side. She seemed to be asleep, the dark of night masking the stain of blood with shadow. Wylla kissed her and stroked her face.

"I love ye," she said. "I will always love ye, dear Freyn. My heart I leave here with ye." Wylla wept and softly spoke a poem.

"I've been on a journey of many milestones, yet my feet dinnae tire.

They've walked dry trails warmed by the sun.

They've tread muddy slopes soaked by dark storms.

The destination is known, yet the trail is misted by many tomorrows, or perhaps just one.

I walk on."

Tears flowed from her eyes and fell to the ground. She stood and nodded to Chyne.

Chyne chanted and wove runes in the air. The outcropping grew over with roots topped with a thick bed of moss bursting with wildflowers.

They said their farewells and continued on to meet up with Ticari, Ticca, Blossom, and the horses.

~~~

"I'm happy for you, Ticari," Ticca said, "and I'm proud to be your sister."

"Gratitude, Ticca. I am surprised by it, but happy, too. Settey"—he let the word sink in—"that means I'll have new classes when we get back. I'll learn new chants and have new duties."

"I know it is wrong, but I wish it were me," she said.

"You just made Osmey, Teek. So, you'll have new classes, too."

"Oh, right." She nodded. "When do you think they'll be back?"

"It's not even sunset."

"They'll be gone for hours," she said and huffed out a sigh of boredom. "Let's eat."

Ticari grinned and the two broke out foodstuffs for themselves and their four-legged friends. Leaning on their bedrolls, they huddled amidst the horses and satisfied their hunger. The sun had set and the full moon rose over the horizon. Sated and comfortable, sleep overcame them both.

A deep boom and the ground shaking under them roused them from the slumber.

"What was that?" Ticca asked.

"I know not," Ticari replied.

They listened but heard nothing further.

"We best pack everything back up," Ticari said, "and light the lanterns."

"It shall be so, Settey," she said.

They waited for what seemed the whole night to Ticca. She wandered to the trail and back every few minutes hoping to catch sight of her grove mates returning.

"They'll be back soon, Ticca."

She turned to reply and saw a man-sized shadow move behind her brother. "Behind you!"

Ticari rolled forward, recovered, spun around, and threw something at the shadow, "*Toir salan magnor rotan.*"

A wide bush with long heavy thorns grew to full size in seconds. A yell of surprise from the darkness preceded a yell of pain. Ticari had hit his mark and turned toward more movement.

Ticca's horse, Cinnacoss, whinnied loudly. Ticca caught a shadow move in the corner of her vision. She quickly ducked under Cinnacoss and pulled out a fungus ball. "*Shushana,*" she whispered and threw it as a dreyg fighter came around the front of her horse. The fungus ball hit him in the shoulder. He laughed as he swept the fungus from his jerkin a second before he fell to the ground unconscious.

"Ha!" Ticca said.

Cinnacoss whinnied again.

Ticca pulled the same maneuver. "*Shushan*—ah!" she screamed as another dreyg fighter grabbed her before she was done.

"A girl?" the man asked. "Oh, yer done, missy—Ah! Ah! Ah!" The man screamed as Cinnacoss bit deep into the crook of his neck and shoulder.

The horse dragged the man away from Ticca and toward Blossom. Cinnacoss let the man go and he turned around in time to face the burro's hindquarters. Blossom looked back over her shoulder at him. Her double-back-leg kick sent the man flying through the air and into the unforgiving trunk of a nearby tree. The horse and burro looked at each other and then at Ticca.

"Gratitude," she said to them.

A third dreyg came after Ticca. Blossom and Cinnacoss moved in and a moment later another dreyg fighter sailed through the air.

Shouts of familiar voices and more lanterns moving through the darkness filled her with joy. Her friends had returned.

Grove Seven harassed the remaining fighters until they fled into the night.

"Are you two all right?" Quinlan asked.

Ticca was so happy to see him she ran up and hugged him.

"Ticca?" Ticari asked.

"Yes, I'm well," she answered. She stepped back and looked at Quinlan, "What of the carraig?"

Quinlan told them of the night's events.

"Both amazing and terrible at once," Ticca said after hearing the tale.

"Yes, love, that be well said," Sovia replied. "Well said, indeed."

"You've packed," Quinlan said. "Good thinking, that. Let us travel a ways through the night and be gone from this place. It is time to close the distance to home."

The group agreed and prepared to mount.

"What's to be done with the cart, Quin?" Sovia asked.

"Leave it," he said. "The tug shafts have to be lashed back on. It will do Blossom good to walk free."

They moved up the trail from Drifting Leaf, but Blossom remained behind.

"Blossom," Chyne said, "thee shan't tarry. Come along."

Blossom laid her ears flat back and looked at the cart and back at Chyne.

"But thee are free to roam," Chyne said.

She stomped a front foot and looked at the cart.

Chyne looked at Quinlan.

He shrugged his shoulders and got down from Biscuit. "Lash up the tug poles. It looks like we're taking the cart."

One of the dreyg Ticca put to sleep moaned as he began to awaken. Therin put him back to sleep with a good old-fashioned five-knuckle lullaby.

"That's for Driftin' Leaf, ya shite," he said.

The cart was assembled and hooked back up to Blossom. Her ears were back up. She pranced in place and appeared ready to leave.

"Let's go," Quinlan said and led the way down the trail.

~~*

Chapter Sixteen

Lord Praven stood calmly now in the provincial chamber of Teivas Keihas. He missed his desert homeland and had grown tired of King Tavish's recent resistance. The king's demands this morning did not meet with Praven's approval.

King Traelin Tavish was now a shriveled and lifeless hulk on the floor of the provincial chamber along with six of his chancellors. Praven did regret the sea captain, Travell, once Prince and now King of Shaan, was not among them.

"Lenistrat," Praven said to the scribe, who was trembling against a far wall of the chamber.

The man stared at the bodies and did not respond.

"Lenistrat!"

He looked at Praven. "M-m-my Lord?"

"Issue a bounty for the life of Travell Tavish, wanted for high treason and the murder of his father, King Traelin."

"I am b-but a scribe, Lord Praven."

"Not any longer, *First Chancellor* Lenistrat."

"The l-lords of the royal houses will not—"

"If anyone objects they can come and see me here," Praven said with a wave around the room. "A squad of the dreyg will escort you."

"Y-yes, my lord. I'll go now."

"No. First, you will scribe a letter to Lord Nemilos." Praven motioned him to a chair at the central table.

Lenistrat tiptoed over what was left of the bodies of King Traelin Tavish and the former first chancellor. He sat down and brought out his writing packet.

"Lord Nemilos, it is my duty to inform you of several setbacks in our occupation of the northern continent. I accept full responsibility for our failures."

Praven waited for the scribe to catch up.

"I have received word Disciple Onidra has been captured in the Cealjin Delta and executed in the Vakerian capital city of Hearth's Port. Vakerian military forces now gather along the eastern border of Shaan."

Praven waited, Lenistrat wrote.

"Our forces in Drifting Leaf have been unsuccessful in completing our mission. The druids have reversed the effects of the shadow parasite infusion. The manner of reversal is unknown at this time. More parasite hulls are being grown and will be ready in a week's time. Mercenaries are being mustered to return and reclaim the watershed. Commandant Kwyett of the dreyg has been killed in the field. A new commandant will have to be appointed."

Praven paused a moment to think.

"A dispatch detailed the loss of Glen Arwe and the defeat of the dreyg forces stationed there," he continued. "MacRory military forces now control Grannagh Province. King Renalth is mobilizing his armies along the border of Raskan and Shaan. We now have threats from both Vakere in the east and Raskan in the north."

Praven watched while the scribe wrote.

"King Traelin and the royal council have been eliminated and the dreyg have control of the capital city. Teivas Keihas is now our central base of operations. The port and surrounding waters are in our control and our ships stand guard at the harbor entrance."

Praven considered one final item.

"Prince Travell has eluded capture and with Traelin dead must now be considered a king in exile. Gone but best not forgotten. I anticipate certain military commanders and loyalists will follow his banner should it be risen in rebellion to our control. I will see him in chains before long."

At last, he peered over Lenistrat's shoulder and dictated his final reassurances to Lord Nemilos.

"Regardless of the setbacks," he said, "I believe we can hold Trossachsmuir long enough for our subterranean forces to achieve the primary goal in the northeast."

He looked over the letter as Lenistrat finished writing.

"Your servant—Praven," he said to close. "Seal it and send it by dreyg courier."

"At once, Lord Praven."

"Then see to the warrant on Travell," Praven said.

"Yes, my lord." He turned to leave.

"Lenistrat."

"My lord?"

"Mention any of this to anyone and I will drain the life force from your wife and children."

He began to tremble again, "U-understood, m-my lord."

"You may go."

"Gratitude, my lord." Lenistrat hurried from the chamber.

Pravus walked to the southern balcony of the tower, looking toward Trossachsmuir's harbor and, far beyond sight, his homeland. Every day, he felt damp and sticky in the moisture-laden air of the coastal city. He longed for the desert, yet the longing irritated him because it was a distraction from his duties. He was angry already at having to deal with the failure of the other disciples.

A knock at the door preceded a dreyg officer announcing visitors.

"Prince Kazim Fahdlam and Commander Marza Malent to see you, Lord Praven."

"Show them in," he said.

Kazim and Marza entered the chamber, both showing signs of their escape from Raskan and the journey to Trossachsmuir.

"Kazim, you were just on my mind."

"Hmm, cheery thought, that. You have been enjoying yourself, haven't you?" Kazim asked when he saw the bodies of king and council lying about the room. "You really must learn to control your temper, Praven."

"I have control of my temper, Kazim. Especially when I must bear the burden of Disciple Onidra, who failed and lies in ashes in Hearth's Port, and of another disciple who was sent running like a cur from Raskan with his tail tucked tight between his legs."

Kazim lost control of his own temper. "I needed more time!"

"You are a fool!" Praven said. "You sat back and waited until Renalth swept in and destroyed your forces like a desert village in a sandstorm."

"I don't know how Renalth managed to move an entire battalion into Glen Arwe without detection," Kazim replied.

"Why did Lord Nemilos endow *you* with the powers of a disciple, Kazim? You are nothing more than a façade of strength hiding incompetence."

"You are calling me incompetent?" Kazim asked. "I am not the one who had an entire watershed stolen from under his feet."

Praven turned an angry look on Kazim. "The watershed is a diversion! The occupation of Shaan is a diversion! Tell me, what are the goals of our efforts here?" Kazim remained silent. "Tell me!"

The muscles of Kazim's jaw stood out then relaxed. "Our goals are to weaken the powers of the goddess Na'veyja, to isolate the druid conclave, and to divert attention from the northeast corner of the northern continent until our main objective is achieved."

"It is your *indulgences* that have brought about your failure, Kazim, and because of it Raskan and Vakere can still come to the druids' aid. We must now work even harder to buy the time necessary."

Kazim poured a glass of port from a decanter on the table along the wall. He offered it to Praven first, who simply stared back at him. He then offered it to Marza, who had picked a spot far from the two of them when they first arrived and had stayed there quietly ever since. She shook her head. Kazim shrugged and drained the glass himself.

Praven stood there with crossed arms, studying Kazim as he finished the glass.

"What do you need of me, Praven?" he asked.

"The subterranean forces have finished their tunneling through the lithosphere and are nearly ready to collapse the structure."

"Have they reached the magma chamber?"

"Yes." Praven leaned over the map table and focused on the druid conclave at the top right-hand corner of the northern continent. "This entire region will become an instant caldera of molten rock. The frozen lands of Kalnu are close, but they are separated by this mountain range."

"And my part in your plan?" Kazim asked.

"Take an insertion force and stop any supplies or aid from getting through here." Praven pointed to a crossroads farther east than Glen Arwe."

"You want me to go back from where I was just routed from?" Kazim asked.

"Your penance for your failure to remain there," Praven said. He turned around in time to see Kazim right behind him and reaching out to drain him.

Praven could feel his life force being pulled from his body. He struggled to maintain possession, but Kazim's attack was too fast. Praven was not only losing the battle for his spirit, all of his powers as a disciple would now belong to Kazim.

The look of satisfaction on Kazim's face turned to a grimace of pain. The draining stopped when Kazim spun to face Marza, backhanding her to the floor. Her dagger was still sticking from his back. He reached his hand out and began to drain Marza to death.

Praven drew upon his powers as a Disciple of Nemilos and locked on to Kazim's life force. He drained Kazim slowly, enjoying every moment. Kazim's glossy hair fell to the floor as the life force left his body. His skin shriveled until it was ashen and wrinkled. Praven focused his attack on Kazim's powers and ripped them away. Kazim's limbs became twisted and grotesque. His legs buckled and he dropped to the floor. When Kazim's powers transferred over to him, Praven stopped.

Kazim moaned in pain as he tried to move his crippled limbs. Cloudy white eyes still held anger even as he searched for his enemy. Praven walked to his side. Kazim tried to grab him, but the gnarled fingers would not open.

"I—curse—you…" Kazim could barely form the words.

"Spit your empty curses, Kazim. They mean nothing." Lord Praven crossed the chamber to help Marza to her feet, but she was already up.

"Guards!" Praven said.

The dreyg guardsmen entered and looked at the moaning horror writhing on the floor, who was dressed in the prince's clothing.

"Remove him," Praven told them. "Have him stripped and thrown in a defecation pit at the piggery."

"Yes, my lord," they replied and hauled Kazim away.

"Why?" Praven asked when the guards had left.

"I was chosen to train as a disciple," Marza answered.

"Until?"

"Until Kazim replaced me." Her look turned sour. "My powers were taken from me and I was assigned a commission as a commander in the dreyg."

"A far cry from being a disciple," Praven said.

"Yes, my lord."

"Your skin color and speech tell me you are from the Kajiji region of the southern continent. Am I correct?"

"Yes, my lord."

"These cold northern lands are a long way from the comforts of home, are they not?"

"Indeed dey are, my lord."

"Perhaps the benefits of being Dreyg Commandant Marza Malent will ease some of the discomfort."

The look that flashed across her face gave him the answer he needed, but he waited to gauge her reaction.

"Indeed dey would, my Lord Praven."

He saw she was careful enough not to assume she had been given the position without hearing it.

"Congratulations, *Commandant Malent*," he said.

"My gratitude, Lord Praven." She bowed formally. "I will prove my value."

"The efforts to distract the druids and the lords of Arden must continue without delay."

"Understood, my lord," she said.

Praven knew he must not fail. "The weak link of Trossachsmuir is the south side facing the bay. The gates have stood open for decades. See to it they are closed and manned from now on. Bring masons and iron workers to reinforce the walls."

"It will be done, my lord."

"Soon our forces will achieve their goal and we will return to our homelands triumphant."

"I look forward to de day we can return home, my lord, but dere is much to be done before dat day comes."

"Indeed, there is." Praven looked out over the bay and the sea beyond. "Send for our sea captains, Commandant. We have plans to make."

Chapter Seventeen

Every moment since their return to Cammachmoor a day and a half ago, Grove Seven had been debriefed, spoken to, and interviewed by more people than they could count. Meetings with the Lords of the Raskan royal houses ran into conferences with druids who answered a summons from Kenri. The tale of Drifting Leaf was told a dozen times over at every meeting.

Quinlan rose early on the morning of their third day back. The grove joined Ronni to eat and then met with King Renalth, his Ministers, and a small group of druids Kenri had formed into a council of sorts.

"I say we move troops ta the far side of Driftin' Leaf in order ta protect the watershed from those dreyg bastards returnin'," Renalth said.

"Nae sayin' yer wrong ta do so, Sire," Modgrin replied, "but 'twould name ye invader in the eyes of some."

"Ni, not invasion—liberation," Therin said. "I guarantee there's ni Shaanlander happy about the enemy destroyin' our homeland."

The Shaanlanders among them, who sat around the table, agreed with Therin.

"Many would even join a liberatin' force comin' through," Cassae said.

Renalth's General of the Armies, Clennen Gilburl said, "A communique sent from Field Marshal Brixal informed us he's movin' the entire Vakerian regular armies ta the Shaan border. If we can free the northern half of Shaan and coordinate with the Vakerian offensive, we'll have those shites trapped between us and the sea."

"There will be more than men, horses, and the engines of war waiting at Trossachsmuir, General," Kenri said. "At least one disciple is there and perhaps two after your victory over the one in Glen Arwe and the routing of the dreyg from Grannagh Province."

"When did this happen?" Quinlan asked.

"Just after ye lot left fer Driftin' Leaf," Renalth said. "Cleared nae only Grannagh Province but ran them all the way out of Raskan!"

"What of the disciple there?"

"Kazim escaped, Quin, along with his dreyg commander," Kenri answered. "The things found done to Lord Grannagh and members of the royal family were—horrific."

Renalth outlined his plan. "Our attack'll be two pronged. An incursion force'll move inta northern Shaan and eliminate the chance of our army bein' flanked. Once we deal with the dreyg, the local militias can defend their own towns and villages as we push ta the south. At the same time, we send troops inta Driftin' Leaf, but we send druids in with them. Then we've steel and mysticism both ta combat whatever comes our way."

"We are not a folk hardy to the battlefield, Sire," Kenri said.

"I'll go," Wylla replied.

Quinlan noticed Kenri and Wylla locked eyes for a moment before the old druid continued.

"Ours would be a more subtle style of eliminating the opposition."

"Oh, subtle lot, are ye?" General Gilburl asked. "Subtle, like growin' an oak tree up a man's arse, that kind of subtle? Folk fear yer kind of subtle, friend Kenri. All we'd have ta do is spread word a druid walks amon' our troops and the dreyg'll be seein' a druid behind every tree in the woods. They'll nae be able to han' their arses over a log and have a shite without fearin' it'll be their last! Ha ha!"

Some of the gathered laughed with him, others did not join in. Quinlan saw Wylla smile briefly, but she did not laugh. Renalth did not laugh along either, yet he let the laughter and general dreyg bashing continue for a minute before he brought a stop to it.

"All right, rein it in, Clennen," he said. "Quiet down, quiet down. I understand Kenri, and havin' ye at vanguard was nae what I had in mind. I was hopin' ye'd lay traps with yer roots and vines and use other such trickery. Like those slings ye made fer yer flyin' fungus balls."

Kenri nodded and indicated some of the druids at the table. "We've developed blowpipes and darts tipped with spinose thorn among other items effective from a distance."

Quinlan looked at Chyne, who knew what he asked and nodded her approval. "We druids stand as children compared to the abilities of the Gwylari. It is they who teach us."

"The farmers?" Clennen asked.

"Farmers, General Gilburl?" Ronni asked and pointed to Chyne. "This wee lass conjured a stingin' nettle out of the ground and sent a man runnin'. What do ye think a group of them are capable of?"

Many of the people were startled when decorative plants around the room suddenly doubled in size. Surprise turned to unease when ivies twisted together into a green-leafed tentacle snaking its way over the table. The green ivy serpent spiraled down to the water decanter and refilled Chyne's glass before receding back to their planters.

"Well now, 'twas impressive indeed, lass." Renalth looked around the table as he continued. "The Gwylari and the druids can use their woodcraft ta slip around unseen and harass the enemy's flanks and eliminate their signalmen. That'll cause a great deal of confusion when the vanguard officers are cut off from their battle commanders. Our main army'll push forward in a coordinated attack with the Vakerians until the vanguard breaks and we take the field in victory."

The discussion continued with ideas from both sides about what they might find and how best to deal with it. The morning passed and the meeting ended with a positive attitude toward the events ahead.

Cassae took Quinlan's arm as Grove Seven left the meeting hall. "I hear the Queen is gonna plant a loom saplin' in Freyn's honor at the memorial."

"Yes, that's right."

"Which is bein' held in the Queen's Garden."

"Yes, it is."

"In about an hour."

"Yeees," he said while he looked at her out of the corner of his eye.

"Just enough time for a walk through the garden before it starts, don't ya think?"

The only answer was, "Yes, of course there is."

"I believe we've waited lon' enough," she said and kissed him openly for all to see.

"Oooh," Chyne said and laughed happily.

"Well, it be about time, I say," Sovia said. "I don't rightly know how the two of you have held off this long."

"We're off to the garden," Cassae said. "Who's with us?"

"I'll come," Wylla said. "It'll do me good."

Ronni shook her head. "I cannae. I must don my finery and do my duty as a lady of the castle, but I'll see ye down there."

The rest of the grove, planning to attend the memorial planting shortly as it was, all went along to tour the garden.

"Nice of Kenri ta have new clothin' waitin' for us," Cassae said along the way.

Quinlan looked down at his sleeve. "Yes, right down to the correct conclave colors and rank braidings. I am pleased and have expressed our gratitude, yet the former will still have its place among my possessions. A tale told with every tear."

"Yi, mine too," she said, "but, I'm happy ta have somethin' not torn and trail worn for the memorial today."

"Why dinnae Kenri wear a raiment?" Kian asked.

"He was once a member of the druid council," Quinlan said. "He spoke out about how the council had come to believe the druids to be the true power of the Great Marsh in place of Na'veyja's grace. It was said he thought the council had grown too prideful of their conclaves and the rest of Arden was paying the price for their arrogance. The council stripped him of his rank and expelled him from the conclave grounds. I had not thought to question the matter until the time we met Kenri and heard what he had to say."

Chyne drew in a deep breath. "Ne'er a more lovely sight hath mine eye beheld."

The entrance to the Queen's Garden, Loko de Belaj Floroj, was covered in blossoms of every imaginable shape and color, from the deep burgundies of the large black dahlia to the bright white of the tiny snowdrop perennial. The mild pastels of echeveria and spiky borage mixed with the eye-catching colors of heliconia and purple passionflower. Élan and other birdlife filled the garden and the sky above. Birds whose wings moved faster than the eye could see buzzed from one blossom to the next, finding sweet nectars to drink.

The garden grounds stood almost as a maze with the plots of colorful flowers and decorative stands of trees too numerous for one to see the far side of the garden. Fountains threw streams of water into the air to splash down into more than a hundred basins and pools that fed the small streams running throughout Loko de Belaj Floroj. Schools of fish sparkled in the sun as they swam from pool to pool.

"Oh, it's so beautiful," Ticca said. "Look at all the dogs."

Handlers strolled around the garden, each walking with a different breed of canine. The traveling duos stopped periodically to give short speeches, which allowed the guests to admire and learn about the breeds.

"Siestrey, what are those?" Ticari asked Quinlan.

A troop of monkeys hung about the rafters of a pavilion. They were small to medium in body size with long noses, human-looking eyes, and scruffy grey hair jutting from the bottom of a wrinkled face.

"They look like old men," Ticca said.

"They are called lesula monkeys, Ticari," Quinlan answered, "and yes Ticca, they appear so human they were once thought to be the *Trauco*, which are gnomelike creatures of Raskanish folklore."

"Look, pavao birds! Oh, they do be my favorite." Sovia pointed to large ground birds with long tail feathers tipped with a design like that of an emerald-and-sapphire eye.

"How cute." Cassae reached out to a hand-sized, fuzzy-faced creature with green-and-yellow-streaked round eyes, grey tabby-marked fur, prehensile feet, and a long ringed tailed.

"A marmoset from southern Vakere," Quinlan said.

"Oh!" Cassae said as the marmoset climbed up her arm and circled her neck once, leaving its tail wrapped around it, and settled down in the crook of her neck. It tucked its chin in its front paws and quietly watched everything go by around them.

Quinlan smiled at the look on Ticca's face as she watched the marmoset cuddle against Cassae's neck. Druid code or not, what young girl would not want to be the one holding a cute and cuddly animal?

"Charming creatures, are they not?" Kenri joined them with a marmoset of his own around his neck. "Hold out your arm, my dear," he said to Ticca, which she did. He rubbed the side of the marmoset's face. "Tuk, tuk, tuk."

The creature unraveled itself, climbed down his arm, and up Ticca's, taking its place around her neck. Ticca's face lit up with a smile.

"If you wish them to go, just say 'tuk' three times and they will wander off," he said. "Loko de Belaj Floroj is a wonderful sanctuary of plants and animals from not only Raskan but all around Arden. Many creatures other than humankind call our world home. They are as much our brothers and sisters as our fellow humans. So much will perish should we not succeed."

"Indeed, and well said," Quinlan replied. "Na'veyja will not let us fail. This I believe in mind, body, and spirit."

"Aye, blessed be the grace of Na'veyja," Kian said. "We shall nae fail."

"What does Loko de Belaj Floroj mean?" Ticari asked.

"It means 'place of beautiful flowers' in an ancient Raskanish language," Kenri answered, "which is no longer spoken, yet the Queen has had an affinity for it since her studies at the royal academy."

"Oh, my word!" Sovia exclaimed. "And not a one on me!"

Therin had birds perched all around him, climbing over him, launching from him, and landing on him. Flit and Singer each sat on a shoulder. He raised his arms and the birds flew circles around them.

"How does that be right, I ask?" Sovia was put out until Flit flew over and landed chittering on her shoulder. "Well, gratitude, Flit, I do love you as well."

"Better grab him, or they'll fly him away," Quinlan said.

A large élan swooped around Therin chatting up a storm before it flew off again. The flock of newcomers on Therin all flew off in the same direction and began to gather in the bushes and trees around a woman who was surrounded by people, too.

"Ah, Queen Aibreann," Kenri said. "She asked to meet the druids who took the artifact to Drifting Leaf. Now, before the ceremony would be an ideal time."

Ticca's face went pale. "Meet the Queen?" The marmoset snuggled around her neck suddenly looked up and turned its head back and forth, barking loudly with its tiny voice. "I'm okay," she told it.

The commotion drew the Queen's attention and she started to walk their way. Guests bowed and curtsied as she walked by.

"Oh, no," Ticca said. "Shh, shh, shush now." The marmoset calmed down but remained alert.

Kenri approached and bowed elegantly. "Your Majesty." All of Grove Seven followed his example.

Aibreann, Renalth's wife and Queen of Raskan, was a woman whose aura Quinlan read as bright and honest. She was dressed in traditional Raskan gowns of state instead of the slim-waisted, crinoline-supported ball gowns that were the latest in court fashion.

Aibreann took the time to hear everyone's names and thanked them warmly for their efforts in saving Drifting Leaf.

"And I do see ye back there, child."

Ticca peered out from behind Kian.

"What're ye doin' back there?" Kian asked Ticca.

"Apologies, Queen Aibreann, I did not hurt it."

"Oh, I know, dear. Pie's only soundin' off because she thought ye needed protectin' is all."

"Pie?"

"Aye, Pie Thief is her name and aptly so.

"Pie Thief, ha, that's funny," Ticca said.

"*Your Majesty*." Kenri reminded Ticca she was speaking to the Queen of Raskan.

"Apologies, Your Majesty," Ticca said quickly.

"Eck, bother all that." Aibreann waved Kenri away. "From here on, dear, ye're ta call me Aibreann. And Kenri, dinnae be such a storm cloud." Kenri bowed in acquiescence.

"Gratitude, y—Aibreann, I'm Ticca."

"Pleased ta know ye, Ticca."

Pie stood up barking and chittering before she hugged Ticca's head and cooed.

"Well I'll be..." Aibreann put her hands on her hips after Pie's demonstration. "Pie seems ta've found herself a new home."

"A new home, Your Majesty?" Quinlan asked.

"Aye, that little dance she did there shows she's chosen Ticca as a loved one," Aibreann answered.

"I can keep her?" Ticca asked and looked at Quinlan who shrugged and nodded.

"She's free ta make up her own mind and it looks ta me she's made her choice," Aibreann said. "Unless ye stand opposed ta such an arrangement, that is. If so, a handler'll take her away."

Pie Thief barked, flattened her ears, and went to hide in the pulled-back hood of Ticca's raiment.

"No!" Ticca regained her composure. "Ah, no, I, ah, I'm not opposed to such an arrangement."

Ticari laughed, but not unkindly, at his sister.

Ticca ignored him. "My deepest gratitude, Queen Aibreann."

"Ye're most welcome, Ticca."

Pie cooed from within the hood.

"And ye as well, Pie. Heed this girl, mind ye."

Pie issued a single coo.

Ticca turned and grinned at her grove mates.

"Bree!" Renalth called out. "It's time."

"Come, friends," Aibreann said. "We've a tree ta plant and a friend ta remember. Wylla, dear, come up front with me, if ye would."

"Aye, ma Queen, 'twould be ma honor."

Aibreann took her arm in hers. "I want us ta start this new life together in Freyn's name."

Wylla broke down in tears.

Aibreann gathered her up in an embrace. "There now."

"I miss her so."

"I know, dear, I know. It'll never go, but after a time it'll nae hurt so badly."

Wylla smiled sadly. "Gratitude, my Queen, fer what yer doin' fer Freyn and fer everythin' ye and the king've done fer our people."

"The Raskan people make it easy fer us ta care about them," Aibreann said, "and we love ta do so."

"Bree!" Renalth called out again. "Sheep farts in aspic, woman! Can ye never be on time?"

"Dinnae get yer knickers in a twist at me, *Yer Highness*!" she called right back and turned to the others. "Ooh, I could leather the arse on him some days. We best be gettin' on or he'll send in the king's guard."

The ceremony got underway as soon as they arrived at the plot with fresh dirt around a hole waiting for a tree to be placed within. Wylla took part in the ceremony and spoke of Freyn after the loom sapling had been set and watered.

Quinlan thought she looked better for doing so. He, too, missed Freyn's presence and energy. He was pleased Kian was not hurt worse and they had no other casualties in the skirmish at Drifting Leaf. He wondered how they would fare in the days to come. Would others of his grove pay the cost with life or limb?

The nearly summer-height sun was bright and warm as the Cetria of Green Rising was coming to a close and the Cetria of Na'veyja's grace was about to begin. Quinlan had an uneasy feeling he should enjoy it while it lasted.

Chapter Eighteen

Primerey Joseah awoke with a little less enthusiasm than usual, but she still loved mornings in the Great Marsh. The flaura mixed with the steam of the wetlands and the view was ignited into bright colors by the morning sunlight. She arose from her bed and prepared for her day.

A young woman waited for her outside her bedchamber as she came out. "Lah ahm, Bekka."

"Lah ahm, Primerey," the woman replied. "Did ye sleep well?"

"Only well enough, I'm afraid, but the night has gone and the chance for more sleep has gone with it. I hope yours was pleasant?"

"Aye, indeed, Primerey, even though youn' Taryl did beat the rooster in both in risin' and in loudness of cry." She smiled happily.

"Ah, ha ha, I remember when my children were newly born. The toughest pleasure a woman could hope to have."

"Right ye are there, ma'am."

"Shall we start our day?"

"We shall, ma'am. Segoney Silari asked ta meet with ye after the mornin' meal."

"Yes, very good."

The clamor of the meal hall grew louder the closer they approached it. Joseah loved this part of the day. She was always pleased to see her fellow druids coming together to share a meal and camaraderie. This morning, the hall was filled with the joyful sounds of laughter and happiness.

Druids greeted her as she walked through, and she greeted them back, even stopping to talk here and there. They selected what they wanted to eat and found a spot at one of the many long tables in the hall. Everywhere she looked she saw bliss and contentment.

We must prevail somehow, she thought but continued to speak cheerfully throughout the meal.

Segoney Silari, her subordinate and close friend, waited for her at the hall entrance.

"Lah ahm, Joseah." He embraced her.

"Lah ahm, Silari, you should have joined us."

"I've nae the stomach fer that now." The look on his face said it all: there was bad news waiting.

"Bekka, please inform my first appointment that I may be delayed."

"Aye, ma'am." Bekka nodded to them before she left for the Primerey's office.

"Walk with me," Joseah said.

They walked into the herb gardens growing outside the meal hall and kitchen. Joseah sat on a bench by a fountain and Silari joined her.

"The Wardens have received word—Freyn has been killed," he said.

Joseah closed her eyes tightly to hold back the tears of grief and frustration. "How?"

"A skirmish with the dreyg."

"Did she make it to see Kenri?"

"Aye, and more. Wylla and Freyn teamed up with Grove Seven out of the Northern West Conclave."

Her eyes snapped open and she looked at Silari. "Yes, and?"

"Driftin' Leaf has been saved." He smiled widely.

"Oh, thank Na'veyja!" Joseah said. "I knew Quinlan's grove was the right one to send, but at such a sad cost. I am heartbroken."

"As am I, but the cause was great and she'd nae be dissuaded."

"Wylla?" she asked.

"Alive. More heartbroken than we, I'd say."

"Yes, to be sure."

"There's more. King Renalth has secured Raskan through and through. The disciple has been driven back ta Shaan. That's two out of three. We may win this thin' yet."

"Encouraging news indeed, my friend," she said.

"The Wardens report two dozen more blendin' pairs have been trained and sent south ta Hearth's Port."

"I must admit the Warden's contingency plan seems to have some merit after all."

"'Twas all. I just thought ye'd want ta know about Freyn."

"Gratitude, Silari, you were right."

They left the herb garden and went about their separate duties. Joseah switched back and forth from being happy about the report and sad about it moments later. The conversations she'd had with Freyn crept into her mind attempting to steal her attention away from the morning's appointments. By midafternoon, the entire conclave was abuzz with the news of Drifting Leaf's salvation.

Bekka came into the office. "Primerey, is it true, about Driftin' Leaf?"

"It appears so, yes. Northern West Grove Seven should be on the way home and I'm sure we'll hear many grand tales of the adventure."

"I cannae wait. I hope there's a gatherin'! I—oh!" Bekka was cut off by a rumble and a slight earth tremor.

A knot of fear formed in Joseah's stomach even though earth tremors had occurred in the region periodically.

"Oh, my," Bekka said after it passed.

"Nothing to fear," Joseah said. "Have the chief of personnel do a rounds check to be on the safe side."

"Aye, ma'am."

Bekka was barely to the door when a stronger tremor passed through the ground. Items on tables and shelves were jostled and tossed about before the tremor ceased.

"Initiate safety proto—" Joseah was nearly thrown to the floor by the force of the next event.

Loud cracks and crashes could be heard all around them.

"Get everyone outside!" Joseah said.

They managed to get to the hallway, telling everyone to evacuate the conclave hall.

Druids poured out of every structure to find safety only to discover the falling trees outside to be just as dangerous. One druid was crushed by a large foundation limb from an upper walkway right in front of them.

"Ah!" Bekka screamed and jumped backward.

Joseah saw Silari close by. "Get everyone out of the trees and into the open fields of the farms!"

"Aye!" he answered and yelled at the panicked throng to head to open spaces.

The ground continued to tremble more frequently and a heavier shudder started up every few minutes.

"Check every classroom. No child will be left," Joseah directed some of her staff. "And clear the infirmary. Get everyone out of the trees! You two, escort Bekka to find her family."

"Gratitude, Primerey!" she said.

"Go! I'll find you later." Joseah saw her off and turned to other urgencies.

"Joseah!" Silari called to her.

The tremors intensified and cracked the foundation trees of the conclave. Areas of the ground snapped apart while others cracked away and shifted in elevation. The heavier shudder made the ground jump under their feet.

"Hurry!" Silari grabbed her hand.

Together they scrambled up a stairway when a tremendous crack and rumble louder than a thousand thunders preceded the stairway falling away from under their feet. The ground they were on fell three stories in a series of rough drops over five seconds' time. They both landed hard each time the ground fell away. Debris of all sizes, freed by the rending, crashed down around them. The tremors subsided and the ground became still.

"Joseah?" she heard Silari call out.

"I'm here!"

Blood ran from a cut on her right forearm. Pain in her head, back, and neck on the left side made her aware of injuries there but none immediately critical.

She got to her feet. "Silari, are you injured?"

"Nae badly," he replied from a ledge above her. He reached an arm down.

She grabbed on and half climbed while he pulled her up to the ledge. They had to climb four more times but managed to make the top before more tremors dropped the section even farther. She turned to look behind them. The Central Conclave lay in rubble spread out down the steep wall of the newly formed gorge.

"What...?" Silari said when he saw the scope of the destruction.

The massive series of earth tremors had consumed all the Great Marsh and the entire complex of the four conclave halls, opening a sinkhole the size of a deep river gorge.

Joseah cried for the hundreds of friends and fellow druids who had to have perished in such devastation, as well as the animals of the forest who had fallen victim to this attack on the druids' complex.

"All of it—gone," Silari said. "How can this be?"

"Fairtheora, they are after the oak tree."

"What? Ye think his disciples did this?"

"Yes, they are trying to free him from under the ground and we are powerless to stop them!"

A deep rumbling began in the ground yet farther away, more from the center of the canyon of rubble that used to be the Great Marsh. Druids, Gwylari, and others gathered beside them, drawn by the horrific scene.

A dome began to form pushing aside rubble as it continued to grow. The familiar glow of flaura came into view when Fairtheora rose above the dome.

"Na'veyja lives!" someone yelled out.

"Blessed be the Goddess!" someone else said.

The dome exploded in an ear-shattering detonation. The force of the explosion threw tons of lava and volcanic debris to incredible heights before it came crashing back down to Arden.

The initial blast was like a whisper in a temple compared to the scream of Na'veyja's despair as her power was broken and Fairtheora was ripped asunder. Her cry echoed to the horizon's edge and back before falling silent.

"No!" Joseah cried out.

People around her fell to their knees; some cried and sobbed, others stared in disbelief.

Na'veyja? Joseah tried to commune with her goddess, but the familiar presence was gone.

A second eruption eclipsed the first in size and power. The blast reached them in seconds and knocked everyone to the ground. A pyroclastic cloud of hot particles and burning ash began to fill the newly formed gorge-sized depression.

The sun disappeared behind huge columns of smoke and ash billowing as high as the eye could see. Bombs of falling lava rained down as jets of molten rock shot into the black-as-night sky.

"Rise and flee!" Joseah had to yell to be heard over the din coming from the eruption. "Rise! Help those who cannot help themselves. Flee! Flee to the west!"

The survivors made it to the farm fields where another band of survivors gathered what goods they could in a wagon hitched to a horse.

Joseah brushed the accumulated ashes from the horse and found a cloth to tie over her head to protect the animal from the ashes.

"She's the only one to survive," the stable master said. A tear cleared a small path through the ashes of his cheek.

"Too many have perished today," Joseah replied. "We will see that she does not. Has anyone seen Bekka or her family?"

"No, Primerey, those here are the only ones to come forth. The ground is ripped apart and we cannot get past to search. Maybe they got out another way."

"Primerey, what do we do?" one of the survivors asked.

"We head for the crossroads and go in whatever direction the ash is not traveling. To the west! Everyone, as quickly as you can!"

The clouds of steam, ash, and smoke stretched far across the sky. Grey flakes fell from the clouds, covering the landscape with heavy and gritty volcanic ash.

"Cover yer mouths and noses," Silari told the group as they prepared to leave. "Try nae ta look up, ye dinnae want this crud in yer eyes, and drink only from closed containers. Put yer children in the wagon and cover them with blankets and such. If there're any who cannae walk, 'tis inta the wagon with ye. We need ta move quickly."

The ragtag group began to move down the roadway as fast as they could if they were to escape the ashes falling from clouds that now stretched out as far as they could see. Many peered back once in a while as they left behind what had been home to the druids for generations.

"Primerey Joseah," one of the children asked, "where has the flaura gone?"

"The ash has hidden it, child," she said. "Now, you get back under that blanket, my dear."

Joseah searched the woods for any sign of the flaura's glow, but not a glimmer shone anywhere. Was Na'veyja one of those who perished in the tragic day's events? She stopped and looked back when they reached the final curve in the road before the destruction was lost from sight.

"Silari, I must try."

"Here? Now?" he asked. "What do ye expect ta see?"

She looked at the volcano that still belched out fire and ash. The clouds around it streaked with lightning. "I must know. Keep them moving. I will catch up."

Silari motioned to two able-bodied druids. "Stay with her. If thin's get any worse, ye're ta drag her out by force, if necessary."

Joseah settled into a seated position and focused on separating her spirit from her body. The chaos around her made it difficult. She focused inward and closed off the outside world.

Her spirit rose up and drifted toward the basin of roiling lava, ash, and smoke. Lava bubbles in the lake of molten rock burst in slow motion while blasts of steam sent smoldering ash particles swirling through heavy black smoke.

She reached the caldera at the center of the basin. There was no sign of either Fairtheora or of Na'veyja. There were only the destructive forces of nature that had been turned against them.

Joseah was about to call her spirit back when a strange motion caught her attention.

A mirage in the heat swirled above the pyroclastic lake of boiling rock and fire. The mirage moved out of the caldera and onto the land. The elements of the world were drawn inward from around it: the dirt, the fire, the air, the steam. The bones of a skeleton formed, organs clustered within, muscle tissue and tendons wove from joint to joint. Skin with the colors of ash and char covered the body as the being strode from the volcanic miasma. Eyes black as coal beheld the physical world once again. Acimasiz was free.

"No!" Joseah cried. The shock of seeing her nemesis for the first time in her life overwhelmed her. The ethereal spirit of her being was snapped back into her body as Joseah passed out in the physical realm.

~~~

Lord Praven needed no introduction when Acimasiz materialized in the provincial chamber of Teivas Keihas. He prostrated himself immediately before his god.

Get to your feet, Lord Praven, the voice of Acimasiz spoke to his mind. *I do not seek worshippers.*

Praven rose and beheld Acimasiz before him. The eyes were pools of black with no visible sclera or iris. His skin looked like black ink misted over with grey storm clouds.

Acimasiz studied a mural depicting a mythical battle between mages and dragons. He touched the image of a mage dressed in lightweight black armor and a mystic cloak, wielding both sword and magic. In the space of a blink, Acimasiz was dressed as the mage was in the mural. He pulled the hood of the mystic cloak up over his head.

You will forgive the intrusion, Acimasiz said.

Praven felt a power grip his spirit stronger than any he had ever known. "Ah!" he cried out when a piercing pain penetrated his mind. Images of Lord Nemilos, the disciples, and the plan to tunnel under the Great Marsh and unleash the magma chamber passed through his thoughts. The events of his life played out as well until the pain ceased and he fell to the floor.

Now I am up to speed.

Praven groaned, but the pain faded quickly and then was gone. He got to his feet and took a breath to compose himself.

She hides, Praven. After confining me for ages, she hides from me.

"How may I serve, Master?" Praven asked.

I wish to continue the hunt for my quarry, he replied. *I can still feel her essence, but it is nearly spent. I need to regenerate my full powers in order to find her. I shall need sacrifices, Praven. Bring me the captive druids. I shall start with them.*

~~*

Chapter Nineteen

The morning after Freyn's ceremony, Quinlan and Grove Seven bustled around the stables seeing to their horses and packing their gear for the trip back to the conclave. Pie Thief and Blossom became great friends in the short time they had known each other. Most of the morning, Pie sat on Blossom's head hanging on to the burro's ears, which were taller than Pie sitting upright. Blossom seemed happy to have her there, especially when Pie would share a purloined bee biscuit with her.

"Ha! Our new grove mate knows how to win friends and influence burros," Quinlan said.

Ticca laughed at the antics. "Siestrey, is she a familiar?"

"I do not believe so, Ticca, but who am I to say? Mine is a walking stick that came to me on a familiar quest three years ago. Askue is capable of channeling the power of the esbat and yet I knew not until this journey. Perhaps this journey has been your familiar quest in the eyes of Na'veyja and you have found yours."

"Have ya tried ta commune?" Cassae asked her.

"No," Ticca answered.

"Let your spirit touch hers and ask her if she hears ya," Cassae said.

Ticca went quiet for a moment and Pie Thief barked three times, ran around the stable, and leapt to her shoulder. She cooed twice and put her paw on Ticca's cheek.

"Looks like ye have yer answer," Swela said who had been watching as well.

Ticca looked like she could not be happier.

A footman entered the stables. "Master Quinlan?"

"Yes, here."

"A message from Master Kenri. I'm ta wait and brin' him back yer answer."

"One moment." Quinlan read the short message. "You may inform him we accept."

"Gratitude, milord." The footman bowed and returned the way he came.

"Kenri would like us to join him before we go," he said.

"He do be setting out the tastiest sweets and breads for his guests, so count me in." Sovia crossed her arms and gave a nod.

"Be mindful we need to be on the trail home by high sun, so don't be shy," Quinlan said. "I know you have trouble in that area."

"I do be a delicate flower, milord," Sovia said daintily.

"Uh-huh," Quinlan replied sarcastically. "Let's finish up before we meet Kenri, so we can leave right afterward."

"It shall be so, Siestrey." She happily started ordering people about.

Grove Seven found Kenri later on one of the terraces of Torr Amhairc along with Ronni MacRory and Wylla.

"Lah ahm, friends," Kenri said as they arrived. "Please, sit with us. We're having a late breakfast and talking about the flaura."

The grove greeted the three and chose seats around the open-air table.

"Lah ahm, and gratitude, Kenri," Quinlan said. "Lah ahm, Ronni and Wylla."

"Lah ahm, Quin, Grove Seven." Wylla nodded.

"Ahh—lah ahm," Ronni said but looked confused.

"Means *good morning*," Kenri told her, "in Gwylari."

"Oh, lah ahm, ta ye all," she said with more confidence. "I was just tellin' them, I always took the glow of flaura fer granted. 'Tis always been there. I never thought ta question it."

"I was the same when I was youn'," Cassae said. "I remember me first years with the Order. I thought the older druids were wizards, truth be told, and that they're weavin' magic."

"What exactly is it, can ye say?" Ronni asked.

"Most certainly," Kenri answered. "Druids can tap into a form of ethereal energy from the goddess we call Na'veyja's grace. Where the environment is alive and healthy, it has a stronger connection to Na'veyja's grace and begins to glow. The flaura shines brighter wherever a group of plants and trees remain strongly connected to the goddess."

"Like the deep woods and the Great Marsh they call home?" Ronni asked. "'Tis why some areas are brighter than others?"

"Yes, and yes," Kenri replied. "In the early days of the Order, two levels of interaction were known of. The typical druid in the Order of Arden can only manipulate flaura, such as fast grow a plant but not without a seed or spore to start with. Other druids, such as a brother or sister of the Dayne Kinship, can create plants by calling the flaura from the world around them without the need of a seed."

"Siestrey Quinlan is a brother of the Dayne," Ticari said.

"You have the right of it, Settey Ticari," Kenri replied. "And congratulations on your recent advancement."

"Gratitude, Master Kenri."

"Before his death, Eldret and I believed a third interface had been discovered. The conduits, as Askue is and as Freyn was, have the ability to access Na'veyja's grace where none is directly available. Perhaps they draw energy from the ethereal plane. I cannot truly say. They can bestow the energy upon other druids who utilize it in many ways, such as—let us say—awakening ancient artifacts in poisoned watersheds. From what Chyne has shared with me regarding her people, I have come to suspect the Gwylari are natural conduits of Na'veyja's grace. They are born with the inherent ability to call the flaura at will and use it in their everyday life."

"The farm communities of the Gwylari are nae what they once were," Wylla said. "And they're fewer and farther between now than in recorded history."

"Yes, truth be told," Kenri said. "I remember the flaura being much brighter when I was a boy playing along the coasts of Vakere than it is today."

"Perhaps the recovery of the Cealjin Delta and Drifting Leaf will help restore it to former glory," Quinlan said.

"Yes, indeed," Kenri replied.

"My curiosity is piqued," Ronni said. "We must speak more of the Order sometime, Kenri. What I saw in Driftin' Leaf dinnae easily leave the mind's eye."

"At length, mi lady, at length," Kenri said. "There was another tale of Drifting Leaf that caught my attention. I heard a tale of a beauty and a beast if you will. Horrendous, what was done to the creature. I imagine the pain drove it into pure mania."

"Truth be told," Ticari said, "it had gone berserk."

"Aye," Kian said. "Even knowin' about her power over beasts, seein' it runnin' at her nearly stilled ma heart."

"Swela," Kenri said, "the tale of you and the Torac in Drifting Leaf intrigues me. Would it pain you to tell me the story of how you got your scar?"

"'Tis painful nae longer, Kenri." She took a deep breath and exhaled slowly. "I was a wee lass of six years. I awoke early one mornin' and went down ta the lake we lived near. I remember a butterfly goin' by and chasin' after it inta the woods. 'Twere summer then and the woods were like a dream, all misty and glowin' in the mornin' light."

The group murmured in appreciation as everyone followed along. Ronni sat forward and paid closer attention to Swela. Quinlan knew Ticari and Ticca had never heard the tale told and they listened intently.

"I was out in the world on ma own fer the first time, just too youn' ta realize there was any danger. A mother bear and her cubs had come down ta forage around the water and I walked straight inta them."

"Oh, no," Ticca said.

Ronni gasped and brought her hand to her mouth. "What happened?" she asked through her fingers.

"The bear roared when it saw me standin' there. The sound of it frightened me so bad, I peed ma bed gown."

Ronni nodded. "Pbff—I probably would'a shite mine."

"What did you do?" Ticari asked.

"I turned and fled, which I know now was the wron' thin' ta do. The bear followed and caught me. She grabbed me here"— Swela unfastened her raiment and moved the shoulder of her blouse down to expose more of a four-lined scar—"and spun me around and knocked me ta the ground." She lifted the bottom edge of her blouse and showed the bottom of the scar lines where it went under the waist of her pants. "Ripped four gashes clear ta ma waist."

"Swela, I never knew!" Ticca became so emotional she ran over and embraced Swela. She pulled a chair closer, dabbed at tears, and looked ready to hear more. Pie peeked out from Ticca's hood, chittered, and remained on alert.

"Did anyone come ta help ye?" Ronni asked.

"Nae, just then," Swela said. "I screamed fer ma and da, but I had wandered too far and they could nae hear me. It hurt so badly where the bear had cut ma side, I cried and cried. 'Twas then I heard the most beautiful and soothing voice. It spoke nae ta ma ears, only ta ma spirit and said, *Swela have nae fear*."

"Who said it?" Ronni asked.

"'Twas Na'veyja," Swela said. "She came ta ma rescue."

"How did she?" Ronni asked.

"The excruciatin' pain was gone. A golden-yellow glow came from ma wounds. They closed over with new skin leavin' only the scar. The bear moved in for another strike, but she stopped within paw's reach. Our spirits blended and she plopped down next to me like I was another cub. Ever since that day, I've been able ta calm the vicious side of angry beasts."

"What happened afterward?" Ticari asked.

"Oh, ye should'a seen my da's face when they come lookin' fer me and find me sittin' next ta that bear."

"Did they kill it?" Ronni asked.

"Nae, I told her ta go and she did," Swela said. "I could nae explain ta ma folks what'd happened until I grew older and reasoned it out maself. Half the village thought me a witch at the time. Da moved us away and we ended up settlin' at the conclave."

"Incredible," Kenri said when she finished.

"Aye," Ronni said. "Quite a tale."

"Swela," Kenri said, "I believe there may be a connec—What in Na'veyja's name?"

The terrace shook under their feet when the castle it was mounted to and the ground underneath the castle shook and rumbled.

"Earth tremor!" Therin exclaimed.

A mighty cracking and a rumbling roar were heard from far in the distance. The noise grew closer and louder in seconds. The force of the sound when it arrived shattered glass panes, terrified animals, and nearly deafened Quinlan before it rolled off toward the opposite horizon.

Quinlan cringed and put his hands over his ears to protect them. The others around him did the same.

"By the Goddess!" Sovia said when it had passed.

"I should go and see if any need help," Ronni said.

"We'll go with you," Quinlan replied.

They reached the castle grounds, which were filling with people as they left the shaking buildings for the safety of open places.

The ground shook more violently than before. The eastern tower cracked and crumbled. A cloud of dust and debris billowed out as the tower collapsed into a pile.

"Clear the castle!" Renalth could be heard as he and Aibreann ran from the castle keep.

The ground shook from deep within, the vibrations building in intensity until one massive shock wave moved through the ground like a flick through a wet towel on laundry day. Afterward the tremors ceased and all seemed quiet except for the occasional rumble falling or shifting.

"Are all well?" Quinlan called out as he got to his feet.

The grove began to sound off and all answered back including Wylla, Ronni, and Kenri.

The next moment tore the hearts from Chyne and the druids when a terrible scream split the air and echoed back across from the four corners of Arden.

"Na'veyja!" Kenri cried and fell to his knees covering his ears. "She is in agony!"

"Aiii!" a yell of pain drew Quinlan's attention to Chyne.

Chyne reached out to him, her face distorted with pain. "Brother, I need thy—aiii!" She collapsed to the ground before she finished.

"Chyne!" Quinlan shouted and ran to her side.

"Ni!" Cassae exclaimed, pointing to the far woods. "The flaura! It's gone out!"

The grove all stared at the woods, which mere moments ago shone with the shifting glow of flaura.

"Nae even a glimmer!" Kian said.

"What evil is this?" Quinlan asked no one in general.

"I don't be liking this, Quin," Sovia said, "not one bit. It bodes great ill."

"Chyne?" Cassae tried to get her friend to respond but to no avail. "At least she still draws breath."

"Sire!" Modgrin yelled from nearby and pointed to the northeast horizon.

The smoke from the volcano could be seen billowing high into the air and stretching out across the eastern horizon with the prevailing winds. Flashes of lightning and flying fireballs were visible even at this distance.

"The conclave?" Therin asked.

"Sure to be," Quinlan said, a thousand questions racing through his head. "It felt as if my spirit was being ripped from me."

Renalth, Aibreann, and Modgrin joined them as they walked through, lending aid where necessary.

"Looks ta be over the valley of the Great Marsh," Renalth said. "I'd say a volcano blew her top, but there's nae one in the valley nor a hundred league in any direction."

"I am sure Na'veyja has been severely wounded," Kenri said. "Something devastating has happened."

"We must ride at once," Quinlan said.

"We'll send an aid caravan as soon as she's loaded, dears," Aibreann replied.

Renalth agreed. "And we'll send a message to Glen Arwe and have them send out scouts ta the east. Maybe they'll know somethin' by the time ye get there."

"Gratitude, Your Majesties, that is most kind," Quinlan said. "Let us hope for the best."

"Here, ye should carry this." Modgrin gave Quinlan a badge of office from his sash. "Gives ye access under my authority in case ye run across any Raskanish military."

"Gratitude, Minister." Quinlan turned to his grove. "No questions, no complaints, Ticari and Ticca, you are to remain here and help organize the aid caravan and accompany it when it leaves. Sovia and Cassae, stay and do what you can for Chyne."

"Quin," Cassae said.

Quinlan shook his head. "You are the best healer I know, Cass. I need you here."

She nodded reluctantly and kissed him. "Come back."

"As fast as the wind," he said.

"Ya mind if I ride with ye?" Wylla asked.

"If you are ready to leave now," Quinlan said.

"Aye, only need time ta throw a saddle on Ember."

"Let's get on," Quinlan said. "Dry rations and water only. We ride light and fast."

~~~

A day and a half of fast travel, resting only long enough to spare injury to their horses, and they reached Glen Arwe.

"'Twere a four-day ride the last time we came through here," Kian said as they checked in with the Glen Arwe patrols, but they arrived before the scouts had time to return.

"Resupply and we ride on," Quinlan said. "Another three days' ride to the conclave if we can make it there."

The second morning after Glen Arwe they saw a Kalnuvian caravan coming from the north down toward the northern crossroads. Quinlan could see the Inn of the Four Winds and the smithy at the crossroads, but no horses roamed the corral and no smoke rose from either building. The closer he got to the crossroads, it became clear the place had been deserted.

The sky from this closer distance was filled with the clouds of ash and smoke coming from what Quinlan could only imagine was a volcano, but it made no sense. A dense layer of clouds covered the landscape. The air under the clouds at the horizon was a hazy grey and becoming darker as it drew closer to them.

"Hail, friend!" A front rider from the convoy rode up and raised an empty sword hand.

"Hail, friend." Quinlan returned the gesture.

"I be Randall Kinworthy, Captain of the Kalnuvian Guard," he said. "We bring healers, medicine, food, and water if you be needing 'em."

"Our gratitude, Captain," Quinlan answered. "We are freshly arrived and know not what lies to the east but what the eye can see. We intend to continue on, at least as far as we can ride."

"I'll have the main group hold at the crossroads and my men and I'll ride with you if you'll be having us."

"Gladly so, Captain."

The reconnoiter group rode east for several hours. The visage of the volcano now dominated the horizon. The central column of smoke rose beyond sight. Bright streaks of blue-white lightning flashed across grey and black patches of billowing smoke. Distant booms went off out of sight and tremors passed through the ground in unison. Flame-red mushrooms of sparkling hot ash surged up through the cooler black smoke.

Grey gritty ash fell heavily and covered the ground as the troop pushed into the darkness of the volcanic clouds. They covered the horses' noses and their own as the ash fell even heavier the farther in they rode.

After only an hour, the men and horses began to struggle against the gritty ash when it worked into their eyes and mouths, down their throats, and under their clothing and saddles.

"How much farther to the conclave?" Captain Kinworthy asked.

Quinlan's heart sank. "Another day's ride."

He looked at Quinlan with sympathy in his eyes. "Master Quinlan..."

Quinlan thought hard on whether to turn back or push on. The clouds above grew darker and the ash fall was almost impossible to see through.

Quinlan looked at the captain, then at his grove mates, and back at the darkening roadway ahead. "I hope you find peace in rest, my friends and loved ones."

The captain turned his men around and headed back the way they had come. The druids slowly did the same.

Quinlan stopped after a few minutes passed. "I must ride down to the next bend, at least," he said to his grove mates. "Ask the captain if he'd wait."

"Quin!" Therin said, but he turned to ride off.

"I'll be right back," he called back over his shoulder.

Quinlan reached the bend in a short time.

"Good boy, Biscuit, only a little longer."

Visibility was low as he rounded the bend and he could make nothing out. He rode a few trots more and still nothing.

"Eh, dung," he said. "All right, boy, let's go."

He turned and rode back to the bend. A last look over his shoulder showed nothing but strange swirls of falling ash. He continued, but for some reason stopped to look again.

The strange swirls began to bob back and forth and then there were more.

"Oh, Na'veyja be praised!" he exclaimed as the swirls turned into the ash-covered survivors from the conclave. He rode back around the bend and signaled to his group to come before he rode on to the survivors.

Three horses, two drawing laden carts, appeared out of the ash with a group of people walking along with them. People began to cheer and wave as he rode into view.

"Blessed be whoever you are," Joseah said when Quin rode up to them.

He dismounted and took down his bandana.

"Quinlan!" she exclaimed. "Ha ha! I should have known it would be you!"

"Primerey Joseah! In Na'veyja's name, it lightens my heart to see you."

"And you, my friend. Silari, it is Quinlan, come to save us."

"Well met indeed, Quinlan. Are ye alone?"

"No, Segoney Silari, a host waits around the bend and the ash lessens not far beyond. Primerey, what happened? Is this all who are left?"

"A longer story for another time, but I must tell you, Acimasiz has escaped. Our fellow druids, their families, the conclave grounds, and everything within—are gone."

"A horrible and sad day for the Order." Quinlan frowned.

The survivors around them cheered as the rest of the rescue group rode around the bend. The Kalnuvian troops dismounted, putting two to three survivors up in their place on the horses, and the druids did the same.

"Wylla!" Joseah called out when she saw her ride in. They met and embraced. "I am so grieved over Freyn passing. How are you holding up?"

"Good enough, Primerey, better than most on this day," she said. "The conclave?"

Joseah shook her head.

They embraced again before they went to help others. The band got moving once again and soon after came to the edge of the falling ash.

People dusted off the grey ash from clothes and hair and used what water was brought along to wash out the grit from their eyes, mouths, and throats. More than one of the survivors retched up the water along with ash from their stomachs.

Joseah told them briefly of what happened the day the volcano swallowed the Great Marsh. How she had seen Acimasiz walk free in her vision and how they gathered together to head out for the crossroads.

"We came upon other groups of survivors and we continued on together." She smiled at a young Raskanish woman holding a newborn swadled against the ash. "I was becoming concerned we wouldn't reach the crossroads until I saw you riding out from the gloom."

Quinlan thought of the day he had seen Lissa before he left for Drifting Leaf. She'd told him, "The Seyna has stood for an age, Quin. It will still be here when you return." How wrong she had been. The memory of her triggered others of Bertrynn, Tomas, Sander, and all the druids he had shared his life with and would never again see in this world.

The Great Marsh, the Seyna, and Fairtheora had been consumed by the destruction. The once-beautiful wetlands had been completely wiped from the face of Arden. All of which, no matter how much it meant to him, was a small concern compared to fact Na'veyja had disappeared and Acimasiz was free.

Quinlan told Joseah about Chyne and the flaura around Cammachmoor going dark on the day of the catastrophe.

"What of Na'veyja?" he asked.

She shrugged sadly and embraced him. "I know not, Quin. Perhaps in time, there will be answers."

"Perhaps," he replied. "For now, let's get everyone to the northern crossroads. The Kalnuvians brought a caravan with physicians and medicines and they have fresh food and water. "

"They are a caring people and good friends of the Order," she said.

"From there, we go to Glen Arwe and then…" He shrugged.

"We will figure that out in time, Quin."

The troop set out for the border of Raskan to see its precious cargo delivered to safety.

Chapter Twenty

Six days after Quinlan found the survivors, the slow-moving caravan reached the Raskan border, with two more days left at walking pace to reach Glen Arwe.

"Dust risin' in the distance," Kian said.

"Let's go see who it is," Quinlan replied.

The five druids walked ahead to the top of the next hill to get a better view. The two figures out in front of an assembly of wagons, carriages, horses, and riders were Ticari and Ticca. They waved and rode faster when they saw Quinlan's group on the hill.

The siblings shared hugs and greetings with them when they gathered.

"A grand sight for sore eyes," Therin said. "How's Sov?"

"She's well," Ticari answered, "and Cassae, too."

"Chyne?" Quinlan asked.

Ticca shook her head. "No change."

"What word of recent events?" Swela asked.

"*Much* word," Ticari said. "Too much for now."

Quinlan felt a great pride swell for the siblings. "I could not be more proud of you both. Well done."

"Aye, lad and lass no longer, ye stand as druids of the Order in ma eyes," Kian said. "Well done, indeed, the twain of ye."

The reunion was short-lived as the relief group reached the hilltop. The rescue force now had more than enough transportation to get everyone off their feet and moving at wagon speed. Ticari had a brief conversation with a Grannagh militia commander and they all rode back to the survivor caravan.

"Gratitude for your efforts, incredible young druids." Joseah embraced Ticari and Ticca both. "I am most impressed."

Ticari bowed. "Gratitude Primerey, but we would have not succeeded without the help of others."

"Well said, Settey Ticari, yet without your help, we would still be walking." She turned to Ticca.

"Gratitude, Prim—" Ticca started to cry before she could finish. Pie Thief popped out and started to chitter.

Joseah stroked the marmoset's cheek. "*Wync*, little one." Pie snuggled up against Ticca's neck and went fast to sleep. Joseah wrapped Ticca in her arms. "I know, Ticca."

"It was to be my first rotation in the Great Marsh," Ticca said between sobs, "and now it's gone. Where will we go?"

"Onward," she said. "For now, we must get these people to shelter and I still need your help to do it. Are you prepared?"

Ticca straightened up and wiped her tears away. "Yes, Primerey."

"Good," she said and climbed into the driver's seat of a wagonful of children and took the reins. "Siestrey Quinlan, if you would be so kind as to take command of our departure."

"It shall be so, Primerey," he said and rode a short distance ahead. "Everyone mount up! Wagons—forward!"

The combined relief forces slowly surged forward, coalescing into a line down the roadway toward Glen Arwe.

Quinlan signaled his grove to ride closer together. "Ticari, tell us what transpired after we left."

"King Renalth sent troops into northern Shaan." Ticari had to raise his voice to be heard over the din of hoof and wheel. "The dreyg forces had already abandoned the northern outposts and withdrawn to the south."

"Yes, of course," Quinlan said, "because it was a feint to keep us distracted. Have they pulled back to Trossachsmuir?"

"Yes, how did you know?"

"I believe they intend to leave the northern continent," Quinlan said. "They are gathering their forces for transport. We must act before they sail."

"And what're ye thinkin', Quin?" Kian asked. "Ride up ta the gates of Teivas Keihas and ask the most evil bastard in the world ta kindly surrender? It took Na'veyja and the Gwylari together ta defeat him in the first place."

"I have not the answers, but all beings have a weakness. We must learn how he was subdued ages ago and somehow attempt to do the same. What else, Ticari?"

"King Renalth and the armies have gone south of Drifting Leaf and are based now at Pinebough. Cassae and Sovia went along and took Chyne with them. They will wait for us there."

"Did they give a reason?"

"Kenri said Chyne's father lives in a village near Pinebough and maybe he could help Chyne. Messages about the calamity have been sent to all druid outposts and replies have returned pledging any assistance necessary. Na'veyja's cry was heard all across Arden and many Gwylari were affected."

"Affected?"

"Yes, but I stand a vexed fool from the explaining. You'll have to seek further answers from Master Kenri."

"Worry not, Ticari, Kenri could vex even the most learned scholars at times," Quinlan replied.

"Kenri," Wylla said, "is *at times* pleased by that, I think. 'Tis rumored there's nae druid raiment big enough ta house his ego."

"A trained druid without the restraint or control of the Order could be a dangerous thin'," Swela said.

"Aye and there's many more like him out there," Wylla added.

"Does the Primerey know?" Ticca asked.

Wylla nodded. "They're out there with her knowledge and blessing."

"How do you know?" Ticca asked.

"Because I'm one of them," she said. "Freyn and I. 'Twere the Primerey and the Wardens of the Woods who sent us ta seek out Kenri. The Wardens heard about Kenri and Eldret findin' the artifact years ago and have been in secret contact ever since."

"Why have you not spoken of this before?" Quinlan asked.

"I was sworn ta silence."

"Then why break yer silence now?" Swela asked.

"Because all those I've sworn ma oath ta were at the conclave and now are naught but ash in the clouds," she answered. "I chose ta serve the Wardens over the Order and now the Wardens are nae more. I'm fated ta become a rogue druid like Kenri."

"Dung!" Joseah said from the wagonful of children she managed to bring up right behind them without anyone noticing. The children giggled when she cursed. "Apologies, young ones, *wync.*" The children all slipped into slumber.

"I owe ye the apologies, Primerey," Wylla said.

"Beetledung! Wylla, I am to blame for all of it. The responsibility rests with me and me alone. You have always remained a druid in the Order of Arden regardless of joining the Wardens. You will always have a place with us."

"Indeed," Quinlan said, "to face what is ahead, we must all band together."

The late afternoon sun shone through the clouds as they reached the border of Grannagh Province and an hour or so later, they dismounted in Glen Arwe. Quinlan helped Joseah unload the wagon of children

"Silari!" Joseah called out.

"Here, Primerey," he said from around the wagon.

"Take charge here in Glen Arwe and see to our druids," she said when he came over.

"Aye, I will, but where do ye think ye're goin'?"

"I'm off to Pinebough."

"Ye need ta get some rest, Jo," Silari said.

"I can rest on the way or when I get there."

"At least change yer robes and wash yer hair afore ye go unless ye intend on scarin' them all away," he said.

"Ha, Silari, I do love you, my friend. Perhaps it will rain along the way."

"Jo."

Joseah turned to him but said nothing.

"Even ye need time ta adjust ta what's happened," he said. "Have ye even tried ta commune with Na'veyja the last day or two?"

She could not meet his eyes.

"Is that nae important ta ye?"

"What"—she lowered her voice—"if she is not there?"

"What if she is and needs our help in some way?"

"Yes, of course, you are right," she said. "You are my blue sky, Silari."

"Aye, well, wise Master Blue Sky says, bath, dinner, commune, rest, and then ye can go." He turned to Quin. "Do ye nae think?"

"Sounds like a good plan," Quinlan said. "I think I shall follow it myself."

"I dinnae think ye had yer ethereal passage trainin' yet, Quin."

"No, Segoney, not officially." He took the opportunity to tell them of the vision during his moon dance and of what took place in Drifting Leaf.

"By the Goddess!" Joseah exclaimed. "Askue is a conduit of the esbat's power? Ugh, right under my very nose and I had not the wisdom to see it. And it took you and Askue *and* Wylla and Freyn combined to awaken the carraig?"

"Yes."

Joseah shook her head. "All I had to do was open my mind and the answers fall to me like ash from the sky."

"Primerey?" Quinlan asked.

"The esbat is an entity of the Vast and Acimasiz is an entity of the Vast," she said. "That may be the key to his weakness. Yes, yes, I must try to commune immediately! Quin, does your group ride for Pinebough?"

"Yes, we leave at daybreak. The Kalnuvian contingent rides with us to join their main force stationed there."

"I shall ride with you as well. I must speak with Kenri."

"We'd be honored to have you along, Primerey," he said, but she had already hurried off.

~~~

The sky was dark in the predawn hours of the next morning and would stay that way until the sun rose over the cloud mass of the volcano to the east. A fair-sized group prepared to ride for Pinebough. There were the eight druids, Captain Kinworthy, and his troop of two dozen Kalnuvian regulars.

An afternoon after a week's travel found the troop at the flower-covered grave mound of the Torac along the northern edge of Drifting Leaf. A group of Gwylari was entering the watershed as they rode up.

"Lah tam, druidae," the unusually somber chieftain wished them a good afternoon.

"Lah tam, Chieftain," Quinlan replied. "I am Quinlan, formerly of the Northern West Conclave."

"Myzani Nal, of Deep Root village. Our hearts weep for thee and thyne. Such tragedy went unlooked for."

"Gratitude, Myzani Nal, and our hearts go out to you and your people as well," Joseah said.

Quinlan noticed more than the one group of Gwylari heading down the trail into Drifting Leaf.

"Where do your people go?" Quinlan asked.

"The great enemy hath shattered the peace of the world once more as thee doth know," he said. "We journey hence to rise against."

"What of Na'veyja, Myzani Nal?" Joseah asked.

"The goddess is elsewhere 'til otherwise," he said. "To Pinebough thee travels?"

"Yes," Quinlan answered.

"Then soon we shall see thee again." Myzani Nal turned and continued on his way.

The troop took the roadway around the watershed turning onto the southwest branch toward Pinebough instead of straight on to the southern crossroads between Shaan and Vakere. The southwest roadway took them into the last mountain range before the coastal lowlands of southern Shaan.

"That peak looks like a wolf's head," Ticca said.

"Yi and it's named such: Wolf's Head Peak," Therin replied. "The hole ya can see through near the top is called the wolf's eye, which is why this is called Wolf's Eye Pass. The village of me birth lies a day ta the west of here."

"Goldenfield," Joseah said.

"Yi, ya know of it?"

"Yes, my husband was from Springsborough."

"Ni!" he said. "That's only half a day's walk from Goldenfield. Did your husband perish in the..."

"Eruption?" She took a deep sigh. "No, he followed some damn fool on an idealistic crusade and returned with an illness that slowly devoured him until he died."

"Oh, me condolences, Primerey."

"Gratitude, Therin."

Quinlan caught what she said and lined it up with what he knew of Kenri and Eldret's quest with a band of rogue druids, which led to the discovery of the carraig. Were they the first Wardens of the Woods? Was Joseah's late husband one of the ill-fated druids?

He looked up and saw her watching him. She smiled sadly and shrugged. He rode close to her and spoke quietly. "Tangetan?"

She nodded.

"I understand so many things now, Primerey."

"All people are responsible for their own choices," she said. "My husband paid for his with his life. Have you never wondered why Kenri is not dead of the same illness that claimed his brethren?"

Quinlan was surprised by the question until he realized he had never thought to ask. "No, until now."

"He took ill and did not go into the black mist, yet he was fine when they came back, claiming he had recovered from a sour stomach."

The truth stung his confidence in Kenri. "He never said anything to us."

"No, but blame him not, Quin. He relived that choice with every day Eldret suffered before his eyes. I did not contact Kenri when my husband died. It did not occur to me to care about what they had found. I was that bitter about it back then. Somehow, Na'veyja guided you to him so Drifting Leaf could be saved and perhaps him as well. The mists of probability cloud over the morrow." She closed her eyes and seemed quite tired.

"Just over this pass, Primerey and we are there," he said.

They breached Wolf's Eye Pass as the last curve of the sun dashed beyond the horizon with a bright green flash. The fine city of Pinebough lay spread out in the valley below the pass. The flame glimmer of hearth fires and candles shone from many doors and windows. Street lanterns lit the lanes silhouetting the city in a warm ember glow against the deep shadows of the valley.

Kalnuvian soldiers lit torches and set riders along the perimeter of the group to light the way, and they rode into the city.

Chapter Twenty-One

A sergeant of the guard greeted them at the gate of Pinebough and needed only a brief inspection of the badge Modgrin Macreeth gave to Quinlan before he granted them entry. They were directed to the Moonshine Inn where rooms had been held for them.

"Quin, Primerey Joseah," Captain Kinworthy rode up as they cleared the gate. "The men and I'll be taking our leave. I must be making my report to the colonel."

"Randall, your company on the trail has been a great pleasure." Quinlan grasped the man's hand in farewell. "Take good care on the battlefield, my friend."

"And you," Randall replied. "We'll be telling tall tales of victory at the end of it."

"Captain, my deepest gratitude for coming to our assistance," Joseah said. "It will not be forgotten."

"My greatest pleasure, ma'am." He tipped his hat. "Column, ho!"

Captain Kinworthy led his troops away down the lane.

"Therin, you know of the Moonshine Inn?" Quinlan asked.

"Yi, it's close by, down this way." He pointed to the right-hand lane. "Kinda tough ta miss."

"An inn?" Quinan asked when they arrived. "Saying such is a grievous understatement. *Ten* inns could not rival this *one* in size."

Two full-sized establishments sat on either side of the reception building, which was backed by a triple-hearthed kitchen. A multifloored lodge in back dwarfed the three-building complex out front and looked like it could house an army.

"Welcome ta the Moonshine Inn, milords and ladies!" a young man said as he strode out to greet them. "My name is Wayn. How may I be of service? Food, drink, lodgin', or all?"

"All!" the druids answered in unison.

"Very good!" Wayn signaled to a group of boys, who took the horses to the stables.

"Quin, I'll go with them and bed the horses," Kian said. "Make sure they get a rubdown and some bee biscuits."

"Yes, gratitude, Kian."

"I'll go with ye," Swela said.

Quinlan and the rest followed Wayn into the reception building.

The lobby's desk and its walls and ceiling were made of polished planks, poles, and beams constructed from different woods. A carved and painted sign reading The Chipped Cup hung on the wall by the left entryway. Another sign over the right entryway made in the same manner but with different colors read The Broken Belt. The tavern was to the left and the brasserie to the right, both of which offered food and drink. The latter just had more tables than the other.

The sound of a band came from The Chipped Cup. The noise of many people talking and laughing coming from both places nearly drowned out the band's music.

"Here we are, folks. Sire Malstrom will book ya in. If ya need anythin' durin' your stay, Wayn is at your service." He bowed and remained there smiling at them.

"Ah, the gratuity," Quinlan said. He took a pinch of something out of a drawstring pouch and placed it in Wayn's hand.

The young man had a skeptical look on his face until he looked down and saw a small red ruby sitting in his palm. The gemstone was not highly valuable but it was worth more than double the amount he usually received. He snatched his hand closed and bowed deeply. "Deepest gratitude, milord. If ya want for anythin', anythin' at all, call for Wayn."

A deep baritone voice rose above the din and sang the last few verses of the band's song. The comedic ballad prompted the patrons to roar with laughter as the singer crooned the final punchline.

"Oh…" Ticca whispered, her eyebrows popping up.

Quinlan turned around to find the most immense man he had ever seen. He was dressed in robes that did not hide the fact his belly hung to his knees. Thick, glossy, black hair bobbed about his head in perfect ringlets and spirals. The cleanly shaven face was red cheeked and slightly sweaty.

"Ha, ha, ha, glorious! Glorious!" the impromptu singer said as he emerged from The Chipped Cup. "Hallooo, my friends! Welcome! Welcome to the Moonshine. My apologies for the wait, but I had to do my civic duty and make sure *the ale had not staled—* and sing some, too. My name's Sire Malstrom. You can call me either or both, your choice. Rooms, I'll bet you're wantin'?"

"Yes," Quinlan said, "they're being held, I'm told."

"Good or I'd have nothin' for you," Malstrom replied. "Booked to the rafters with Raskans as they say, and they do love a good ale." He took down the last three keys from hooks on the wall. "Here we are." He read from a note. "I'm to tell Quinlan, Cassae has your key, and, Therin, Sovia has yours. These are for Ticari and Ticca, Kian and Swela, and Joseah." He put a key down for each set of names.

"Gratitude, Sire Malstrom," Quinlan said. "What do we owe you for the rooms?"

"Not a thing," he answered. "King Renalth has more than covered all costs for those in his party, which is the entire inn and half the city. I think I shall cry when you folks go. The lodge is straight through here to the back"—he pointed to a hallway leading to a set of doors—"when you're ready. The bottom floor of the lodge is reserved for the lords and war masters of Raskan. The stables are on the far side."

"Your kindness is appreciated, Malstrom," Quinan said.

"Kindness is a currency that never loses value. I hope you enjoy your stay, my friends."

"Ticca?" Sovia exclaimed as she walked out of The Broken Belt with a load of four covered baskets in her arms. "Oh, and there be every druid else! Na'veyja be praised. Therin-love, you be a looked-for sight. Get down here." She kissed him soundly when he bent down. "And here, you can be taking some of these baskets while you're here."

Ticari stepped up to take some as well.

"Gratitude, Ticari," she said. "Blessed be your heart, love. Primerey Joseah, lah quen, I'm Sovia. If there be anything you need, please ask, no matter what. My heart be torn open by the tragedy."

"And mine, Sovia. It has touched us all with shadow. Together we shall walk in the light again. Gratitude for your concern. Whatever is in those baskets smells delightful."

"Dinner for Cassae and me to go up to the room. Quin, you be a sight for sore eyes, too. Give us a hug. Ahh—best bring more dinner now you all be here. Ticca-love, come and help, if you would." Sovia held her arm out to her.

"Of course." Ticca hugged Sovia so hard it made Pie Thief squeak.

"Oh, hush Pie, and you be keeping your paws to yourself, you riscally-rascally-roustabout," Sovia said. "Come, the kitchen be this way."

"Sov!" Therin said as they walked off.

"What?" she stopped and asked.

"The rooms?" he asked.

"Oh, ha! Right, they all be together." She came back and pointed to the doors in the rear. "Go out through there, then they be all the way up and all the way south."

They followed her directions and found the rooms. The commotion of them sorting out rooms must have drawn Cassae's attention. The door at the end opened and she looked out.

"Quin!" She flew out of the room and into his arms where they stayed for a minute.

"I've missed you more every day since we parted," he said.

"I missed ya too," she replied as they separated. "Primerey Joseah, it does me heart glad ta see ya."

"Cassae, my dear, how are you?" She embraced her. "I have missed our time together at the conclave, but I rejoice in your healing."

"I couldn't have done it without your help. I am well because of it."

"How is Chyne?" Quinlan asked.

"She appears ta sleep yet will not awaken," Cassae said.

"Show me to her. Let us see what healing is left in these old hands," Joseah said.

Cassae showed them in and greeted the rest of her grove mates. Chyne lay on the bed in a room off the common area. Quinlan thought she did not look at home on a bed in a room. She needed to be out among nature and under the sky.

Joseah went work, immediately pulling the bedsheet down. She inspected Chyne's eyes, ears, mouth, and even the withered plants on her clothing. She listened to Chyne's chest and felt the side of her neck.

She straightened up and faced them. "Right, Cassae, I shall need your help. We shall require sprigs of slippery elm, echinacea, calendula, peppermint, eucalyptus, elder, burdock, lavender, and yarrow. Also, for the tincture, we need plantain and comfrey, chamomile and rose hips, and cayenne and nightshade. First, though, we will need to eat. We must be strong. This is going to take some time."

Sovia, Ticca, Swela, and Kian all came in with the rest of dinner. The grove enjoyed a quick meal together for the first time in weeks. The tale of finding the survivors was told before splitting off to find or grow the herbs Joseah had requested. They reconvened shortly at the inn's kitchens.

"Gratitude, Malstrom, for allowing us the use of a hearth," Quinlan said as he brought some of the herbs into the smaller kitchen of the Moonshine Inn.

"My pleasure, Master Quinlan, my pleasure. I'll have that cot for your friend brought around straight away. I've never seen magic before. You're sure nothin's goin' to blow up?"

"Ah—fairly sure." He acted concerned but then grinned.

"Ah! Ha ha! I do like you, Master Quinlan. You're a good man. Ha!"

Quinlan told the truth. He was *fairly sure* nothing would blow up. Two inn employees carried in a cot with a thin mattress. Therin followed them in, carrying Chyne. Joseah told them where to place the cot and Chyne. The grove had gathered everything required for the healing ritual.

Joseah looked at them all as they stood around the table of herbs, oils, and powders. "I feel the presence of Acimasiz in the world. It burns like a hot coal dropped into an open sandal. I still feel Na'veyja's presence too, but she feels far away. If you attempt to seek her, you will not find her. Instead, clear your minds and open your spirits to her as an invitation. We will persevere. Now, let's bring our loved one home, shall we?"

"What do you need us to do?" Quinlan asked.

"First, we need to brew the extract, so we need to make a *much*," Joseah said. "We need to mash and macerate the combined ingredients into a mass of plant matter and juices. So, Ticari, we need eight chamomile blossom buttons. Pick all the white petals off and pluck the stem, leaving only the central yellow disc. Put them into the kettle."

"What is the much for, Primerey?" Ticari asked.

"We must bring out such things as the alkaloids, inulins, nutrients, and proteins from the plants and strain the broth containing them. Ticca, you chop sixteen plantain leaves, nice and fine, and into the kettle they go."

"Yes, Primerey. What do we do then?"

"We steep the much until it bubbles, then we pour it into a cloth bag and twist it to extract the juices from the much, leaving the plant matter called the *pomace* in the bag to be discarded. Swela, if you would chop eight comfrey plants—root, stem, flower, and all—in the same manner, please."

"Aye, Primerey."

"Cassae." Joseah handed her a wrapped bundle. "You are a skilled healer. The nightshade is yours to deal with. Sixty-four leaves need to be mashed. Take care with it."

"I will, Primerey."

"Sovia, warm a flagon of water and add sixty-four drops of the rose hip oil and eight smidgeon-spoonfuls of cayenne powder into it."

"It shall be so," she said.

"Therin, we'll need a bucket of water from the well. Would you get it?"

"At once, Primerey."

"Wylla, we're going to need twenty forearm-length strings of twine to tie the sprigs."

"I'll take care of it, Primerey." Wylla nodded.

In short order, all of the plant ingredients lay in the bottom of the kettle and the flagon was warming.

Joseah looked at Quinlan. "Well, are you going to sit around all night and watch the rest of us work, or are you going to macerate the ingredients?"

"Ah—apologies for my laziness," he said. "I shall do so immediately."

"Kian, will you stoke the fire good and warm?" Joseah asked.

"Aye, Primerey."

"Sovia, stir in the flagon as Quinlan mashes the ingredients."

Sovia added the rose hip-and-cayenne elixir while Quinlan mashed it into the plant ingredients.

"Now, we fill the kettle three-quarters and let it bubble for an hour or so," Joseah said. "Quin, if you would please?"

"Of course." He placed the kettle on the hearth hook and poured in the water.

For the first time, Quinlan noticed faces and bodies filled the windows and doors of the kitchen. Word of what they were doing had spread and they had drawn a quiet audience including Ronni and the Lords of Raskan.

"Ronni!" Ticari said and grinned before he caught himself. "Lady Ronirah, I mean."

"Greetin's, Ticari and Grove Seven." She came forward and embraced them all. Quinlan thought Ticari might float right out of his moccasins.

"Hope we're nae interruptin'," she said. "We're all pullin' fer Chyne ta come through."

"Nae ta mention a chance ta watch druid magic bein' done should never be passed over," Renalth said. "Dear Joseah, 'tis been too lon' since ye walked in Aibreann's Garden."

"Renalth, how good it is to see you." She welcomed his hug. "I would love nothing better than to wander Loko de Belaj Floroj for the rest of my days, but sadly, it shall not be soon."

"Aye, Joseah, we have a difficulty of grand proportions ahead," he replied.

"We may have discovered something, Renalth. I believe we may hold an advantage."

"I'd like ta hear more. I'm holdin' a council with the Vakerian and Kalnuvian commanders and the Gwylari chieftains in the mornin'. Would ye come?"

"Yes, of course. You'll want to hear from three, maybe four others as well."

"Brin' who ye need."

Talk of recent events took up the time until a murmur went through the crowd outside and six Gwylari appeared at the door, one of which was Chieftain Myzani, the one they had met near Drifting Leaf. He stood behind another man whose clothing bore different markings than the others.

"Grymni Kai-Nal!" Joseah said.

"Joseah, *sha kin Druidae-Nal.*" He touched foreheads with her. "Mine eyes rejoice to behold thee."

"And mine, dear friend Grymni." She turned to the druids. "This is High Chieftain Grymni of the Gwylari." She went around the room and introduced everyone there.

"Blessed be thee and thyne for thy caring of Chyne," Grymni said, and the other chieftains all echoed his sentiment.

"We hath come to blend with thy rhythms, Joseah," Grymni said.

"Gratitude, friends, one and all," Joseah replied.

"Primerey?" Kian said from the hearth. "Ye may want ta have a look."

"Oh, yes it is ready. Sovia, grab the bowl. Ticari, dear, hold this cloth sack over the bowl. Kian and Therin, grab the kettle—mind the hot handles—and pour the contents into the bag."

Ticari struggled to keep the top of the sack open and hold it at the same time. Ronni stepped up to help hold it while the mixture was poured in. Quinlan noticed she and Ticari locked eyes for a moment through the steam of the hot pomace before she turned her attention to the sack.

"Good, now twist hard. Squeeze all the juices into the bowl," Joseah said.

The Gwylari lined the wall behind Chyne's cot, holding brands of wood and whispering chants. Quinlan was sure they floated and swayed just above the ground when not watched and quickly stood grounded and still when looked at.

"Sovia, Wylla, Swela, Ticca, come help Cassae and me," Joseah said and looked at the male remains of Grove Seven. "Apologies, boys, this one will take a woman's touch. In the meantime, you may lay out ten piles of hand-length sprigs. Lay one sprig of slippery elm, echinacea, calendula, peppermint, eucalyptus, elder, yarrow, burdock, and lavender in each pile, please."

"It shall be so, Primerey," Quinlan said.

The women gathered around the bowl and each took up a piece of twine, except for Joseah who held a tri-brand wand. Brands of cedar, osage, and birch were lashed together at the ends with green cord and engraved with small script druidic runes.

"Hold each twine in the extraction for two verses of the chant while speaking the chant with me. Are you ready?"

They all were prepared to begin.

"Sistren, the song of renewal." She held her tri-brand out over the bowl.

"*Yara vuu nasan beteth drath su in,*" they spoke in unison. "*Lacas geen ova liv drath su in.*"

The women repeated the chant one more time and drew the twines out of the extraction. Ethereal bubbles of ghostly white rose into the air from each twine silently bursting after a second's time.

"It tingles," Cassae said.

The reaction was not lost on those who watched from around the kitchen. Conversations struck up almost immediately. Renalth had to shush the crowd.

They repeated the process thrice more together completing twenty bindings.

"Now, any who wish to may help tie the bundles," Joseah said.

"May I?" Ronni asked.

Joseah motioned to a chair. Several others, both druid and non, stepped up to each take a place.

"One binding at each end of the bundles," Joseah told everyone, "making sure all bundles have one of each sprig tied within."

The twine lengths continued to give off the effervescent sparkles as they were tied around the bundles of sprigs. The people involved all commented on the tingling sensation. Joseah took the finished bundles over to Chyne.

"Now, the sprig bundles must be placed over these areas of Chyne's body. The forehead to clear her mind. The neck to cleanse the blood running through. The heart to guide her home. The solar plexus to stimulate the breathing. The abdomen to bring health to the organs. The pelvis to initiate rebirth. Plus one over each ankle and wrist to clasp on to her spirit."

The sprig bundles now bubbled from the ten areas around Chyne's body. Joseah brought a palm-sized crystal laced with light blue, purple, and white from her possessions. She placed the gemstone above Chyne's head.

"Cassae, take these and lay them by her ears, shoulders, hands, waist, and feet."

She gave Cassae ten discs of willow wood, each one engraved with a druidic rune of healing. She placed them where Joseah told her to.

"Settle down on the other side of her, across from me," Joseah said. "Good, get comfortable and take my hands."

Cassae readied herself and took Joseah's hands over Chyne's torso.

"Prepare your spirit, Cassae. We must continue to sing the song of renewal until we see a response from Chyne."

"I am ready."

"Then let us sing."

They repeated the chant over and over. "*Yara vuu nasan beteth drath su in. Lacas geen ova liv drath su in.*" The bubbles of ethereal energy descended into Chyne instead of rising into the air.

Two hours passed. The effort of the continued singing brought forth sweat, which soaked through their clothing, yet still, they sang. The Gwylari as well had whispered the chant along with them since they began.

Chyne drew in a sudden breath and slowly let it out. She blinked a few times and focused in on her surroundings.

Joseah and Cassae ceased their vigil and both nearly collapsed. Quinlan grabbed Cassae, Therin grabbed Joseah, and they helped them up to chairs.

"Father mine?" Chyne asked.

"Daughter mine," Grymni answered and knelt by her cot.

"What hath occurred?" she asked and the room almost shook with relieved laughter and cheers.

Grymni helped Chyne into a chair as well and she was told of all the events that had occurred since she fell ill. Sovia and Ronni helped fill in some events that took place after Quinlan's group had left Cammachmoor.

Many emotions passed over her face during the telling. She wept openly when she heard the conclave had been devastated. Many others joined her and the moment helped to ease the grief for them all.

Chyne looked greatly saddened by what she had heard. She went around and hugged all of her friends and anyone else in the kitchen before returning to her seat. Joseah and Cassae had recovered and Grove Seven was reunited once more.

Chyne noticed the condition of what she was wearing, and sniffed. "Eww, me thinks mine clothing hath expired."

Another round of laughter sounded off and all, for the moment, was well.

~~~

Ronni MacRory stayed to talk with Renalth and Modgrin after witnessing the incredible healing ritual. She walked down by the lake to unwind from the night's events before going to her room.

Ticari walked up from the beach clutching his clothes in one hand and holding a drying sheet around his waist. He smiled and nodded to her.

Eck, I should nae've come this way. She swallowed and quickly looked away.

"Fine night for a swim," he said, coming up next to her.

"Aye, 'tis." She nodded and continued on her way.

"Lady Ronirah."

"Good evening, druid Ticari!" she said and kept walking.

"Ronirah, wait."

She stopped and immediately wished she had not.

"Ronni, I know you feel the same."

A knot formed in her stomach, telling her to walk on, yet her heart begged her not to.

"Do you not?"

She spoke over her shoulder to him, "Nae, Ti, I—I dinnae have feelin's fer ye, so..."

"Liar, I saw the spark of if it in your eyes earlier."

"Even if 'twere true, and I'm nae sayin' 'tis, I've duties as a lady of the royal court of Raskan and I'm nearly ten years yer senior ta boot." She started to walk away.

"Who'd rather run around the countryside in rags—and likes to pretend she's much older." He caught up to her again. "I know there's not even four years between us."

She turned on him, hands on hips. "Just how'd *ye* find out how old I am?"

"The answers are out there. You just have to know where to find them." He cocked his head. "You pretend to be older, so you feel accepted around lords and kings and all, yet who's there with you when you simply want to be a woman, young and free? Anyone?"

Ticari's remark struck a nerve even though there was no way he could know how she longed for someone to be with, to be next to, and to lie with. "Ti—"

"Ronni, I cannot keep your face from my mind," he said quickly. "I try not to think of you, but then I see a rose and I think of your hair. I think of your hair and I see your face all over again. I'll be eighteen by the turn of the year. I'm nearly a man—I *am a man* and I love you."

Oh, dinnae say that. She swallowed hard and looked at him, fully intending to end the matter and walk away. A man's eyes looked back stealing away her resolve. A man's body trimmed and toned from his life as a druid stalled her voice. A warmth deep inside began to build into a yearning.

Nae, nae, nae, nae, I cannae sleep with him.

Ticari leaned in and kissed her tenderly, just once.

Shite! She fought to let it pass, but the touch of his lips ignited a passion that burned through her body like wildfire across a dry grassy plain. Her inhibitions were melted away by the white-hot heat of her desire. She snatched the clothes from his hand and the drying sheet from his waist, throwing them to the ground. They wrapped each other in passion and fell into the secrecy of nearby shadows.

Chapter Twenty-Two

The first light of dawn fell on Quinlan's face as he sat outside his room listening to Pinebough waking up. The city sat in a valley below the pass, but the south end of the valley was open and dropped away offering a panoramic view. The spires and towers of Teivas Keihas glistened from Trossachsmuir along the horizon. The quietness of it all sat contrasted to the turmoil of the recent weeks.

"Quin?" Cassae asked from the doorway. "Is all well?"

"Yep, just enjoying the sunrise."

She stepped out wrapped in a blanket and looked to the south at Trossachsmuir.

"Do you think he's really there?" she asked.

"Joseah said she saw him walk from the volcano in her mind's eye and he certainly is not in Fairtheora anymore."

"I still can't believe it's all gone, the Great Marsh, the conclave hall, Bertrynn and the others," she said.

"Me, either," he replied. "I hope every day it is nothing but a dream and I'll soon awaken."

The sound of others moving about below drew their attention to the kitchen. Quinlan's stomach growled.

"I agree." Cassae nodded. "Let's go eat."

The breakfast idea must have hit everyone at the same time. The Broken Belt brasserie was almost full when they got there, but members of their grove had already secured a table in back. Ticca shared a piece of banana with Pie as they walked up.

"Where's Ticari?" Quinlan asked her.

"I know not," she answered. "His bed was empty when I awoke. I thought he would be here."

Ronni MacRory walked in right then looking a bit disheveled. She waved heartily at them as she joined Renalth's table. Ticari walked in a few moments later. He and Ronni appeared to be trying not to look at each other—it wasn't working. Ticari's hair was a mess and his clothes were sandy and wrinkled. He smiled at them as he sat down and grabbed a biscuit.

"What?" he asked and tried to smooth his hair. "I fell asleep on the beach after a swim last night."

The sudden quiet smiles and lack of responses from his grove mates were almost deafening.

"I did." Ticari almost held it together, but he could not stop his cheeks from reddening and then the grin broke through his defenses.

"Uh-huh," Kian said. He and Swela snickered quietly.

"What is going on?" Ticca asked and looked at her brother. "What did you do?"

Ticari went red to the ear tips.

The look on his face, the fact he did not sleep in his own bed, and the smiles of her grove mates must have clued her in on what took place last night.

"Ticari!" she exclaimed loud enough for all to hear. Pie Thief barked.

Quinlan saw Ronni bring her hand up to her face and look the other way. Most of the other patrons of The Broken Belt seemed not to notice much beyond their own conversations.

The breakfast continued until it was nearly time for Renalth's meeting.

"Swela, Wylla, and I have been requested to attend the meeting," Quinlan said. "All others are welcome if you so choose. Chyne is visiting with Grymni, so someone will have to tend the horses and Blossom this morning."

Therin raised his hand. "I'll do it."

"And I'll be helping," Sovia said.

"And me," Ticca said and looked at Ticari.

He cleared his throat. "I thought I might, ah, attend the meeting." He focused on finishing his meal. "You know, keep up with what's being planned and all."

No one bought what he was trying to sell. The grove split to go about their respective days.

Joseah met them outside the meeting room on the bottom level of the lodge.

Lah ahm, Primerey," Quinlan said. "We missed you at breakfast."

"Lah ahm all," she said. "That was the first solid night's sleep I've had in weeks. I was not about to ruin it for anything."

They entered the meeting room and Kenri was near the door. He saw Joseah and walked over.

"Lah ahm, Joseah, you are as lovely as ever. My heart is glad to see you."

"Lah ahm, Kenri," she replied. "I seem to remember calling you vilely conceited the last time we saw each other. It has been a constant regret, my apologies."

"Hmm, yes, well you were right," he said, "and my self-centeredness cost me the life of my most beloved and now there is nothing left within. I am old and fearful the deeds of my life will drag my spirit into eternal shadow with no time left for redemption."

"And I the same, but for deeds left undone. Kenri, let us help each other atone for our deeds, both done and undone."

"Yes—yes." He took her hands. "Yes!"

"We will rebuild the Order together!" she said happily.

"Rebuild the Order?" He took his hands back. "Jo, the close-mindedness of the Order is the root of the problem."

"Not even close, Ken. It is druids with talent who run amuck playing god who are the problem." She scowled.

Quinlan cleared his throat.

They both stopped arguing and smiled.

"Old habits," Kenri said.

"Indeed," she added.

"Perhaps it is time you two put your combined and considerable energies to better use," Quinlan said.

"Apologies, Quin."

"Mine as well," Kenri said.

Modgrin Macreeth called people in to the meeting. Renalth and Ronni sat at the table. The other Gwylari chieftains were there but not Grymni or Chyne. The Gwylari seemed to present an odd area of calm in the busy room.

Captain Kinworthy and his superior, Colonel Declan Stone, both white-haired and pale-eyed like Sovia, represented the Kalnuvian forces. The captain's hair was long and pulled back. Colonel Stone's hair was trimmed short and stood straight like little soldiers at attention.

Field Marshal Brixal had traveled from the Vakerian encampment on the east side of Trossachsmuir to attend. The man looked a lot like Quinlan: tall and broad chested with unruly black hair but a full beard instead of a goatee.

Military aides and scribes from all sides filled the room to capacity.

"Quin!" a familiar voice called out.

"Lissa! Na'veyja be praised," he said and wrapped her up in a bear hug embrace. "When did you arrive?"

"Just this morning with Brixal." She looked sad for a moment. "I spoke with the Primerey already. I cannot imagine the Great Marsh was simply swallowed by the ground. We heard Na'veyja's shriek and saw the clouds rising to the north then received the first messages from Kenri in Cammachmoor. Where will we go? The conclave is gone."

"First," Quinlan said grimly, "we must attend to matters in Trossachsmuir."

"Right." She nodded.

The meeting came to order and the druids sat together. Renalth took the floor and talked about the dreyg forces they would face in battle.

"Oh, I almost forgot." Lissa leaned toward him and whispered, "Bertrynn, he is alive."

"Gratitude, Na'veyja!" Quinlan exclaimed loud enough to stop Renalth's lecture. "Apologies, King Renalth."

Lissa motioned that they would talk later.

Renalth continued, "Lady Ronirah will give us the reconnaissance report."

"Milords and ladies." She nodded to the group as she stepped up to an improvised map table. "Major alterations have been made ta the city. All trees and brush have been cleared from Trossachsmuir ta the base of these mountains."

She indicated the mountain range where Pinebough was located. Angry murmurs circulated at the razing of one of Arden's largest and oldest growth forests.

"Trossachsmuir has sprawled. They've built four new walls beyond the old city boundary. Outside of those walls is where the dreyg have set up the new line of defenses. They've piled mounds of rubble everywhere. They're taller than a man on horseback. Ye'll never mount a direct charge against the gates. The barbicans and bastions are made of thick stone and the gates are nae big enough ta get even a catapult through."

"We'll nae be able ta hit the castle with siege engines from such a distance," Modgrin said.

"The root grows mighty," Myzani Nal said. "Gates of stone tremble."

"Apologies," Ronni replied. "What was that?"

Kenri said, "He means the Gwylari have the ability to move great weights and the stone gates will be thrown aside as a child tosses a pebble."

"Oh." Ronni grinned. "Well, that'll come in handy."

Comments of agreement and some snickering went around the room.

"That's basically it," she said. "Troop movements and patrol routes and times're here should anyone need them."

"Gratitude, Lady Ronirah," Renalth said. "Field Marshal Brixal has teams of fighters trained in *shadowcraft* and we've spoken at length. Ye should hear from him. Brixal—"

The Vakerian stood up to address the gathering. "Gratitude, King Renalth. We propose putting druids in with our subversion squads. These teams would sneak through enemy lines and eliminate the signal corps. The front line commanders depend on the signalmen for orders critical to any war effort. Disrupt that communication and the united defense of Trossachsmuir will fall into chaos." Brixal took his seat again.

"We're all aware the dreyg will nae be able ta stand against us, but they're nae the real problem, are they? We can deal with the dreyg. Acimasiz, however is the purview of the druids and I'd like ye ta hear from them now. I give ye Joseah, Primerey of the Order of Arden."

Joseah stood and thanked Renalth. "Greetings, friends. I can tell you firsthand of the power Acimasiz holds. Where the Great Marsh once was, a volcano now spews ash and smoke. Acimasiz will not stop there—no—he will not stop until all of Arden is in ruin. We still have a chance, my friends, but we must act quickly, or we may lose the opportunity that lies at hand. Hear, from those who were there, the events in Drifting Leaf."

Quinlan, Swela, and Wylla told them about what happened in the watershed. They told them about the carraig, what it was, and how it functioned. They related what steps had to be taken to activate it. Ticari even found some tidbits to add.

Joseah outlined her idea about Quinlan and Askue and how the connection to the esbat may be the key to Acimasiz's weakness.

"Because they both live in the Vast?" Brixal asked.

"Yes," she answered. "I believe it would—*disrupt*—the cohesion of his physical being."

"Joseah, that is absolutely brilliant!" Kenri exclaimed.

"Master Quinlan," Renalth said, "that puts a great deal of importance upon yer shoulders. Are ye capable of it?"

"Yes, but I need to be close and I need time unhindered to perform the ritual."

"How do we manage that if Acimasiz be as powerful as you say?" Colonel Stone asked.

"Diversion upon diversion," Kenri said.

"Master Kenri," Renalth said, giving him the floor.

"Sire, we use however many of the druid conduits that are left and team them up with the Gwylari forces. We need to sack the city and surround the castle with as much plant life as we can fit on the walls. This will isolate Acimasiz and force him into the open."

"And ye think an angry god is gonna let ye saunter up and zap him with yer magic?" Modgrin asked.

"No, he will have to be bound to the ethereal plane, which is possible, but I need a second druid to complete the ritual," Kenri answered. "One with abilities level to my own." He looked at Joseah.

Joseah looked back at him, straightened herself tall, and nodded her agreement.

"Joseah, it will..." Kenri started to say something.

Joseah finished, "Likely take all that we have to give. Yes, I know and I will gladly give what is necessary."

"And I," he replied. "Now all we have to do is figure out a way to get beside him without being seen."

"I may be able ta help."

"Swela, nae," Kian said. "'Twill nae work. Acimasiz is nae just some mad beast in the woods. He'll rip ye ta shreds."

"Swela?" Quinlan asked.

"Quin, please, nae," Kian said. "Dinnae let her do this."

"But I know I can do it, Kian," she said. "I feel it deep in ma heart. 'Tis why I am the way I am, hon. 'Tis why Na'veyja chose me." She turned to Quinlan. "I can take his rage. I can hold his attention long enough for Joseah and Kenri to get close and bind him."

"Quin," Kian said, "he—is—a—god! She could be killed."

"How many've died already?" Swela asked. "If I can keep more from dyin', I will. I'm gonna do it anyway, so ye'all may as well come and help."

The gathered people had to be told of Swela's ability to control the rage of beasts and to calm their spirits.

"Yes, of course," Joseah said. "I see it now. There is a will and now there is a way. Na'veyja must have foreseen this and doled out bits and pieces of her essence to us all. Now, we have gathered them together again. That's what she was trying to tell me in the beginning and I could not hear it through the sound of my own chanting. You may have been right, Kenri. Perhaps I was wearing blinders all along." She paused for a moment. "King Renalth, I believe we have the advantage."

"What's in yer mind, Primerey?" he asked.

"We must attack on the next full moon when the power of the esbat is strongest. The armed forces will engage the dreyg. The Gwylari and the druids, including some blending pairs, will overrun Trossachsmuir with plants trapping Acimasiz in the tower. Acimasiz will be forced to show himself. Then we move into our respective positions. Swela will divert the energy of Acimasiz, giving Kenri and me time to bind him to the ethereal plane. Once he is bound, Quinlan and Askue will channel the esbat, breaking down his molecular cohesion and banishing him from the physical plane."

"Sounds about as easy as goin' down ta market," Renalth said, which got a laugh from the group.

"The full moon is only three days away," Brixal said. "We have a lot of plans to make in a short time."

"Then we best get to it." Renalth spread out the strategy maps.

The meetings lasted most of the day. When they were done, Quinlan and the others found the rest of the grove in the courtyard between the kitchens and the lodge. Chyne rode her horse around showing Ticca and some others how to improve their horsemanship.

Quinlan stopped to watch awhile and Cassae stood by him. "Such simple play makes life worth living."

"Is there hope for our world when so many're out ta destroy it?" she asked.

"As long as there is one druid left to care about the plants, trees, and animals of the world there will always be hope."

~~*

Chapter Twenty-Three

The main armed forces of Vakere, Raskan, and Kalnu had tightened the military noose and the city of Trossachsmuir stood blockaded from the east, north, and west. A forward operating base was set up a short way behind the front lines. The combined forces peppered the city's outer defenses with siege engines and archers starting late morning and continued into the afternoon, but no major offensive had been launched.

Quinlan sat in on a strategy meeting while the commencing attack could be heard in the background. Modgrin Macreeth had the floor.

"The subversion squads have another two hours ta get inta position," Modgrin said. "We'll keep the dreyg busy with the initial assault 'til then. The main assault'll begin at nightfall. The subversion squads will disrupt battlefield communications upon our attack. Once the city's breached, we'll surround Teivas Keihas, and the Gwylari and the druids can move in and work their magic. At the same time, Grove Seven with Kenri and Joseah will be escorted by Vakerian subversion troops inta the castle. If all goes as planned, we'll have contact with our main objective somewhere within."

"Are there contingency plans?" Joseah asked.

"Nae as such, Primerey. Our underlyin' priority is the protection and timely placement of our main objective force, namely yerself and the others tasked with achievin' our main objective."

"The main objective," Quinlan said, "sounds tame enough."

"I dinnae think throwin' the name of a godlike enemy around was the best idea, especially with him bein' so close by and all."

"Point taken," Quinlan replied.

"Now, with the location of our main objective bein' unknown, our force must be ready ta enter the city and go inta action at a moment's notice."

"Hope fer clear skies," Ronni said, "so, ma friend here with the magic walkin' stick can tell our main objective what ta go do with himself."

"Aye!" Modgrin said. "Best get yerselves rested. We've a long night ahead and hopefully, another day'll dawn at the end of it."

Quinlan and Grove Seven left the meeting to make the final preparations before heading down to the staging area.

"Wylla wasn't at the meetin'," Cassae said.

"No, she joined one of the subversion squads and left before sun up to meet them," Quinlan replied.

"She took a life when one was taken from her, yet she thirsts for more blood. It's a dark trail ta walk."

"What was the poem she spoke in Drifting Leaf?" Quinlan asked.

"'Tis a Raskanish burial verse ta be spoken at graveside by survivin' kin," Kian answered and recited the poem.

"I've been on a journey of many milestones, yet my feet dinnae tire.

They've walked dry trails warmed by the sun.

They've tread muddy slopes soaked by dark storms.

The destination's known, yet the trail's misted by many tomorrows, or perhaps just one.

I walk on."

"Beautiful, yet lonely," Ticca said.

"Indeed and sadly it doth suit Wylla," Chyne replied.

"There will be many tomorrows for Wylla and for us all," Quinlan said. "Remember to take one of Kenri's dart pipes and a satchel of darts. Leave the balsa caps tight until you are ready to load. Bring slings and a good selection of seeds and fungus balls. Prepare and practice your chants so they come without effort. Na'veyja is still out there somewhere and she will hear your call."

"Na'veyja watch over you tonight, Siestrey," Ticca said.

"And you, whom I love as my own daughter," he replied and wrapped her briefly in a bear hug. "Mind Sovia and stray not from her side. Ticari, you and Ticca must shield Sovia, Therin, and Chyne from discovery so they have time to launch their attacks. Once one attack is complete, you need to move quickly and silently to the next attack position." Quinlan looked around at his grove. "I could not be more proud. Blessed be you all."

Grove Seven returned his blessing.

"The horses and Blossom're stabled and set fer the night," Swela said. "We're packed and set ta shove off."

"Very good, we walk to battle." Quinlan pulled up the hood of his raiment. "Grove Seven, packs on, hoods up, let our feet be swift and our tread be light."

The grove reached the Raskanish staging point of the multipronged siege effort. A large group of druids had already gathered, Joseah and Kenri among them. The druids greeted Grove Seven like brethren and sistren, whether they knew them previously or not. Quinlan felt good being among so many of his fellow druids again and had not realized how much he missed it.

"Lissa!" Quinlan said when he saw her, "you never told me of Bertrynn."

"Apologies, Quin, the day got away. He would be here today, bloody stump and all, if the physicians hadn't slipped him sleeping powder."

"Bloody stump?" Cassae asked.

Lissa nodded, clicked her cheek, and sliced her hand across her leg at the knee. "Rock fall during the—event. He and a few of the others here managed to escape to the south. Vakerian scouts found them and brought them to Hearth's Port."

"I guessed such was the case," Quinlan said. "I should have looked farther for more survivors."

"No, Quinlan," Lissa replied, "you were on the west side of ash fall and they to the south. You would've had to cross the ash field to have found them. You would have perished like all life there has, plant and animal alike."

A blond woman in druid clothes and raiment joined them slipping her arm around Lissa's waist. Lissa did the same and they shared a kiss.

"Rose, these are my friends, Grove Seven," Lissa said and introduced each of them. "Rose is my wife. We were wed this morning, we and ten other couples in a group ceremony."

"Shin Lahqui, Grove Seven," Rose said. "I am honored."

"Na'veyja be praised! Welcome to the family, love." Sovia gave her a hug, and the rest followed suit.

Ronni MacRory rode up dressed in maroon-and-red light armor. She wore a wooden brigandine cuirass, metal arm and leg plates, plated gloves, and a close-fitting helmet. A dirk and a sword were belted around her waist and a teardrop-shaped medium-sized heater shield bearing the MacRory crest hung from her saddle horn. Her horse wore brigandine barding and chanfron of the same wooded armor. She removed her helmet as she stopped and dismounted.

"Is that kingswood?" Therin asked her, nodding to her wooden tile-reinforced cuirass and barding.

"Aye, 'tis," she replied. "Lightweight and stron'."

"Stron' ya say?" Therin asked. "They don't call it 'axe-breaker' for nothin'."

"May it live up ta the name this night," she replied.

"What's the word?" Quinlan asked. Others gathered around.

"We're about ready," Ronni said, her voice loud enough for the others to hear. "Everyone should take their positions." She looked at Grove Seven. "Luck in battle, ma friends. Na'veyja be with ye."

The grove bid her luck as well and she mounted up again. She looked down at Ticari as he stroked her horse's neck. She held his eyes and touched his hand. "Fare thee well, druid."

"Fare thee well, lady warrior." He grasped her hand. "I will find you afterward."

She nodded, quickly turned away, and donned her helmet. Urging her horse forward, she rode off to join the battle.

The sun had dropped below the horizon and Renalth must have given the order to commence with the main assault on the city's defenses. Catapults and trebuchets doubled their assault, sending boulders of fire into the air, the flames crashing down onto the wall, gate, and soldiers.

"Find your places, druids!" Joseah called out from nearby. "Na'veyja will guide you through the dark night!"

"May Na'veyja protect you and aide you in your quest," Lissa said to Quinlan. "We all fight with you."

Quinlan only had time to wave as she and Rose ran to join their group. His grove watched him for instruction.

"Go and blessed be you all," he said.

Sovia, Therin, Chyne, Ticari, and Ticca parted from their friends and joined the druid assault groups.

Quinlan stood with the remaining members of Grove Seven watching the others disappear in the growing darkness. The battle for Trossachsmuir had begun. Quinlan's small force of druids met a subversion squad at the staging area.

"Quinlan of Calamere!" a voice from the past called out.

"Ha ha!" Quinlan did not turn around. "Crack of lightning."

"Clap of thunder," the man said.

Quinlan turned to face him.

"Let no man break we friends asunder!" they finished in unison and embraced warmly.

"Edwynn Gerlynn, your face rekindles glad memories," Quinlan said and introduced the others. "Edwynn and I grew up together playing on the piers of Calamere."

"Seems ages ago now, old friend," Edwynn said.

Quinlan noticed the uniquely reinforced black leather armor his friend wore. He bore two crossed short swords on his back and was loaded with daggers and throwing knives. A crossbow was slung over his shoulder and quivers of bolts were strapped to each thigh.

Edwynn bowed low. "I'm your guide for tonight's festivities."

"Subversion squad?" Kian asked.

"Yep," Edwynn replied. "My boys and I will get you in there safe and sound, don't you worry."

Quinlan could barely make out the rest of Edwynn's men standing behind him in the growing darkness.

"The idea is to follow the main incursion force as soon as the wall is breached. We stay out of the fighting and stick to the shadows. Our mission is to reach Teivas Keihas not fight in the battle. Understood?"

A Gwylari courier reported to Joseah.

"The Gwylari and druid forces are in position and ready to proceed," she said. "Let us move to where we can observe."

Quinlan could see two other staging areas to the east and west of Trossachsmuir preparing to initiate the same attack. The Vakerian encampment fires lit up the eastern hills. The Kalnuvian encampment did the same for the fields west of the city.

Catapults and trebuchets filled the sky with giant stones and firepots of naptha and nails. The moon had not yet risen and war masters of Trossachsmuir had darkened the city. A dozen large fires dotted the high towers where colored flags shone in their light. Trumpeters sounded coded instructions to the commanders of the city's defenses. One of the fires went out as they watched from a hill near the Raskanish offensive.

"That was one of our teams," Edwynn said. "Now the fun begins. Come, it is time."

The main objective force took their position behind and to the side of the host of Gwylari and druids. Somewhere in the host ahead was the rest of Grove Seven preparing to do their part. In front of the host was a line of troops pushing carts mounted with large shields toward the walls of Trossachsmuir.

The main host began to move up with them. A dim glow came from many different spots in the darkness as the druid conduits channeled the energy of the world around them, passing it on to fellow druids. The sound of chants mingled together when the first of the giant rubble piles was encountered. The Gwylari and the druids used the channeled energy to fast grow trees with mighty roots.

The advancing force reached the giant rubble piles outside the gate. Massive roots rose from the ground reducing the piles and pushing the rubble from the main roadway. The trees grew along the road and their roots reached the barbicans standing on each side of the portcullis. The foundations of both gate and the walls around it crumbled with a crash in the distance.

More fires around the tower had darkened as the subversion squads succeeded in their missions.

"Torch arrows!" a commander called out from the darkness.

Small fires sprang to life ahead of them and a volley of flaming arrows streaked toward the gate area. Dozens upon dozens of burning arrows illuminated the scene ahead

"Advance!"

The row of shielded carts moved forward while squads of archers provided suppressing fire along the castle's parapets and ramparts. The main host moved in behind the row of massive shields. Teams of oxen pulled the siege engines closer now that the rubble piles were out of the way.

"Engines loose!"

The barrage of stones and firepots began their work on the next line of walls.

"We move up," Edwynn said. His men had already taken perimeter positions around Quinlan's group.

The force reached the first gate just as the main host had torn down the gate and portcullis, clearing them from the path

"Infantry!" the commander called out.

A large group of fighters surged past them and through the opening. They swept into the bailey beyond the wall, engaging dreyg wherever they were found.

The first of four walls had been breached and the dreyg were pushed back. The method of attack was used three more times and three more times the walls of Trossachsmuir crumbled.

The soldiers of Raskan entered the city and quickly gained footholds in strategic areas. The dreyg were forced to abandon their positions and retreated to the castle keep. Signal corps fires no longer burned along the keep's thick crenelated walls. The plan was working.

Quinlan's group waited with Edwynn's subversion squad and advanced each time the war effort advanced. They moved in to the keep and climbed siege ladders to the top of the curtain walls, which stood as the keep's first line of defense. The castle, Teivas Keihas, rose from the center of the keep a long arrow shot from the outer walls.

The infantry forces broke through the curtain wall gate with a battering ram. Dreyg archers and troops with ballistae let loose from the keep's higher advantage, raining death on the infantry soldiers trying to make it through the gate. Dozens of clay pots were flung into the advancing army shattering and splashing oil in every direction. Archers from the keep sent flaming arrows into the oil, filling the courtyard with fire.

"Taking the keep will prove to be a tough fight," Quinlan said.

"Yes, but look there, Quin." Edwynn pointed to the sea illuminated by the moon cresting the horizon. A fleet of ships sailed into the bay engaging the opponent's ships and blasting the city's unprotected south side with cannon fire. "The Shaanlander navy under King Travell Tavish sailing with Vakerian privateers and they bring warriors from the southern continent. Apparently their chieftain has somewhat of a large beef with the disciple, Lord Praven."

"Vakerian privateers?" Quinlan asked.

"Yes, a group of former fishermen hired by the Order to find sailing routes to the southern continent. We're moving out! Heading for the south wall!"

The group eventually made their way around to the south side of the keep.

"The esbat rises," Swela said.

Quinlan looked to the east and saw the moon fully above the horizon. "And so it begins."

The Vakerian and Shaanlander ships hammered the southern gate and the walls around it with cannon fire crumbling the structure to the ground.

"There it goes!" Edwynn exclaimed. "The keep has been breached!"

The cry could be heard transferring from person to person that the keep was vulnerable from the south.

Hordes of black-skinned warriors streamed into the keep grounds. Dressed in crimson uniforms and wielding long curved swords, they screamed terrible battle cries and attacked the dreyg forces.

"The *Onomali*, warriors of the southern continent," Edwynn said as they watched. "I've never seen such ferocity before. We need to climb down and cross the courtyard to the castle."

They started across to Teivas Keihas when a group of dreyg burst through a door, locked sights on their group, and attacked. Edwynn's men readied their crossbows, but the druids were faster with their dart pipes and their foes dropped to the ground.

"They'll be out for hours," Quinlan said.

"Hmm, pretty handy those things," Edwynn replied.

The next wave of attack required both parties to act and some enemies dropped unconscious and some dropped dead. More dreyg headed their way.

"This is not where we want to be," Edwynn said. "We must get to the castle!"

Advancing dreyg fighters blocked the way in to the castle. The way back was clogged with fighters in a close quarters melee. More dreyg forces poured from the castle gate.

"Stay behind us," Edwynn said to Quinlan's group. "Shield us with your mysticism if you can."

"Ready your crossbows!" Quinlan replied. "Druids, green gas!"

The seven druids drew small pods from pouches and whispered, *"Sanath"* before throwing them in front of the advancing soldiers. The pods grew in size and began to fester.

"Strike them!" Quinlan said.

Edwynn and his men shot bolts into the pods. The green pods burst and released a green gas into the air. The front of the enemy mass fell to their knees, vomiting and choking. Another volley of crossbow bolts dropped another group of dreyg. The druids used fungus balls, nettle attacks, and dart pipes to mount offenses and defenses. The subversion squad worked with the druids where they needed and dealt with the overflow in expedient military fashion with bolts and swords. Fight as they may, even more dreyg charged into the courtyard.

"We'll hold them as long as we can, Quin," Edwynn said. "You must get to the castle."

The clash of weapons drew their attention and that of the dreygs' even more to a charge by Kalnuvian infantry. The dreyg attack faltered and fell apart. The front line tried to engage the trained military forces of Kalnu and the back turned and fled.

The sight of the Vakerian ground forces coming in from the east halted the dreyg's forced retreat. The enemy host turned south and straight into a horde of screaming Onomali warriors. The dreyg soldiers of fortune were no match for the trained fighting forces of Arden.

"Regroup!" Edwynn called out. The subversion squad closed in and reformed the perimeter around the druids.

"Everyone good?" Quinlan asked his group. All of them showed signs of the exertion of battle, yet all stood ready to continue on.

Edwynn pointed to the castle entrance which was clear of enemies for the moment. "Leave the fighting! We make for the castle!"

The main objective force fled the courtyard, reached the castle gate, and entered Teivas Keihas.

~~*

Chapter Twenty-Four

Ronni MacRory walked in the courtyard of the keep in time to see Quinlan and his group heading for the castle entrance. She heaved her breath in and out but was well within her comfort range. Bumps, bruises, several small cuts, and a medium gash were the extent of the costs she paid to get this far. Those who had stood in her way had paid a dearer price. Her horse took a mild injury, so she left him behind with a squire.

Ronni surveyed the battle scene with a keen eye. A woman fighter of skill in dreyg armor pursued Quinlan's group cutting down any allied soldier who confronted her. She dispatched them quickly and continued the hunt.

"Oh, nae, ye dinnae go after ma friends, ye bitch," she said and took off in pursuit of the dreyg huntress.

The woman was almost upon Quinlan's group, who was unaware the dreyg was in pursuit, and Ronni was still too far to catch up. She picked up a fist-sized rock and flung it with all her might. The rock sailed through the air and cracked the woman in the back of the head. She had a helmet on, but the impact knocked her to the ground face-first.

"Oh!" Ronni yelled out, did a little dance, and charged.

The woman rose from the ground and turned to face her. Blood trickled from abrasions on her nose and chin. A black-and-grey herringbone-weave aiguillette ran from left shoulder to left breast.

Ronni circled her, sword in sheath. "Ye better get that looked at, dearie, blood'll stain ye know."

"Raskan cow!" the woman screamed and drew sword and dirk in one smooth movement.

Ronni drew sword, set stance, and raised shield.

The dreyg fighter lunged forward with her sword only to spin aside at the last moment, deftly slipping her dirk behind Ronni's shield and up toward her neck nearly scoring a fatal strike but leaving only a slash up Ronni's jaw and cheek.

Ronni instantly went defensive and spun in the opposite direction smashing into the woman with her shoulder. The impact knocked the dreyg backward, but not down. The two women circled each other with a little more wariness.

"Commandant Malent!" A dreyg fighter ran to defend her before an arrow flew into his chest. In a glance, Ronni saw Modgrin with his bow.

"Yer in the clear, milady," he said.

"Commandant Malent?" Ronni asked. "Commandant of the Dreyg, are ye? The turd at the top of the pile."

Marza sneered at her. "Marza Malent, and I know you, Lady MacWhore-y."

"Oh, ha ha, you'll pay fer that one, ye shite-eatin' bitch." Ronni thrust her sword at her opponent.

Marza crossed her dirk and sword, deflecting Ronni's thrust and started to slice her dirk upward.

Ronni was a step ahead of her and smashed her in the face with the edge of her shield.

Marza staggered backward but recovered, grimaced, and closed the distance.

The two fighters traded blows and parries stalking each other beyond a dozen encounters. Each woman drew the other's blood on several exchanges. One fighter used dual-blade fighting techniques against the other who was a single-sword-and-shield fighter.

Marza thrust with her sword. Ronni deflected it down with hers. Marza spun toward the two swords and inside Ronni's defenses. She stabbed backward with her dirk before quickly spinning back out. The blow landed in the unreinforced area under Ronni's shield arm. Marza immediately came in with a cross-body sword strike catching the inside of Ronni's shield and slicing across her forearm.

Pain seared the left side of Ronni's chest. Marza's sword edge opened a gash to the bone across her forearm and she could barely grip her shield. She never saw the kick to her chest, which knocked her flat to her back. She looked around for last-minute help, but Modgrin was fighting his own battle and no help was in sight.

Marza moved in and thrust down with her sword. Ronni managed to sweep her shield across to block the strike, but Marza knocked the shield down and stepped on it. Ronni stabbed upward with her sword. Marza's cross block sent her sword flying out of reach. Ronni raised her right hand up to Marza, who stepped over her and drew back her sword. Ronni planted the toe of her armor-plated boot right between the woman's legs with all her strength, Marza doubled over and toppled from the shocking pain.

Ronni pulled her bleeding arm free of her shield and rolled on top of Marza. She pushed the woman's own dirk into the side of her neck and pulled it back out again. She laid on Marza as she struggled and her life's blood ran from the wound. The pulsing of the blood flow slowed and stopped as Marza Malent, Commandant of the dreyg forces, died in battle.

Ronni rolled over onto her back thoroughly exhausted. A strange man in a turban with a tail to the left shoulder stood over her, smiling. He reached out his hand to her and she suddenly could not breathe. Her body felt like it was being torn apart from the inside out. Through the haze of pain she saw Ticari nearby chanting and as fast as the sensation started, it came to an end.

The man attacking her was being encased with vines and roots that were constricting around him as well. A calm look was on his face as he chanted in return and the plants began to wither and die. Sneering, he turned his power on Ticari, and Ronni could do nothing but watch as the stranger killed the one she had come to love.

"Nae," she whispered, "Na'veyja..."

The turbaned man was suddenly snatched from his feet and thrown sideways. The cause was not an answer to a prayer but the weight of a thrown spear. Ronni watched as an Onomali warrior walked up to the man and pulled the spear from his body. The black-skinned man of the southern continent thrust the spear into the turbaned man one more time before he came over and began to apply pressure to Ronni's wounded arm.

"Gratitude," she said.

The man nodded. "Welcome. I am named Jua Kali."

"Ronirah—MacRory," she said.

"Ah, Raskanish, eh? Very good."

"Ronni!" Ticari said as he regained consciousness and came over to them.

"Ti," she whispered.

"Hold on," Ticari said and dug through his possessions. He brought out several herbs, chewed some of them, and smeared them on her arm. *"Cala vasayr huut abnas."* The bleeding stopped as the herb poultice sealed the injury.

"A druid?" Jua Kali asked. "A very good day indeed."

"Yes," Ticari replied and turned to Ronni. "Here, eat this, it will give you energy." He turned back to the man. "The raiment didn't give it away?"

"What is raiment?" he asked.

Ticari wiggled the edge of the raiment he wore.

"Ahh—no, de druids of my land, dey do not wear such garments."

Ronni felt her senses return. She slowly got to her feet and to a nearby bench with the help of the two gentlemen.

"Gratitude, lads," she said.

"The dreyg have surrendered," Ticari said. "We came in with the Gwylari to mount an offensive on the castle when I saw you and"—he pointed at the body—"whoever that was."

"Lord Praven," Jua Kali said, "Disciple of Nemilos and overlord of Acimasiz. He and his kind are de sworn enemy of my people."

"You know of Acimasiz?" Ticari asked. "And who are you?"

"Jua Kali, second son of Chieftain Kali San."

"Ticari, Settey in the Order of Arden."

"Most pleased."

"And gratitude for your timely arrival." Ticari held out his hand, which Jua grasped.

"I am honored it was my spear dat took his life."

"Physician, over here!" Ticari called out to a medico. "Lady Ronirah needs attention!"

The battle doctor worked on Ronni's wounds while troops of every land mingled in the courtyard and Gwylari and the druids encircled the castle and began to chant.

Tendrils of green snaked their way out of the ground. The green sprouted between the courtyard tiles and seams spreading everywhere. The perimeter base of Teivas Keihas's four wings became solid green. The mystical work of the Gwylari and the druids sent the green rising up the walls until a moat of living plants surrounded the castle.

A dim glow of flaura like a steaming mist of colors rose from the gathering of plant life. The cloud began to drift and flow becoming a river of flaura running around the castle's exterior. The more they chanted, the higher the flaura rose. It twisted, churned, and spun into a vortex of colors.

"Druid magic," Jua Kali said as they watched the gathering of mystics do their work.

The rest of Grove Seven joined them in the courtyard minus Quinlan's group. Ticari introduced Jua Kali to his grove mates and told them of what happened.

"A disciple and the dreyg commandant," Sovia said. "Be a couple of points for our side, there."

Ticca looked at the bodies and at the carnage all around them. "I care not for battle."

Ticari held his sister. "Nor do I."

"Ronni!" Modgrin exclaimed as he came by. One arm hung limp and he bled from the side of his head. "Apologies, lass, are ya all right?"

"Aye, Modgrin, I'm fine. Naught ta worry about," she answered while Chyne worked on Modgrin's wounds.

"The moon is high," Modgrin said. "What happens if our friend dinnae want ta come out and play?"

"Then we need to be a bit more persuasive about our invitation," Sovia said.

People around them muttered as a black mist slowly moved from the top of the tower toward the moat of green. The black mist and the flaura cloud tore at one another like thousands of gaseous vipers fighting over territory. The mist crept over the plants and began to smother the life from them. The Gwylari and druids responded by chanting stronger. The moat of plant and energy held, but could go no higher. They had reached a stalemate.

"It be up to Quin and the others now," Sovia said, hands on hips and tapping her foot. "Och, I'll die if I has to wait any longer. I'm going up to be of help to Quin. Who be with me?"

"I am with thee, Cetrey," Chyne replied.

"And I," Jua Kali said.

"I'm goin'," Ronni said, which met with the immediate disapproval of Modgrin and Ticari.

"Hey, ye there! Vakerian!" Modgrin called out. "Have ye seen Brixal?"

The man pointed to a large group of men by the east end of the courtyard.

The group found Field Marshal Brixal organizing troops to do a final sweep of the city and rout out any remaining dreyg.

"Well met, friends," Brixal said when the group arrived. "Victorious so far, but it seems we've woken the lord of the manor."

"Indeed," Modgrin said. "Brixal, would ye have a spare subversion squad ta send inta Teivas Keihas with these druids in case they meet armed resistance?"

"Certainly, we planned on entering the castle momentarily as it was. Come along with us. Jua Kali, it is good to see you again."

"And you, Brixal. De plan went exactly as you said it would. You Vakerians are *very* sneaky. Most pleasing."

An aide reported to Brixal that all was ready. "Very good," he replied. "Subversion squads, move out!"

"Ye stay put," Modgrin said to Ronni. She looked down but nodded.

"Na'veyja be with ye all," Ronni said to her friends and embraced them before they left.

She watched the host head off to the castle. Modgrin had gone as well with a dozen Raskanish fighters. She waited until no one was watching and quietly slipped away after them.

~~~

Quinlan and the main objective force encountered dreyg as they entered the castle. They dealt with them easily using mysticism and might.

Edwynn laid out the next phase of the plan. "We must go up through one of the corner towers and cross over to the central tower from there."

An ornate wide flight of stairs split off into two smaller stairways going in opposite directions. The subversion squad led the way up the stairs and to the right with crossbows up and ready. Many dreyg fell dead silently as the squad cleared the way until they found the next flight of stairs.

"We are running short on time," Joseah said.

"There." Quinlan pointed to an alcove with a spiral stairway going up.

Dreyg fighters waited at the top of the stairway and fired crossbows whenever squad members peeked around the corner. The engagement would be difficult to win. One group was under cover with clear shots at the entryway and the other safely behind the entryway wall but unable to move ahead.

Quinlan moved up to the edge and grabbed a handful of seeds from a pouch. "*Mundi jala tarquath*," he said and threw them down the hall. "Stay back."

Questions and comments preceded several popping sounds and yells of pain. Glossy spikes stuck into the stones of the wall across from them.

Edwynn started to move, but Quinlan stopped him. "Wait."

The glossy spikes began to wilt and decompose.

Quinlan nodded to Edwynn. "Clear."

The dreyg were semiconscious and moaned in pain from blisters growing all over their skin.

Edwynn looked at Quinlan as they passed by the dreyg. "I'm glad you didn't know how to do that when I stole your fish that day."

"Yes, as you should be," Quinlan replied. "I might have used it on you."

They reached the gleaming steel gates of the bridge to the central tower. The crenelated structure was wide enough to line a hundred horses in the allure between the parapets. Four of the bridges spanned the gap between the corner towers and the twice-as-tall central tower.

"Too quiet." Kenri shook his head.

"He's right," Edwynn replied. "I expected more resistance. I smell a trap."

"Have we any other choice?" Quinlan asked.

"Nope," Edwynn answered and opened the gates.

Quinlan looked down and saw the green of plants gleaming in the moonlight. The glow of flaura swirled around the four wings of the castle and up the sides of the central tower. A black mist began to descend, engaging the flaura and attacking the plant growth.

"Acimasiz is here!" Joseah said.

"We must hurry," Kenri said

They no sooner reached halfway to the central tower when the expected ambush took place. Dreyg fighters poured from the four corners and out from the central tower. They were surrounded by the enemy.

"Circle up!" Edwynn said.

The subversion squad took positions around the group. Their defense did not need to stand long before the dreyg turned to defend their rear flanks from a new attack. Druids, Gwylari, subversion squads, and armed forces from across Arden stormed the four bridges. An all-out melee ensued in every open space of the four allures.

The scene changed instantly as Acimasiz materialized on the bridge before them—a giant among men. He drained the lives from those around him, friend and foe alike. He drew a sword swathed in black mist and lifted fighters off the ground without touching them. Draining them dead, he cleaved them in two.

"Engage!" Quinlan said.

Edwynn's subversion squad spread out to give them room. Quinlan moved to where he could see the moon. Cassae and Kian joined the subversion squad to protect Quinlan and the others. Joseah moved to one side of the allure and readied her tri-brand. Kenri moved to the opposite side of the allure and brought forth a hand-sized green-and-brown-streaked adder stone.

Swela walked forward and confronted Acimasiz when everyone was set.

"I feel yer anger, beastie," she said and held her arms out wide.

The power of Acimasiz shook the bridge as he turned his attention on Swela and advanced.

Her scar began to glow with golden-yellow light.

"Ease yer anger," she said calmly. *"Talath on hongna."*

Acimasiz stepped up unhindered by Swela and raised his blackened sword.

"Talath on hongna..." she let her voice trail off slowly and focused her spirit.

The sword did not fall. Acimasiz looked angry but seemed frozen by her words.

"Talath on hongna..." she spoke calmly and smoothly.

Joseah moved into position and began to chant. Kenri did the same. The blending of their energies created an emerald-colored ethereal web over their enemy. Acimasiz was bound to the ethereal plane.

Quinlan focused his spirit. He lifted Askue high and pointed it at the full moon.

"Esbat nom krayla nom talsa. Rynn nom krayla nom talsa. Na'veyja nom krayla nom talsa."

The moonlight once again was drawn to Quinlan and Askue. The shimmering silver glow around Askue sparkled with thousands of tiny bright white shooting stars. The silvery-white starfield traveled down Quinlan's raised arm, flowed across his body, and toward the ensnared Acimasiz.

The power of the esbat clearly caused Acimasiz discomfort. The sword arm dropped and he fell to his knees. A deep growl grew into a mighty roar as the moonlight dealt him great damage.

The dreyg surrounded the subversion squad and pressed the attack. Three dreyg fighters broke off from the melee and attacked Quinlan. He had to stop his channeling to defend himself.

When the moonbeam stopped, Acimasiz recovered. "Foolish animals!" He turned his visage upon Kenri and screamed.

Kenri's adder stone charm exploded sending shrapnel in every direction. The shards tore through Kenri's body. He fell to the stones of the allure and did not move again.

The ethereal web dissipated and Acimasiz was free again. He turned next to Swela and began to drain her life force. Swela staggered under the effort to continue her defense and calmed her spirit. "*Talath on hongna...*" she whispered peacefully.

Acimasiz faltered but only for a moment before he advanced again.

Joseah ran in between the two with her tri-brand raised. She stood boldly before her enemy and blocked his attack on Swela.

Quinlan kept one eye on the objective and the other eye on defending against his attackers.

Ronni came up from behind and ran one dreyg through with her sword. With one arm bandaged and slung, she faced the other two.

Quinlan swung Askue and clipped one of the dreyg at the base of the skull; he went down in a heap. Ronni took only a minute more to dispatch the last fighter.

Quinlan strode back into the open and called to the esbat once more. *"Esbat nom krayla nom talsa. Rynn nom krayla nom talsa. Na'veyja nom krayla nom talsa."*

The channeled beam of moonlight struck Acimasiz causing him to turn from Joseah and Swela and toward Quinlan. He fought against the moon's power and slowly moved closer to Quinlan. Swela and Joseah continued their efforts, but it seemed to have less effect than before, now that the binding was broken.

The glowing form of a woman took shape in the swirling flaura cloud generated by the Gwylari and the druids below. She reached forth with arms of ethereal energy wrapping them around Acimasiz. He struggled to be free of Na'veyja's embrace and his defenses dropped.

Joseah and Swela moved up and continued to blast Acimasiz with their powers. The tiny stars of Quinlan and Askue's channeled moonlight penetrated his skin and began to erode his physical body. The robes burned away and the skin underneath drifted away in flakes of ash. Muscles rotted, decayed, and peeled from his bones. The bones disintegrated into molecular dust.

The burning spark of Acimasiz' physical presence that remained suddenly detonated and threw off a massive shock wave of black, green, and white energy. Everyone on the allures was blasted off their feet. The energy ring from the blast disappeared past every horizon leaving only its echo to remain.

Quinlan got to his feet and looked around. Acimasiz was gone, but so too was the swirling cloud of flaura. The troughs of Askue's wood grain pulsed with bluish-white light that slowly faded away. He and Ronni went to Swela's side.

"Swela?" Quinlan asked.

She came around quickly and he helped her to her feet. Kian ran over with all of Grove Seven. Cassae went to check Kenri, but she shook her head.

"Quin," Sovia said from Joseah's side.

Quinlan knelt by the Primerey's side. Her breathing was ragged and blood trickled from her mouth.

"We—did—it," she whispered and smiled.

He smiled back and tried not to cry. "Yes, Primerey, we did."

"Croaker, we need a litter here!" Edwynn called to the squad medic.

Chyne knelt down and placed her hand on Joseah's abdomen then withdrew it and began to cry.

Joseah took her hand and squeezed it. "Worry not, Chyne. We all must leave this world. My time comes."

The subversion squad carefully loaded Joseah onto the litter and carried her down to the courtyard. Others did the same with Kenri's body.

The mass of armed forces, Gwylari, and druids gathered around the triage area where Vakerian physicians tended to the wounded.

"Tenderfoot," someone said as Quinlan walked by. Even through his surprise, he knew the voice well. He turned to greet his smiling brother.

"Lanry!" Quinlan said and embraced his brother. "By the Goddess, what brings you here?" Lanry stepped back and showed off his outfit.

"You're with the Vakerian privateers?"

"I'm not the only one."

An older man dressed similarly walked up, holding his arms out.

"Dad?"

Riklan hugged his son. "Quin, I could not be more proud. Word has already spread throughout the city of you and your friends' deeds."

Jua Kali joined them. "I should have known de savior of de day would be a child of your loins, Riklan of Calamere."

"Jua Kali, meet another son, Quinlan. Quin, this is Jua Kali, Prince of the Onomali, from the southern continent."

"I am most grateful to you and de northern druids, Quinlan," Jua Kali said. "De natural world rejoices."

"We paid a dear price," Quinlan said, looking at Joseah and Kenri.

Joseah held a hand out to him and he sat by the bed they'd placed her in.

"Acimasiz is not gone, Quin," she said, "but he has been rendered powerless for some time. I fear the same for Na'veyja."

"What must we do?" he asked.

"Seek out Azuria Norr," she replied.

"I know of dis sorceress," Jua Kali said. "It is said she lives deep in de jungle, at de bottom of de Misted Gorge."

"On the southern continent?" Quinlan asked.

Jua Kali nodded. "Far from de coast."

"She'll know how to find Na'veyja," Joseah said.

Quinlan looked down at her. "We will find her, Primerey."

Joseah shook her head. "*You*—are Primerey now, Quinlan. My time is at hand."

"No, I have not the knowledge to be Primerey," Quinlan replied. "You must live, Joseah. You are the last of our elders. If you die, who will be left to learn from? What of Segoney Silari?"

"He would agree that you must find Azuria Norr. She will guide you to Na'veyja. Trust in yourself, Quin, and in your grove. Blessed be..." Joseah whispered and passed from the physical world into the beyond.

Many cried, but all mourned the passing of Joseah. She was the last druid council member of the Order of Arden to survive the destruction of the conclave. The era of the Great Marsh and the druid conclave that had existed there for generations of time had come to an end as well.

"Oh no," Cassae said.

"What?" Quinlan asked.

"Wylla…" Cassae said as two soldiers laid her body to rest with the others and covered it with a sheet.

The grove went over to pay respects and pay their farewells to their fallen friend. Quinlan pulled the sheet back from her face and straightened blood-soaked hair. He recited the poem she had spoken over Freyn's gravesite.

"I've been on a journey of many milestones, yet my feet do not tire.

They've walked dry trails warmed by the sun.

They've tread muddy slopes soaked by dark storms.

The destination is known, yet the trail is misted by many tomorrows, or perhaps just one.

I walk on."

"Wherever you are, I hope you find the peace you could not find here." He smiled at her before replacing the sheet.

"What be your orders, Primerey?" Sovia asked with all respect intended. Flit and Singer chittered a happy song back and forth to each other, which lightened the mood.

The grove came together to hear what he had to say.

Quinlan simply looked at them and did not know what to say, so he chose what he knew how to do best. "Help others."

Pie Thief barked her agreement and chased away some more of the gloom.

The gathered people split off to deal with the grief in their own way. The assembly, Grove Seven included, pitched in to help tend the wounded or clean up the debris and bodies.

"So, what's next?" Quinlan asked his father as they looked over the ships in the harbor from the keep walls.

"Go visit your mother, of course. She'll be sore with me for being gone this long." They shared a laugh as they both knew her scowl well. "After that, we sail for the southern continent to help Jua Kali free his city from the dreyg."

"Then we will sail together for the first time in years. I look forward to it."

"As do I," Riklan turned to his son. "Who would have thought those many years ago when we rode to Telovin things would turn out such as they have?"

"I followed the druid way and felt Na'veyja's presence, yet in my heart I did not see the threat existed until it was too late."

"That's the nature of evil, Quin. It sneaks in even when you think you're the most secure. Enough talk of dark things. Today we are victorious over the sahdow."

"Agreed!" Quinlan began to process the recent events. The battle was over, they had won the day, and at least for now, life could return to a more normal course.

~~~

A destitute cripple with shriveled skin, stinking of pig feces, teetered over Praven's corpse and began to pee all over the face and head. The deed being done, he laughed and shuffled off back to find a place among the beggers on the streets of Trossachsmuir.

The former Disciple of Nemilos had resigned himself to his new existence until a presence he had not felt before touched his mind.

Kazim…

~~*

Epilogue

Quinlan, Grove Seven, and a group of others looked out over the bay from the walls of Teivas Keihas.

"The ships're nearly done, laddie," Bertrynn said as he wiggled a bit to adjust the wooden prosthetic of his right leg and tighten a strap.

"It astounds me how fast the Gwylari work," Quinlan replied.

"And de way dey build deir ships," Jua Kali said. "I have never seen such a ship. Dey are constructed of living timbers dat grow food during de journey. I am envious of druid magic."

"The Gwylari're nae druids—technically," Kian replied.

"Dey are de druid's druids."

"Aye, that sounds about right." Swela nodded.

"Joseah would have loved the ships," Ticca said. "They look like giant log rafts with sides and masts and branches with fan leaves for sails and tievines for ropes."

"Thrice the size of any of ours," said Travell Tavish, newly crowned King of Shaan.

"Are the stories true?" Ticari asked. "They are said to be stormproof."

Therin had a gleam of a dream in his eye. "We're goin' ta find out."

"Thyne ears hath heard truth, Ticari," Chyne answered. "Only a third doth show above the waves. Great ballast below wilst keep the vessels upright."

Cassae sighed dreamily. "Ta ride the wind with not a thin' on your mind but where it takes ya. Sailin' like a great bird across the sea."

"Och." Sovia wrinkled her nose. "Bounced back and forth and up and down like you be no more than the last tater in the sack. Where be the fun in that, I ask?"

"Aye, this highland girl dinnae belon' on the sea," Ronni said, "but ta lay ma eyes on the southern continent, fer that I'd gladly set sail."

"I am just the opposite," Lanry replied. "Land feels strange to my feet and I yearn for the open water."

"As do I," said Riklan. "It has been two moons since the battle and the siren's song calls to me louder with every passing day."

"My people are ready to return to deir home," Jua Kali said.

"The ship's near completion and then we set sail with you," replied Quinlan. "Your homeland shall soon be free of the dreyg, Jua."

"Dat will be a day of great rejoice, my friend."

"How long will we bob about on this fleet of flotsam 'til we get there?" asked Sovia.

"Seventy days, there about, to reach the Onomala River Basin on the southern continent," Riklan answered.

Her eyes grew wide. "Seventy days?"

Riklan nodded. "About half of that will be pure open water. Then we'll be able to make landfall and resupply."

"The Gwylari ships can grow food," Ticca said.

"Indeed they can, but our ships cannot," Lanry replied. "Anyway, every ship on the sea should carry enough food and water for their crews."

"Dere is anodder fortnight of rough seas beyond my homeland to reach de shores of Kajkara." Jua Kali extended his arm to the horizon.

"How much farther inland does this druid, Azuria Norr, live?" Bertrynn asked.

"Dree moons will go by during de journey," Jua Kali replied. "De *Maharamatswi* is an ancient jungle where it is said danger hides in every shadow. In Onomali, 'Maharamatswi' means 'place of angry spirits.'"

Bertrynn grimaced. "Three moons of angry spirits? Sorry I asked."

"The Misted Gorge lies beyond Maharamatswi?" Cassae asked.

Jua Kali shook his head. "In de heart of de jungle."

A footman approached Travell and bowed. "Dinner will be served shortly, Your Majesty."

"Very good, gratitude," Travell replied. "My friends, Trossachsmuir stands whole again. Let us have food, drink, and tales to fill the night!"

The announcement met with happy enthusiasm from all and Travell led the way to the newly rebuilt dining hall of Teivas Keihas.

Quinlan and Cassae walked side by side, hanging back a ways behind the others.

"So, the Order of Arden journeys ta the southern continent?" Cassae asked.

"Only part of it," Quinlan said. "Silari and Lissa remain to rebuild the Order on the northern continent."

"Isn't that the job of Primerey Quinlan?"

"Teasing me?"

"Yeah." She snickered a little. "I know ya need ta try and find Na'veyja. I feel the same. We'll find her."

"Joseah said Azuria Norr will guide us to Na'veyja," he said. "I have never read or heard of Azuria Norr in my time at the conclave."

"And what of Acimasiz?"

"That is a question of which I dread the answer."

"Have ya seen the mural the young artist did?"

Quinlan nodded. "He has remarkable talent."

Cassae cuddled up to his side. "All the liberatin' forces gathered together in triumph under the esbat. I love how he put the fallen as spirits in the night sky above."

"Yes and the memorials spared no effort in recognizing them either. Joseah, Kenri, Wylla, Freyn, and all who gave or lost their lives were remembered."

They watched the assembled group as they laughed, swapped tales, and laughed even more. Flit and Singer had collected a permanent entourage of other birds that constantly cavorted around the group like crazy moons circling their home world.

"Do ya think we have it in us ta succeed?" she asked.

"Oi!" one of the cooks yelled from somewhere out of sight. "Come back here with that, you!"

Pie Thief raced from the serving room with a small tart tucked in the crook of her arm. She was of great amusement to all but the cook.

"No question," Quinlan answered her. They shared a smile at the antics and went, arm in arm, to join their friends.

Watch for the continuing adventures of Grove Seven in book two of The Druids of Arden series – *Southern Winds*.

May your trails be clean and your forests be green!
AZK

Acknowledgments

The writing of a story, for the most part, is a solitary work for the author alone. The development of a novel, on the other hand, might require a small crowd to achieve. I am both lucky and grateful to have such a wonderful crowd of supporters not only for the *Green Rising* project, but the works of AZ Kelvin in general.

My deepest gratitude to you all for your support!

The AZ Kelvin All-Stars

Sunny Lee
CJ Lee
Evelyn & Bill Lee
Matt Metzler
Amy Stahl
Brandy Lowrey

The story and the book containing it, both require that several different aspects come together in order to produce a well-designed and well-written novel. *Green Rising* exists today because of the skills and creativity of the people involved with the project. My thanks to everyone!

Nikki Busch Editing

Nikki Busch Editing took on the task of editing *Green Rising*, which represents the fourth time we have worked together. A top-quality editor does not work *for* the writer, they work *with* the writer. Nikki does her job with excellence.

Thank you, Nikki!

Find her at www.nikkibuschediting.com

Lee Companies, LLC.

Lee Companies, LLC did a terrific job with publishing *Green Rising*. The Lee team checked the storyline for consistency and designed both the interior content and the cover illustrations.

CJ Lee – Interior and exterior design, cover illustrator.

Sunny Lee – Story wrangler and creative consultant.

Beta Readers

Green Rising had a fantastic group of beta readers give the book its pre-release reading. Beta reading is a very important part of the publishing process and I am very glad to have had such a great group to work with. My thanks to every one of you for a job well done!

Louann Dresden

Laura Whitcomb

Gabriel Strump

Steve Gannon

Rod Kroes

Randy Healy

And, Thank You!

Thank you, reader, for your support as well, through your purchase of this book. I hope you enjoyed the story and if you did, please consider telling your friends or posting a short review. Word of mouth is an author's best friend and is much appreciated!

Cheers! – AZ Kelvin

Look for more on the *Druids of Arden*, along with other stories like *The Altered Moon Series* and *Here We Ghost*, at:
www.azkelvin.com

Glossary

The following glossary lists a majority of both common and uncommon pronunciations found in *Green Rising* and throughout the Druids of Arden story line.

Format: word/name, (phonetic), [**emphasis**/syllable], {note from author}

Na'veyja (nah-vay-zha) [na/**vey**/ja]
Acimasiz (ah-kim-ah-seez) [**a**/cim/**a**/siz] {Aztec flavor}
Quinlan (coo-in-lah-n) [**quin**/lan]
Cassae (cass-ay) [cassae]
Chyne (ch-eye-n) [chyne]
Swela (sway-lah) [swela]
Kian (kee-ahn) [kian]
Ticca (tee-kah) [**ti**/cca]
Ticari (tee-kar-ee) [**ti**/cari]
Sovia (sew-vee-ah) [sovia]
Therin (th-air-in) [therin]
Joseah (jo-say-ah) [**jo**/seah]
Nemilos (nem-ill-os) [**nem**/il/os]
Flaura (flaw-rah) [flaura] {think "flower aura"}
Gwylar (gu-eye-lar) [gwy/**lar**]
Gwylari (gu-eye-lar-ee) [gwy/**lari**]
Raskan (raz-kan) [raskan]
Raskanish (raz-kan-ish) [**raskan**/ish]
Shaan (sh-on) [shaan]
Shaanlander (sh-on-lan-der) [**shaan**/lan/der]
Vakere (va-care) [vakere]
Vakerian (va-care-ee-in) [**va**/kerian]
Kalnu (cal-new) [kal/**nu**]

Kalnuvian (cal-new-vee-in) [kal/**nu**/vian]
Sairyn (sair-eye-n) [Sair/**yn**]
Aibreann (eh-bri-anne) [**ai**/bre/ann]
Kwyett (coo-eye-et) [kwyett] {Just say "quiet"}
Edwynn (ed-win) [edwynn]
*

Ilywodre Dronjida (Ill-ee-woe-dray) (der-on-zhee-da)
[il/**y**/**wo**/dre] [dr/**on**/ji/**da**]
{helps to sing-song this one a little bit, kind of like a fancy
royal announcement}
*

Druidic circles of rank:
10th (highest) Primerey (pry-mur-ay) [**pri**/mer/ey]
9th   Segoney (say-gon-ay) [**se**/gon/ey]
8th   Tretjey (tret-zhay) [**tret**/jey]
7th   Cetrey (set-ray) [**cet**/rey]
6th   Siestrey (see-ess-tray) [**si**/es/trey]
5th   Cinquey (seen-coo-ay) [**cin**/qu/ey]
4th   Settey (set-tay) [settey]
3rd   Osmey (oz-may) [osmey]
2nd   Novey (no-vay) [novey]
1st (lowest)   Tiatey (tee-ah-tay) [tiatey]

I hope this glossary helps out. If you have any questions
and/or comments on *Green Rising* or any *AZ Kelvin* story, please
contact me through my website, www.azkelvin.com. I am more
than happy to talk with my readers.

AZ Kelvin